the Hawaiian DISCOVERY

the Hawaiian

DISCOVERY

SEQUEL TO *The Hawaiian Quilt*

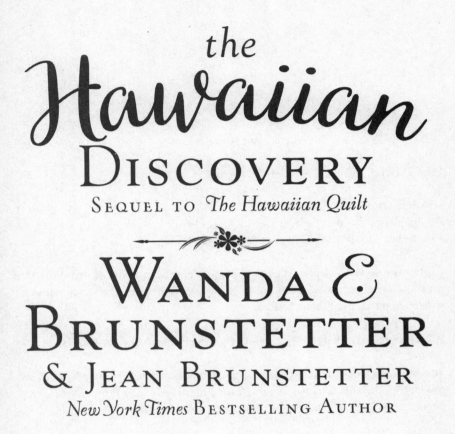

WANDA E. BRUNSTETTER

& JEAN BRUNSTETTER

New York Times BESTSELLING AUTHOR

SHILOH RUN PRESS

An Imprint of Barbour Publishing, Inc.

© 2018 by Wanda E. Brunstetter and Jean Brunstetter

Print ISBN 978-1-68322-447-1

eBook Editions:
Adobe Digital Edition (.epub) 978-1-68322-449-5
Kindle and MobiPocket Edition (.prc) 978-1-68322-448-8

All scripture quotations are taken from the King James Version of the Bible.

This book is a work of fiction. Names, characters, places, and incidents are either products of the author's imagination or used fictitiously. Any similarity to actual people, organizations, and/or events is purely coincidental.

Cover Design: Buffy Cooper
Cover Photography: Richard Brunstetter III; RBIII Studios

Published by Shiloh Run Press, an imprint of Barbour Publishing, Inc., 1810 Barbour Drive, Uhrichsville, Ohio 44683, www.barbourbooks.com

Our mission is to inspire the world with the life-changing message of the Bible.

ecpa Member of the
Evangelical Christian
Publishers Association

Printed in Canada.

DEDICATION

To our special friends from Kauai—Nathan & Rebecca Cotter,
Tristan Dahlberg, and Randy & Primrose Rego.
May God bless each of you.

Cast thy burden upon the LORD,
and he shall sustain thee.
PSALM 55:22

PROLOGUE

Middlebury, Indiana

*E*llen Lambright finished sweeping the kitchen floor and paused from her work to brew a cup of tea. Since the Pleasant View Bed-and-Breakfast currently had no guests, she and her friend Mandy had spent most of the day giving each of the guest rooms a thorough cleaning. While they worked, Mandy's husband, Ken, made a few repairs on the front porch.

Mandy and Ken had purchased the B&B two years ago, soon after they were married. They'd hired Ellen to help out, since she'd had previous experience working at another bed-and-breakfast in the area. Ellen enjoyed her job and was glad her friends' business had been doing well. Many tourists came to the area, looking for lodging, and information had quickly spread about their B&B. Mandy, having been raised in an Amish home, was an excellent cook. Ellen knew her way around the kitchen too. With their culinary skills, every guest woke up to a tantalizing breakfast.

As she sat at the table, sipping the soothing lavender tea, Ellen's thoughts took her back to Hawaii, where she'd had her first taste of what quickly become her favorite beverage. It seemed like yesterday when Mandy, Ellen, and their friends Sadie and Barbara went on a cruise to the Hawaiian Islands.

When Ellen and Mandy became stranded on Kauai, it turned into quite an adventure. Thanks to a caring Hawaiian couple who owned a bed-and-breakfast in the town of Kapaa, the young women were taken care of. It was during their stay on the island that Mandy fell in love with Ken, whose family owned a business raising organically grown chickens. At first, Ellen hadn't understood her friend's infatuation with Ken, but as time went on, she realized the couple had fallen in love. The most difficult part was trying to understand

Mandy's decision not to join the Amish church. However, by the time Ken moved to Indiana and married Mandy, Ellen had accepted the changes.

A chilly January breeze blew outside, and Ellen rose from her seat to put a log on the fire in the adjoining room. Things had slowed down at the B&B since the holidays. But that was okay. It would give Ellen more free time to spend with her parents and siblings.

The phone rang. "Good evening," Ellen answered. "Pleasant View Bed-and-Breakfast."

"Hello. This is Vickie Williams. Is my son available?"

"Yes, he's around somewhere. Would you like me to see if I can find him?"

"Please do. It's urgent that I speak with him right away."

Ellen heard the anxiety in Vickie's voice. *I hope nothing bad has happened.* Just then she heard a noise in the kitchen and looked up.

"Oh, wait. Ken just came inside." Ellen held the receiver out to him. "It's your mother."

Ken reached for the phone. "Hi, Mom. How are things on sunny Kauai?" He shifted the receiver to his other ear. "What was that?"

Mandy moved closer to him.

"Oh, no!" The color drained from Ken's face as he lowered himself into a chair. "I'll book the next flight available. And don't worry, Mom. Just pray."

Ken hung up the phone and leaned forward, his face in his hands.

"What's going on?" Mandy put her hands on his shoulders. "What did your mother say?"

"Dad had a heart attack. He's in the hospital being prepped for surgery." Ken looked up, slowly shaking his head. "It sounds serious. I have to go to Kauai, Mandy. My folks need me right now."

"Of course they do, and I'm going with you." Mandy's brown eyes darkened as she turned to face Ellen. "Do you think you can manage the B&B while we're gone?"

"Of course." Ellen slipped her arm around Mandy's waist. "Now that it's winter, things are likely to be slow here anyway. So don't worry. Everything will be fine. It shouldn't be difficult to run the place by myself."

CHAPTER 1

Two weeks later

*E*llen was up by six and ready to face the day. After Mandy and Ken left for Kauai, she'd brought some of her things from home before new guests arrived. With people coming and going, someone had to be in the house at all times.

Once in the kitchen, Ellen fixed a piece of toast with apple butter and heated a cup of her favorite tea. She appreciated the door separating the kitchen from the dining room. The noise of her breakfast preparations would hopefully go unnoticed, and neither of the guests would be disturbed.

Ellen nibbled on the toast and watched the sun slowly climb into the sky. *The Lord can surely create beautiful sunrises and sunsets. But I can't sit here all day, taking in the view. Ken and Mandy are depending on me, and it's time to start breakfast for the guests who arrived last evening.*

After she finished eating and had put the dishes in the sink, Ellen spotted the neighbor's cat darting through the yard with a sparrow in its mouth. *Poor little bird. Wish that feline would go after mice and leave our feathered friends alone.*

When the cat disappeared, Ellen double-checked the menu she'd planned for the middle-aged couple who'd checked in last evening. She would serve them scrambled eggs and sausage, sliced bananas mixed with vanilla yogurt, and blueberry muffins with sweet creamy butter. There were also two kinds of juice in the refrigerator.

She glanced at the clock. *I need to hurry.*

✳

After spending most of the morning and a good chunk of the afternoon scurrying to get everything done before another set of guests arrived, Ellen felt tired. She went into Ken and Mandy's room, where she'd been sleeping since they left, to freshen up before her friend Sadie Kuhns arrived.

Two boxes of Christmas decorations sat in the corner. A few days after New Year's, Ellen had helped Mandy and Ken take down the simple holiday trimmings and box them up for next year. But in the rush to get Ken and Mandy packed and to the airport, some of the boxes didn't get put away. "In one of my spare moments, I'll need to get those in the attic."

Turning from the decorations, Ellen eyed the bed longingly. She wished she could take a short nap. But with Sadie coming soon, there was no time for rest.

Things hadn't slowed down as much as she'd expected, and Ellen had soon realized it would be difficult to run the place without Mandy's help. So she'd asked Sadie to help out whenever she could. Since her friend worked weekdays at the hardware store in Shipshewana, she was available most evenings and Saturdays.

Ellen smoothed a few wrinkles in the lone-star quilt covering the queen-sized bed. Mandy's mother had made it, as well as several others for the guest rooms. Most of the rooms were decorated with an Amish theme, so it was appropriate to have homemade quilts on all the beds.

Ellen glanced at the calendar on the far wall. It was hard to believe Ken and Mandy had been gone only two weeks. It seemed much longer. But it was a good thing they left when they did. Ken's father had died three days ago, and his mother and brother needed emotional support, as did Ken.

When Mandy had called the other day, she learned that Ken's brother, Dan, had taken their dad's death harder than anyone, and he could barely function. This meant most of the duties at the organic chicken farm fell on Ken's shoulders. Mandy had also mentioned that it could be a few months before they returned to Indiana. Ellen hoped they'd be back before spring. Things slowed down during the winter months, but tourists flocked to the area during the rest of the year, keeping hotels, B&B's, restaurants, and gift shops in Elkhart and LaGrange Counties very busy.

With only two guests in the house this morning, Ellen's load had been a little lighter. But this afternoon, another couple checked in, so Ellen was glad she could count on Sadie for extra help.

After changing into a clean dress and apron, Ellen stepped into the hallway. Glancing at her reflection in the entryway mirror, she saw the telltale signs of exhaustion beneath her blue eyes, in addition to worry lines creasing her forehead. Even her blond hair didn't look as shiny as usual. Truth was, Ellen wasn't sleeping well, and her energy level was at an all-time low. How much longer would it be before Mandy and Ken returned? Could Ken's brother handle the family business on his own, or would he end up hiring someone to help out?

Ellen hadn't said anything to Mandy, but she hoped Ken's mother might sell the organic farm and move to Indiana. Ellen couldn't imagine living so far from her parents and siblings. She figured it must be difficult for Ken too. Someday, when he and Mandy had children, it would be nice for the little ones if they lived close to both sets of grandparents.

Studying her reflection, Ellen tapped her chin. *I wouldn't want to be separated permanently from my family or friends.*

The months Ellen had spent with Mandy on Kauai had been difficult, despite the beautiful scenery surrounding them in every direction. Had it not been for the companionship of Mandy, as well as the kindness of Luana and Makaio Palu, Ellen would have given in to depression during their unexpectedly long stay. She'd always been close to her family and missed them terribly during the months she'd been gone. Ellen had developed a special bond with Luana. The generous Hawaiian woman was as beautiful on the inside as her outward appearance. Her caring, gentle spirit was exactly what Ellen needed, being so far from home.

Mr. and Mrs. Hanson stepped into the hall from their guest room, pulling Ellen out of her musings.

"We're going out to eat an early supper." Mrs. Hanson, a silver-haired woman in her midsixties, gave a rosy-cheeked smile. "Do you have any restaurant suggestions, Miss Lambright? This is our first time visiting the area, and we're not sure which establishment to choose."

"If you're looking to stay fairly close to the B&B, then I would suggest Das Dutchman Essenhaus. They have many good choices on the menu, as well as a buffet with a variety of delicious food. Of course," Ellen added, "there are several other nice places to eat as well."

"We appreciate the suggestion." Mrs. Hanson put her hand in the crook of her husband's arm. "Shall we seek out the closest restaurant, dear?"

He nodded agreeably, then called over his shoulder as they moved toward the door, "Thank you, Miss Lambright. When we get back, we'll let you know how we liked the food."

Ellen smiled as the pleasant couple stepped outside. Of course, most of the guests who came here were kind and polite. Ellen couldn't recall anyone saying anything negative during their stay at the Pleasant View Bed-and-Breakfast.

"Guess I'd better head for the kitchen and fix myself some supper." Ellen snickered as she padded down the hall to the kitchen. Since no one else was in the house, it didn't matter if she talked to herself. But she'd have to be careful not to do that when guests were present.

✳

Soon after Ellen started washing her supper dishes, Sadie knocked and entered through the back door.

"Sorry for being late. I had some errands to run for my *mamm* after I got off work, and it took longer than I expected." Sadie's hazel eyes, with flecks of green, seemed to sparkle as she removed her heavy jacket and hung it over the back of a kitchen chair. Her pretty auburn hair couldn't be seen under the black outer bonnet she wore on her head.

"No problem." Ellen lifted a soapy hand. "As you can see, I haven't started the breakfast casserole I'm planning to serve to the guests tomorrow morning."

"I've eaten your delicious casserole before, and I'm sure they will enjoy it as much as I did." Sadie removed her outer bonnet, placed it on the chair, and picked up a dishcloth. "I'll dry and put the dishes away, unless there's something else you need me to do."

"I could use your help with the casserole, but let's get the dishes done first."

As Ellen and Sadie completed the task, they talked about the weather.

"It's sure nippy out there," Sadie said as she placed a plate in the cupboard. "Makes me wonder if it might snow yet this evening."

Ellen glanced out the window at the darkened sky. "I hope not. I have another set of guests coming in later, and the roads could get icy if it snows."

Sadie bumped Ellen's arm and gave a playful wink. "It is winter you know. Most people expect a little snow this time of the year."

"True." Ellen sighed. "I wonder if Mandy has been able to take a little time to enjoy the beautiful weather they're no doubt having on Kauai. I should have asked when she called the other day."

"I'm sure even though she's busy helping Ken's mother with things, she's been able to spend some time outdoors in the sun." Sadie reached for a glass to dry. "The balmy weather was the one thing I enjoyed most when we visited the Hawaiian Islands."

"Same here. Although the beautiful flowers and colorful birds made it special too." Ellen pulled the drain plug, letting the water out of the sink. "Well, that chore is done. Guess I'll set out the ingredients for the breakfast casserole." She made her way to the refrigerator and paused. "Unless you'd like to have a cup of tea before we start the preparations."

"That does sound nice. I'll put the teakettle on the stove." Sadie got the water heating, while Ellen placed two cups and some slices of banana bread on the table.

As they ate their snack and drank the tea, Sadie brought up the topic of Mandy again. "You don't suppose Ken and Mandy will decide to stay in Hawaii permanently, do you?"

Ellen shook her head. "I'm sure they have no plans of staying. If they did, Mandy would have said something when we last spoke." She reached for a piece of the moist bread and slathered it with creamy butter. "She did say Ken's mother really needs their help right now, so it could be a month or two before they return to Indiana."

Sadie raised her pale eyebrows. "That's a long time for you to run the bed-and-breakfast on your own."

Ellen pointed at Sadie. "You're here helping me, so I'm not completely on my own."

"But a lot of work will fall on you when I'm not able to be here. Have you considered hiring someone full-time? Maybe one of your sisters could help out."

"With the exception of my younger sister, they all have jobs, and Mom needs Lenore at home to help with chores." Ellen took a sip of tea and set her cup down. "Besides, so far I'm able to manage on my own. And once Mandy and Ken get back, we won't need anyone else."

"You have a point." Sadie fingered the edge of the tablecloth. "Let's hope they get back before too many people make reservations and you end up with more responsibility than you can handle. Not to mention that with me working at the hardware store all week and helping out here evenings and Saturdays, it could end up being too much for me too."

The phone rang, and Ellen excused herself and stepped into the hall to answer it. "Pleasant View Bed-and-Breakfast. Ellen Lambright speaking."

"Hello. This is Tammy Brooks, and I'd like to make a reservation. It will be for my husband and myself, as well as our little one. Do you have any vacancies for this Friday and Saturday night? We'll be attending my aunt's funeral Saturday morning, and we haven't been able to find suitable accommodations."

Ellen found it hard to believe that all the hotels and other B&Bs in the area could be booked, but she gave the woman the benefit of the doubt. The fact that the couple had a baby might be a problem, since the policy here was to rent only to adults. And she couldn't lie to the woman, because four of the six rooms were vacant this weekend.

"Umm. . .would you please hold on while I check on this?"

"Yes, of course."

Ellen set the receiver on the entryway table and rushed back to the kitchen. "There's a woman on the phone who wants to make a reservation for this Friday and Saturday night." She moved closer to Sadie. "The only problem is, they have a baby, and we're not set up to accommodate children here."

Sadie rubbed the bridge of her nose. "You could borrow a crib and set it up in the parents' room."

"*Jah*, but what about the policy of no children?"

"Did you tell her that?"

Ellen shook her head. "She sounded desperate for a place to stay, so I thought I'd get your opinion before I responded."

"What do you think Mandy would do if she was here?"

"I'm not sure, but I believe she might make an exception."

Sadie patted Ellen's arm. "Then my advice is to follow your convictions."

"Okay, I will. After all, it's only one little child. What could it hurt to let them stay a few days?"

CHAPTER 2

*E*llen was surprised when she heard a vehicle pull in at ten thirty Friday morning. Check-in for guests wasn't until three in the afternoon, and she wasn't expecting any deliveries.

Going to the front door, she watched as a young couple got out of a minivan. The dark-haired man opened the sliding back door and took a small boy out. As the family headed for the B&B, Ellen stepped out and greeted them on the front porch. Thinking they might be lost and in need of directions, she asked, "May I help you?"

"I'm Tammy Brooks, and I made a reservation with you earlier in the week." The blond woman gestured to the man beside her, holding the little boy's hand. "This is my husband, Ned, and our two-year-old son, Jerry. We're a few hours early, but if it's possible, we'd like to check in now."

Ellen rubbed her forehead, wondering what to do. The Brookses' room wasn't quite ready. Worse yet, their child was not the baby she had expected.

She continued to massage her temples. *How would Mandy handle this is if she were here? She probably wouldn't have to deal with it, because she would have said no in the first place.*

"Well, your room isn't ready, but I suppose it would be all right if you wait in the living room while I make the bed." She glanced at the little boy. "Will your son be okay sleeping in a crib? I set one up in your room, because when we talked on the phone you said he was a baby."

Tammy shook her head. "No, I said we have a little one."

"Sorry. I assumed you meant a baby." Ellen couldn't remember when she'd felt so rattled. She had gone against the "adult only" policy, and now she would be hosting a couple with a toddler, not a baby.

She opened the door wide and stepped aside so the guests could enter. "Please come in."

"I'll go out to the van and get our luggage." Ned looked at his wife. "You and Jerry need to get inside out of the weather."

"Yes, it is a lot colder here than I expected." Clasping her son's hand, Tammy led the blond-haired boy into the foyer. Ellen took their coats and hung them on the coat tree. They followed her into the living room.

"This home is lovely. I like the Amish theme." Tammy gestured to a quilted runner on the coffee table. "I guess it makes sense, with you being Amish, that you'd have this type of item here."

Ellen shook her head. "I can't take credit for any of the decor. My friend, Mandy Williams, and her husband, Ken, own the B&B. I just work here."

"Oh, then I look forward to meeting them." Tammy took a seat on the couch and lifted Jerry onto her lap. He leaned his head against her chest and stuck his thumb in his mouth.

"Actually, Ken and Mandy are in Hawaii right now," Ellen explained. "I'm in charge of the B&B until they get back."

Tammy heaved a sigh. "They're lucky. I'd give anything to be on vacation in Hawaii right now."

"They're not on vacation. Ken's parents live there, and his father died of a heart attack recently."

Tammy lowered her gaze, stroking the top of her little boy's head. "That's too bad. I'm sorry for their loss."

"Yes, it's been difficult for them."

"As I mentioned when I made our reservations, my aunt passed away. I'm sure there will be lots of tears shed during her funeral tomorrow."

Ellen slowly nodded. Saying goodbye to a loved one because of death or even miles of separation was never easy. She thought about the loneliness she'd felt when she and Mandy were in Hawaii, so far from their Amish family and friends. At one point, Ellen had begun to feel as if she was never going home. Mandy, however, seemed to adjust well to her Hawaiian surroundings. For a while, Ellen had wondered if her friend might end up staying on Kauai. She was glad when they both returned to their homes in Indiana. Then Mandy found Luana and Makaio's missing quilt by a strange coincidence, so she returned to the island for a time. That was when Ken proclaimed his love for Mandy and decided to move to the mainland so they could be married.

Ned entered the house with their suitcases, bringing Ellen and Tammy's conversation to an end. "It's clouding up out there." He cupped his hands and blew on his fingers. "Might get some snow while we're here."

"January and February are usually our snowiest months." Ellen rose from her chair. "If you'll make yourselves comfortable here, I'll get the bed made up and then show you to your room."

✳

When Ellen returned to the living room, she spotted Ned in front of the fireplace with hands outstretched toward the heat, while his wife slouched on the couch with her eyes closed. Ellen figured the poor woman fell asleep. She was surprised to see little Jerry kneeling on the floor in front of the coffee table. The little guy had his mother's comb, and pulled it across the exposed part of the table.

Ellen gasped when she looked down and saw a gash in the wood. She was sure it hadn't been there before. *Oh, dear, how am I going to explain this to Mandy when she gets home? Should I say something to the boy's parents or let it go?*

She didn't have to think long, for Jerry's father turned around and grabbed the comb from his son's chubby little hand. "That is a no-no, Son. You're not supposed to get into your mommy's purse."

Ned didn't say anything about the scratch on the table. He either hadn't seen the mark or chose not to mention it.

Ellen decided not to say anything about the scratch, either. She would work on it later and try to buff it out. "The room is ready for you now."

Ned shook his wife's shoulder. "Wake up, honey. Our room is ready, so you can take a nap on the bed if you want."

Her cheeks colored as she looked up at Ellen and blinked a couple of times. "Sorry for dozing off. Guess I'm more tired than I realized."

"It's all right. If you'll follow me down the hall, I'll show you to your room."

When they entered the room with a king-sized canopy bed, Tammy commented once again on the Amish décor. "What a lovely quilt on the bed. Was it locally made?"

Ellen nodded. "The owner's mother, who is Amish, has made several quilts for the B&B. This one, however, my own mother quilted, so it's special to me."

Tammy fingered the stitching along the top of the covering. "It must have taken many hours to produce something this intricate. I can't get over how tiny and even the hand-stitching is. I do a little sewing, but could never tackle anything this big or with such a complicated design. What is this pattern called?"

"It's the log-cabin pattern."

Ned leaned close to the bed, as though scrutinizing the quilt. "Doesn't look like a log cabin to me."

"Oh, the design is there all right," his wife said. "You just can't see it."

Squinting, he shook his head. "You can't see what's not there."

Deciding it was time to end this conversation, Ellen pointed to the crib across the room. "Will that be adequate for your son?"

"Since it's a full-size crib, I'm sure it will be fine. We recently put Jerry in a small bed at home because he kept crawling over the rail and getting out of his crib." Tammy picked the boy up and carried him across the room. "I bet you could use a nap too, little man." As soon as she put him in the crib, he started to howl.

Ellen hoped Jerry wouldn't cry a lot while they were here. It would disturb the other guests, not to mention herself.

She turned toward the door. "I need to get some things done now, so I'll let you folks get settled in. Let me know if you need anything."

"Thanks, we will," Ned shouted above the boy's screams, which grew louder by the minute.

Ellen wanted to cover her ears as she exited the room. Had she done the wrong thing by allowing this couple with a child to rent a room? Well, it was too late to worry about it now. She'd make the best of things and hope little Jerry didn't cause too much of a disturbance while he and his parents were here.

✳

Ellen woke up Saturday morning, rolled onto her side, and looked at the alarm clock on her nightstand. It read 6:00 a.m. A few seconds later, Ellen heard the old clock chime faintly from the other room, confirming the hour. She felt tired and out-of-sorts because Jerry's frequent crying kept waking her. She hoped the guests occupying two of the upstairs rooms hadn't been disturbed too. If word got out that the Pleasant View Bed-and-Breakfast was noisy, business could suffer. The one thing Ellen could do for her friends during their absence was to make sure their establishment ran smoothly and without complications.

After Ellen got dressed, she headed for the kitchen to get breakfast ready for her guests. This morning she planned to serve baked oatmeal, French toast, and a bowl of fresh apple, orange, and banana slices. Between the three items, Ellen felt sure everyone would have something they liked for breakfast. She would also serve apple and orange juice, as well as coffee and tea for the adults. For little Jerry and anyone else who wanted it, she had plenty of milk.

Ellen glanced at the clock on the kitchen wall. It was six thirty, and Sadie should be here any minute. She heard a soft knock on the back door and, opening it, found Sadie on the porch, holding a wicker basket.

"It feels good in here," Sadie said when she entered the kitchen. "The temperature dipped during the night, and the ride over with my horse and buggy was chilly. I half expected to see snow when I looked out the window this morning."

"Well, I'm glad you're here, because I could use your help with breakfast." Ellen kept her voice low so she wouldn't wake any of the guests.

"I saw three cars parked outside, so I figured you must be busy." Sadie put the basket on the table. "I made two apple pies last night. Thought you might want to serve them for breakfast this morning. They'd go nicely with the baked oatmeal you mentioned you'd be fixing today."

Ellen's mouth watered. "Yum. I love apple pies, especially this time of year. Maybe I'll forget about making French toast and serve the pies instead."

Sadie removed her outer garments and hung them up. "How'd things go after I left here last night? Did the little boy settle down and go to sleep?"

Ellen shook her head. "He fussed and cried well into the night. I probably didn't get more than a couple hours of sleep."

"I can tell. Your eyes look bloodshot, and there's no spring in your step." Sadie moved closer to Ellen. "Are you wishing now that you'd said no to the parents' request to book a room here?"

"Yes and no." Ellen rested her hips against the table. "It's nice to have more business in January, but at the same time. . ."

Sadie leaned closer to Ellen. "Sounds like someone is up already. I hear a muffled conversation down the hallway."

Ellen retrieved a bowl from the cupboard and placed it on the counter. "I wonder which guest is up."

"Oh, there you are Miss Lambright; I hoped you were up." Deep wrinkles formed across Ned's forehead. "I'm afraid we have a problem in the bathroom."

"Oh?" Ellen tipped her head. "What sort of problem?"

Ned glanced at the floor, and when he looked back at her, his cheeks reddened. "My son dropped my keys in the toilet then gave it a flush. Now they're stuck inside where I can't reach."

Ellen cringed. Walking along the beach in Hawaii sure sounded like a nice alternative about now.

CHAPTER 3

Island of Kauai
Kapaa, Hawaii

As Mandy approached the Palms Bed-and-Breakfast, she heard music drifting from the open windows and knew Makaio must be playing his ukulele. It brought back memories of times he'd taught her how to play the instrument. Makaio had even given Mandy a ukulele for her birthday when she and Ellen stayed with him and Luana. Mandy still played it during her free time, and the music always brought her back to the days spent on Kauai.

Stepping onto their lanai, Mandy set the box she held on a small wicker table. She was about to knock on the door, when it opened and Luana greeted her with a hug. "*Aloha*, my dear friend. How are you today?"

"I'm doing all right, but Ken's still having a hard time. Between dealing with his father's death and trying to keep the organic farm running, he's pretty stressed out."

"Isn't Ken's brother helping?" Luana asked.

Mandy shook her head. "Dan's taken his dad's death the hardest of all, and he's sunk into depression. His wife, Rita, said it's all he can do to get out of bed."

Luana's dark eyebrows rose. "Does that mean Ken is doing all the work by himself?"

"Pretty much. I'm helping him with the chickens as much as I can, and of course, doing inside chores to help Ken's mom. As you can imagine, neither of us has any free time." Mandy gestured to the box. "I brought the four-dozen brown eggs you requested."

"*Mahalo*. With all the guests we have scheduled in the next few weeks, the eggs will be gone quickly."

"Let me know when you need more. The layers are producing a lot right now."

"Good to know." Luana gestured to the wicker chairs on the lanai. "Do you have a few minutes to sit and talk? I have some fresh papaya and pineapple cut. It might be a nice pick-me-up."

Mandy moistened her lips. "That does sound good, but I can't stay long. Ken needs my help this morning, cleaning out the rest of the chicken houses."

Luana gently rubbed Mandy's back and shoulders. "You know what I think?"

"What's that?" Mandy felt her tension ease a bit.

"I think Ken's mother should hire someone to work on the farm. She'll have to do that anyway, once you and Ken go back to the mainland."

Sighing, Mandy sank into a chair. "It doesn't look like we'll be leaving here anytime soon. But you're right—Vickie should hire someone—if for no other reason than to help Ken right now. He's so tired at the end of the day that he can barely muster up the strength to kiss me goodnight."

Luana slowly shook her head. "That's not good. Why, you two are still basically on your honeymoon. Instead of wading through piles of chicken manure, you should both be swimming in the ocean and enjoying the mesmerizing sounds of the surf."

"I wish we could spend time relaxing on the beach, but as you know, that's not the reason we came to Kauai." Mandy gestured to the cardboard container. "Would you like me to take the eggs inside for you?"

"No, I'll do it." Luana picked up the box. "Just sit there and rest. I'll be back with some delicious fruit."

When Luana went inside, Mandy leaned her head back and closed her eyes. She drew in a deep cleansing breath of air, relishing in all the pleasurable scents from vegetation blooming in the Palus' yard. Back home, the only flowers around were the poinsettias left over from Christmas. So Mandy's senses were piqued by all the colors and fragrances on the islands.

The sound of birds chirping in the trees nearly lulled her to sleep. *Luana is right. I do need some time to relax. Ken needs it too. I bet he wishes he had time to go surfing with his friend Taavi.*

When Luana returned to the lanai, Mandy opened her eyes and yawned. "It's a good thing you came back when you did, or I'd probably be counting sheep."

Luana tipped her head to one side and chuckled. "Silly me. I took you literally for a moment there." She placed a plate of fruit on the wicker table and handed Mandy a glass of guava juice. "I'm glad you had a few minutes to yourself. It's not good to work all the time."

Luana plucked a piece of pineapple off the plate and took a seat in the chair beside Mandy. "I spoke to Makaio when I was inside and asked if he knew of anybody who needed a job or might like to work at the Williamses' farm."

"What'd he say?" Mandy took a sip of juice.

"Not off hand, but if he hears of anyone, he'll be sure to let Ken or his mother know."

Mandy nodded slowly, before taking another drink of the succulent juice. She wished they sold guava juice in the stores at home, because their bed-and-breakfast guests would enjoy it as a nice change from the usual orange, apple, or grape juices she offered.

"How's Ellen doing these days?" Luana asked. "Is she managing the B&B on her own?"

"When I spoke to her earlier this week, she said she's been quite busy. But she's managing okay with our friend Sadie's part-time help." Mandy shifted in her chair. "Ellen ran into a little problem last week, though, when she rented a room to a couple with a two-year-old boy."

"So I'm guessing your bed-and-breakfast has an 'adult only' policy like we have here?"

"Yes, but Ellen made an exception and regretted it later. Would you like to hear what happened?"

Luana nodded as she nibbled on a piece of papaya.

"Well, in addition to scratching the coffee table in the living room with his mother's comb, the little guy dropped his father's keys in the toilet, and they got stuck."

"Oh, my! Were they able to get them freed without calling a plumber?"

"Yes. The boy's dad bent a coat hanger and fished them out." Mandy helped herself to a piece of pineapple. "Ellen was so apologetic. She thought I'd be upset, but I told her not to worry. It could have happened if Ken and I had been there. We both like kids, so we would have probably made an exception and let the couple stay too."

Luana grinned. "Running a B&B does have its challenges. Believe me, over the years of owning this business, Makaio and I have faced many unusual situations. We are thankful each day for the Lord's help in everything we say and do."

"One thing is certain. You two are the kindest, most hospitable couple I've ever met. It's because of you that Ken and I decided to open our bed-and-breakfast in Middlebury."

"Well, thank you. It's nice to know we had a positive influence."

Mandy reached over and clasped her friend's arm. "You certainly have, and in more ways than one." She set her empty glass down and stood. "As much as I'd like to sit here all day and visit, you have things to do, and I need to get back to help Ken."

Luana rose and gave Mandy a hug. "Please keep in touch, and we'll let you know if we hear of anyone who might need a job."

✳

Middlebury

"I'm glad you were able to take a little time off and join me and your *daed* for lunch today," Ellen's mother said as she sat at her kitchen table. "We don't get to visit much since Mandy and Ken left you in charge of their bed-and-breakfast. I think you're working too hard."

Ellen's father looked at Ellen and winked.

"I'm fine." She smiled, hoping to reassure her mother and thankful that Dad understood her position. Mom had enough going on with Lenore, Ellen's youngest sister, close to finishing up her last year of school. It seemed as if she worried about everyone in the family—including Dad and how hard he worked at his shoe store. She also fretted over Ellen's other two sisters, who were away in Sarasota waitressing at a restaurant until they returned in the spring. Ellen didn't want to cause Mom more concern.

"Sadie's the one who's working too hard, being at the hardware store all day and helping me out in the evenings and Saturdays. I don't know where she gets all that energy."

Mom took a sip of water. "I'm sure your friend does work hard, but you do too, and—"

"Now Nora, don't start mothering our oldest *dochder*," Dad spoke up. "Ellen's a grown woman. I'm sure she knows her limitations and can handle most any situation."

Ellen bit the inside of her cheek. "Actually, I do have a problem I can't seem to resolve on my own. Sadie hasn't been able to figure it out either."

"What's going on?" Dad leaned his folded arms on the table.

Ellen explained how the little boy had dropped his father's keys in the toilet. "Even though his dad managed to get them out, the toilet hasn't been running right since."

"Does it still flush?" Dad questioned.

"Jah, but it keeps running, unless someone jiggles the handle. And I sure can't expect any guests staying in that room to be subjected to the inconvenience."

Mom looked at Dad. "I bet you could fix it, Nathan. You've always been handy with things like that."

He nodded, running his fingers through the sides of his thinning reddish-blond hair. "I'll come over sometime later today and take a look-see."

"*Danki*, Dad. I'm sure if anyone can fix it, you can."

✳

Ellen finished washing her supper dishes when Sadie arrived to help with preparations for breakfast the next morning.

"How'd your day go?" Sadie asked after removing her outer garments and hanging them up.

"It went well." Ellen dried her hands. "I had lunch at my folks' place, and my daed said he'd be over later today to check on the toilet that keeps running." She glanced up at the clock. "I figured he would be here by now, though."

"Maybe he got delayed at the shoe store. Sometimes customers come in a few minutes before the hardware store closes, and we have to stay open till they finish shopping."

"Jah, that could be what's happened. It wouldn't be the first time he's had to work late either."

A knock sounded on the back door. "I bet that's my daed now." Ellen hurried to the door, but when she opened it, she jerked her head back, surprised to find Ezra Bontrager on the porch, holding a tool box.

"Hello, Ellen." Ezra's cheeks reddened. "I'm guessin' I took you by surprise, showing up here when you expected your daed." He gave her a half-smile, glanced down at his boots, then looked back at her.

"I am a bit surprised," she admitted.

"Your daed's still at the shop, so I hope you don't mind, but I'm here to take a look at your *briwwi*."

"Oh, okay." Ellen felt a little funny about her dad's employee coming over to fix the toilet, but she needed it done, so she showed Ezra the way.

"You work in a nice place, Ellen." Ezra paused before entering the guest room. He glanced around, as though trying to take it all in, and then he stared at her a little longer than normal.

Ellen noticed Sadie poke her head into the room and give her a silly grin. Then she disappeared into the kitchen, hopefully, undetected by Ezra.

"Uh. . .thanks, Ezra." Her chin dipped down. "I like working here. I'd be disappointed if I ever had to quit."

"That speaks volumes to me." Ezra shuffled his feet. "I like my job too. Your daed's a good boss. I don't mind assisting him and enjoy the easy-going pace at the shoe store."

Ellen smiled. "Dad's mentioned several times how glad he is that you're working for him. He says you're a good worker."

"That's nice to hear." Ezra blushed as he looked down at his boots again. "Guess I'd better get busy fixin' your problem in the bathroom."

Ellen led Ezra into the small connecting bathroom and watched as he set his tool pouch in front of the sink. "It's sure a waste of water when a toilet runs all the time, and the noise it creates can get annoying," he commented.

"I'm glad it still worked after those keys got flushed, but I began to worry when it started doing this." She rested her hand against the door frame.

He flushed the toilet, jiggled the handle, and lifted the lid off the top.

"I think I know what the problem is, so you can go back to whatever you were doin', and I'll get to work."

"Okay. Let me know if you need anything." Ellen returned to the kitchen where Sadie mixed muffin batter.

"Did Ezra find the problem?" Sadie asked.

"I think he may have, but now he has to fix it." Ellen took a carton of eggs from the refrigerator. "Think I'll mix the eggs and milk now, so tomorrow morning all I'll have to do is cook and scramble the egg mixture."

Ellen and Sadie worked in silence until Ezra came into the room. "All done," he announced. "The briwwi shouldn't keep running anymore." Ezra glanced in Ellen's direction, giving her a shy kind of grin.

"Danki for taking care of it. How much do I owe you?"

He held up one hand. "Don't worry about that. Your daed said he'd take care of it, since I did him a favor by coming over in his place." He shuffled his feet once more. "Guess I oughta get going."

"Okay. Thanks again, Ezra."

"No problem," he mumbled before heading out the door.

Sadie snickered.

"What's so funny?"

"Didn't you see the way Ezra looked at you when you two chatted?"

Ellen shook her head. "I don't know what you're talking about."

"Oh, boy. . . How could you miss it?" Sadie snickered again. "I think Ezra's interested in you. Jah, I'm almost sure of it."

"No way!" Ellen took out a wooden spoon. "I've known Ezra since we were in school. Besides, he's two years younger than me."

"A few years one way or another doesn't mean a thing." Sadie poked Ellen's arm. "I wouldn't be surprised if Ezra doesn't ask your daed if he can start calling on you."

Ellen shook her head. "Even if Ezra wanted to, it'd be kind of hard for him to come calling on me when I'm here at the B&B working all the time."

"Well, you know what they say—'where there's a will, there's a way.'"

Ellen rolled her eyes. "Come on, Sadie. No more talk about Ezra Bontrager. Let's get to work."

CHAPTER 4

*E*llen sat at the desk in the kitchen, looking at the computer to confirm upcoming guests. It was hard to believe it was the last day of February. But on the other hand, the outside thermometer reading was a clear reminder that winter was far from over.

Ellen thought about the warm tropical breezes in Hawaii, and wondered if Mandy and Ken were outside, doing something fun today. They certainly deserved a little enjoyment. She knew from having visited the Williamses' organic chicken farm that the work could be tiring and demanding, so some relaxation was certainly needed on occasion.

Ellen remembered the day she and Mandy had gone over to swim in the Williamses' pool. She was a good swimmer and enjoyed herself, but poor Mandy, unable to swim at the time, feared the water. Ken volunteered to teach Mandy, and she caught on fairly quick. Those days had been fun and carefree, despite Ellen's longing for home.

Returning her focus to the upcoming B&B reservations, Ellen reflected on how things had been slow at the bed-and-breakfast the last few weeks. She wasn't complaining. It was only temporary and gave her more time to spend with family and friends. Last night she and Sadie had visited their friend Barbara Eash and enjoyed supper together.

Clicking the ballpoint pen in her hand, Ellen continued, deep in thought. *It's funny how things turn out in a way one never expects.* Barbara was happily married to Mandy's ex-boyfriend, Gideon, and they had a one-year-old baby girl they'd named Mary Jane. Had it not been for Mandy falling in love with Ken when they were stranded on Kauai, she might very well have married Gideon and be living here. Maybe not at this bed-and-breakfast, but somewhere in Middlebury.

Ellen turned off the computer and went to get a drink of water. As she stood looking out the kitchen window, the scene was breathtaking. Fresh-fallen snow coated everything in a powdery, glistening white, and big puffy clouds slowly parted to reveal an azure sky of blue.

A squirrel caught her attention as it bounded through the fluffy snow, leaving a small trail of tracks behind it. Then the critter stopped under a pine tree and stood on its hind legs to look around. His bushy tail was bent in a position reminding Ellen of a question mark.

I wonder what that little guy is thinking. Ellen watched as a slight whiff of breeze lifted and blew through the squirrel's thick gray tail.

Her gaze shifted higher in the tree, where she spotted something red. It was a beautiful cardinal sitting on the end of a pine bough, and even though muffled by the closed window, its *cheer, cheer, cheer* song reached her ears.

Ellen took the last gulp of water and gave one more glance out the window. "Oh my!" She watched in amazement as the cardinal flew off, sending a sprinkling of snow from the branch, down over the squirrel. Ellen giggled when the squirrel jumped up and took off running. "I'll bet that was cold. Wait till I tell Sadie about those critters."

It was moments like this that were fun to share. *Poor Mandy. She's missing all this winter beauty.* Ellen walked back to the desk and reached for the phone. *I need to call her and see how they are doing. They've been gone almost two months. Surely they must be ready to come home soon.*

✳

Kapaa

"Mandy, you're wanted on the phone," Vickie called from the kitchen. "You can take it on the living-room extension."

Mandy set the dust rag aside and picked up the receiver. "Aloha."

"Hi, Mandy, it's Ellen. I haven't heard from you in quite a while and wondered how you are doing."

Mandy took a seat in the recliner. "We're getting by, just busier than ever it seems." She paused and took a drink from her bottle of Hawaiian filtered water. "I'm sorry for not keeping in better touch, and I'm glad you called. I planned to call you as soon as I finished helping Vickie clean the house. Luana and Makaio are coming over for a barbecue this evening, so we wanted to get the cleaning done before we started getting things out for the meal."

"Sounds like fun. I thought about you earlier. Do you have time to talk now?"

"Yes, I have a few minutes," Mandy replied.

"I'm glad you're taking time out to do something enjoyable. How are Makaio and Luana?"

"They're both well, and keeping busy with the B&B. Are things busy there too?"

"It's slowed down a bit, but I'm sure things will pick up with spring just around the corner. Oh, and we had some snow overnight. You should see how beautiful it is right now. Your yard looks like a pretty Christmas card."

Mandy sighed. Along with missing everyone back home, she missed Indiana's winter beauty. Making snow angels didn't compare to making them in the sandy beaches of Hawaii—not that she had any free time to spend along the ocean's shore.

"Any idea when you'll be coming home?" Ellen asked.

Mandy clasped her knees tightly together. The back of her throat ached, making it hard to swallow. She reached for the bottle and took a drink.

"Mandy, are you still there?"

"Yes, I'm here."

"Oh, good. Thought maybe we'd been disconnected. Did you hear my question about when you might return to Middlebury?"

"Yes, I did—it's just that. . ." Mandy's voice trailed off.

"What's wrong? You sound *umgerennt*."

"I'm not really upset. I just dread giving you this news."

"What news? Is everyone there all right?"

"We are fine physically, but everyone's emotions are still scattered all over the place."

Mandy twirled a piece of hair around her fingers, then touched the flower pinned behind her left ear, signifying she was married. "You see. . . well, the thing is. . . Ken and I have discussed this at great length, and we feel a responsibility to stay here and help out."

"I understand, but for how much longer?"

"Indefinitely. Ken's mother can't manage without us, and Ken's brother wants her to sell the farm, because he doesn't want to run it anymore. In fact, he's talking about moving to California, where Rita's parents live."

"That's too bad. Would Vickie consider moving to Middlebury with you and Ken?"

"No, she is determined to keep the place. It's all she has left to remind her of Charles, and she feels he would not want her to sell out." Mandy spoke quietly, hoping Vickie couldn't hear her conversation from the kitchen. The last thing she wanted to do was make her mother-in-law feel guilty for keeping them here.

"So in order for us to stay on Kauai, we'll need to sell the B&B there."

Silence on the other end. Mandy knew her friend wouldn't take this news well. "Ellen, please say something."

"I...I'm stunned. When you and Ken left for Hawaii, I never dreamed you wouldn't be coming home. I thought..."

"We thought we'd be coming back too. But our circumstances have changed, and we feel it's God's will for us to stay on Kauai."

"I understand about family obligations, but what about your family here? Your parents and siblings will be disappointed when they hear this news."

Mandy's vision blurred as tears sprang to her eyes. "I'm going to miss them all terribly, but Ken and I can't be in two places at the same time. Maybe someday Mom and Dad, or one of my siblings can take a cruise and come here to visit. I'm sure they would fall in love with the island the way I did."

"Maybe, but they won't be able to stay. Their home is in Middlebury."

Mandy drew a couple of deep breaths, hoping not to break down. *Why does Ellen have to make this so difficult?*

"I don't mean to be selfish, but it's hard to think I may never see you again." Ellen sounded like she too was close to tears.

"We'll come home for visits," Mandy assured her. "Ken will have to hire someone to help out on the farm, and even if Ken's not free to leave the island, I'll fly home whenever I can."

"I'm sure you both feel like you're doing the right thing."

"Yes. Oh, and there's a couple more items I need to mention."

"What's that?"

"You're the first person we've told about this. None of my family knows our plans yet." Mandy cleared her throat. "Would you please not share this with anyone until I've let everyone else know?"

"Sure, Mandy. So what was the other thing you wanted to tell me?"

"We'll be contacting a Realtor to sell the B&B, but we'd like you to keep running the place—at least until the new owners take over. When that happens, then maybe you can continue working there if you want to."

"Oh, I see."

"If you'd prefer, we can close the bed-and-breakfast while it's up for sale." Mandy held her breath, waiting for her friend's answer. She hoped Ellen would be willing to keep the place open. She and Ken needed the extra income to help them pay to ship their personal things from the mainland to Kauai, and she didn't want Ellen to be out of a job.

"If it doesn't sell quickly, I may have to hire someone to help full-time. Sadie's been most generous to assist me in her free time, but with her working at the hardware store, I can't ask her to keep doing it indefinitely. I'm surprised she keeps going like she does."

"I understand. Feel free to use your discretion about whether to hire someone to help you there. Since Sadie is still helping you, go ahead and tell her our news, but just keep it between the two of you, until we've told my family."

"Okay."

Mandy heard the door to the kitchen open and saw Vickie enter the living room. "Umm, I'm sorry, Ellen, but I'd better go. I'll call you again soon and let you know how things are progressing."

"All right. Take care, Mandy, and tell everyone, including Luana and Makaio, I said hello."

"I will. Bye, Ellen." Mandy hung up the phone and sat slumped in her chair. As much as she loved it here on Kauai, she would miss her friends and family back home. It was hard to tell her best friend the sad news and even harder to ask Ellen to keep all this information a secret for some days ahead. Mandy would call her folks tomorrow and let them know the new plan. She dreaded hurting her parents, but it couldn't be helped. This would be a big adjustment for several people in her life. But Mandy felt confident she was supposed to be on this island, so she would take one day at a time and trust God to guide her and Ken.

✳

Middlebury

Ellen hung up the phone, leaned over, and bent into the pain. She couldn't imagine Mandy and Ken selling their beautiful bed-and-breakfast, much less making what could very well be their permanent home in Hawaii.

Ellen tried to soak it all in as the tears ran down her cheeks. When the B&B sold, she would probably be without a job, because the thought of working here without her friend, Mandy, was not pleasant. She never imagined this would happen. Just thinking about this change brought an ache to her heart. *Why do I have to lose one of my best friends? We had such a good thing here. Why, Lord?*

Ellen wept for several minutes and then forced herself to sit up. *It isn't right for me to be thinking only of myself. I could tell from talking to Mandy that she felt sad about selling the bed-and-breakfast. She and Ken are making a sacrifice to stay on Kauai and keep his parents' organic farm running. The least I can do is offer them my full support.*

Ellen reached for a tissue, dried her eyes, and blew her nose. Then another thought popped into her head. *Will I have to show the B&B to prospective owners, or will the Realtor Ken and Mandy hire do that? And if that's the case, how's it going to work if there are guests here?*

There were so many things to think about; it was hard not to feel overwhelmed. Ellen knew, however, that the best antidote for stress was prayer. So she bowed her head and closed her eyes. *Heavenly Father, You know what is best for Mandy and Ken, as well as Ken's mother and brother. I want to seek Your will in my life, so help me keep a positive attitude and remember to trust You in all things. Perhaps there is something better for me than working here at the Pleasant View Bed-and-Breakfast. Help me to be open to the plans You have for my life. Please watch over my dear friends in Hawaii, as they serve and trust You for their future.*

When Ellen opened her eyes, a sense of peace settled over her like being covered with a warm quilt. She didn't know what the future held for any of them, but felt confident that through it all, the Lord would be their guide.

CHAPTER 5

I still can't believe Mandy and Ken are selling this place," Sadie said Friday evening as she and Ellen put on their aprons, in preparation for baking.

"I know. The Realtor they contacted is coming by tomorrow morning to do a walk-through, which will help her figure out how much they can ask for the B&B." Ellen sniffed. "I'm trying to keep a good attitude, but I struggle not to cry every time I think about it. Everything went along so well, and now this."

"I don't understand why they couldn't keep the B&B and let you run the business like you're already doing." Sadie's chin jutted out. "A lot of people own a business in one state when they live in another. Besides, they might move back here someday. And if they sold the bed-and-breakfast, they'd have to start over."

"Mandy and Ken will need the money from this place when it sells to help out with their expenses staying on the island." Ellen pressed her palms against her chest. "I don't think they have any plans of coming back."

"I wonder if they'll come home for visits."

"Mandy said they would, but with a business to run, it will be difficult for them to get away very often."

"Maybe we could take another cruise and go see them sometime." Sadie's round face offered Ellen a hopeful-looking smile. "It's something to think about and maybe start planning for now."

"Guess we'll have to wait and see how it goes." Ellen gestured to the baking pans sitting on the counter. "In the meantime, we'd better start mixing, or the harvest loaf will never get done."

✳

At ten o'clock on Saturday morning, a dark blue car pulled up the driveway of the Pleasant View Bed-and-Breakfast. It was Ken and Mandy's Realtor, and Ellen wished she didn't have to answer the door. The woman had phoned the night before, saying she'd be coming by this morning to do a walk-through of the B&B. While this was necessary in order to put the place on the market, Ellen dreaded the process. It was one more reminder that Mandy and Ken weren't coming back. Nothing would be the same without them.

If whoever buys the B&B lets me keep working for them, maybe I won't feel so bad, Ellen thought as she made her way to the front door. *At least I'll still be doing the kind of work I enjoy, and in familiar surroundings.*

Ellen put a smile on her face and opened the front door just as the woman stepped onto the porch.

"Good morning, I'm Polly Stapleton."

"Please come in. I'm Ellen Lambright." She opened the door wider and stepped aside.

Polly paused in the entrance until the door was shut. "I didn't realize this place was run by Amish. I'm sure the business does nicely in our tourist area."

"Ken and Mandy are English, but I am Amish."

"Oh, I see." Polly looked about the room.

"During tourist season the B&B does a good business." Ellen put her best friend's interest ahead of her feelings. She wouldn't say anything to detract from the sale of the home.

"The bed-and-breakfast is in a good location and quite easy to find." Polly looked at the floors. "Is this wood flooring throughout most of the house?"

"Yes. Ken and Mandy had the kitchen floor sanded and finished after they moved in." Ellen watched the Realtor write down the information.

"I understand there are six bedrooms in this house." Polly turned to face Ellen. "How many of them are actually used for guests?"

"Five. There are three bedrooms down, and three upstairs. The owners have their own room and bath on one end of the house, and the other two downstairs rooms are for guests. Each of the rooms has its own bathroom," Ellen added. She gestured to the living room. "Would you like to look in there first, or do you want to start with the bedrooms?"

"Let's start with the kitchen, then work our way through the rest of the house."

"Please excuse the disarray. I cleaned out the utensil drawer earlier and haven't quite finished the project," Ellen commented.

"No problem." Polly placed her expensive-looking leather purse on the side table.

Ellen led the way, her heart sinking. This walk-through made selling the bed-and-breakfast official, and her resolve to keep a positive attitude was weakening.

✳

That evening, when Sadie showed up, Ellen's burden felt heavier. She tried to put on a happy face, but her friend saw right through it.

"Okay, what's wrong?" Sadie placed her hands on Ellen's shoulders. "I can see by the lines in your face and your slumped posture that you're upset about something."

"The real estate agent Mandy and Ken hired to sell the B&B was here this morning." Ellen sank into a chair at the kitchen table. "She'll put the place on the market within the next few days, and then it's just a matter of time before someone buys it." A deep sigh escaped her lips. "If I had enough money I'd purchase the B&B myself, but there's no way I could come up with a decent down payment, let alone make monthly payments. Even if I could afford to buy this home, it wouldn't be the same without our friend, Mandy."

"I understand the feeling. I'm not dealing well with this either." Sadie took a seat beside Ellen. "It's hard to accept change, isn't it?"

"Jah." Ellen's throat constricted. "It's difficult to trust God for my future."

Sadie rapped her knuckles against the table. "A few years from now we might both be married. Then we'll be focused on raising a family and feeling hopeful about our children's futures."

"Maybe so. Although right now, neither of us has a boyfriend, so marriage seems a long ways off—much less raising a family."

Sadie clasped her hands under her chin. "You may not have a steady beau now, but there's one young man who I believe would like to be your suitor."

"Who would that be?"

"Ezra Bontrager."

Ellen swatted the air. "Oh, not that again. If Ezra is looking for a woman to court, I'm sure it would be someone younger than me." She pushed her chair aside and stood. "Now let's get busy planning tomorrow's breakfast for the two guests that checked in this afternoon."

"All right, I'll change the topic for now." Sadie stood up and repositioned her *kapp*.

"What do you mean 'for now'?" Ellen's brows drew inward.

"Until Ezra is around here again, talking sweetly to you." Sadie giggled.

"Okay, you've had your fun." Ellen smiled and poked her friend's arm.

The phone rang, and Ellen picked up the receiver. "Pleasant View Bed-and-Breakfast." Since the computer wasn't on, she glanced at the guest reservation book lying next to the phone. Not fully trusting the computer's scheduling program, she used the book as a backup. "Yes, Mrs. Adams, the date you requested is confirmed. I have two rooms reserved for you and your family, and will look forward to seeing you next month."

When Ellen hung up the phone she looked over at Sadie and groaned. "What's going to happen if the B&B sells quickly? What if the new owners decide not to accommodate any of the guests that have reservations? They'll need time to settle in, won't they? What if they make all kinds of changes around here?"

"There, there, try to relax." Sadie patted Ellen's back. "You *druwwle* about things that may never happen. I'm sure whoever buys the bed-and-breakfast will be happy to have guests coming right away, because without people booking rooms, there would be no income."

Ellen moved her head slowly up and down. "You're right, Sadie. I do have a tendency to worry about things. I need to remember what

Psalm 55:22 says: 'Cast thy burden upon the Lord, and he shall sustain thee.'" She smiled. "If necessary, I'll quote that verse every day to remind myself not to worry, but cast my burdens on the Lord."

✳

Kapaa

"Are you sure you don't want something more to eat for lunch?" Mandy placed her hand on Ken's arm as they sat at the table on his mother's lanai. "You hardly ate a thing."

"The heat of the day's taken away my appetite," he replied. "I'm good with the fruit salad you served." Ken rose from his chair. "Besides, I want to check on those raised beds I built and see if I need to make any adjustments."

"That's fine, but could I say something first?"

"Sure. What's on your mind?" Ken sat back down.

"Since the B&B will be going on the market soon, I think it would be good if I go back to Middlebury and box up some things to be sent here. Most of our clothes are still there, as well as many personal items. I'd like to make plane reservations right away. Can you manage without my help for a week or two?"

"Yes, I'll manage. And you're right—we do need the rest of our clothes, not to mention anything else we don't want to sell with the B&B." Ken leaned over and kissed Mandy's forehead. "I wonder sometimes how I ever got along before I met you. The fact that you're willing to leave your family and friends on the mainland and relocate here to help mine speaks volumes."

She patted his arm. "My place is with you, Ken. Wherever you are is where I want to be." Remembering her wedding vows, Mandy whispered, "My sacred promise is to stay by your side as your faithful wife, in sickness and in health, in joy and in sorrow, through good times and bad. I further promise to love you without reservation, comfort you in times of distress, encourage you to achieve your goals, laugh with you and cry with you, grow with you in mind and spirit, always to be open and honest with you, and cherish you for as long as we both shall live."

Ken drew Mandy into his arms. "I thank the Lord for bringing you into my life. Had you and Ellen not become stranded on this island, I would never have experienced the joy of knowing you, my beautiful wife."

Mandy gazed into her husband's vibrant blue eyes. "I am thankful God brought you into my life as well. And I am confident that wherever we go and whatever we do, with you by my side and God at the center of our lives, we will find peace and happiness."

CHAPTER 6

Middlebury

Jt's so good to see you." As soon as Mandy entered the bed-and-breakfast, Ellen gave her a welcoming hug. "It seems like you've been gone forever."

"I know." Mandy swallowed hard, hoping tears wouldn't let loose and she'd be unable to stop crying. Being back in Middlebury, in the home she and Ken had bought soon after their marriage, was bittersweet. As much as she loved Hawaii, it was hard to think about leaving her family and friends once again.

The prospect of selling the B&B was also difficult. Their lovely home had been on the market for two weeks, and so far they'd received no offers. At least with Ellen running things, the business would stay open for guests while it was for sale. Mandy hoped when a buyer came along that the people would continue using the home as a bed-and-breakfast.

"How long can you stay before you have to go back to Hawaii?" Ellen asked, following Mandy into the living room, after she'd taken off her coat.

"My return flight is in two weeks, so that should give me enough time to go through everything, get it boxed up, and sent off to Kauai." Mandy blew out a noisy breath. "It could be a while before either Ken or I will be able to come back for another visit, so I'll want to spend some time with my family and other friends while I'm here too." She moved close to the fireplace, rubbing her hands. "Brr. . . I've been enjoying the warmth of Hawaii long enough to forget how cold it can be here this time of the year."

Ellen nodded. "I assume you've already seen your folks?"

"Oh, yes. They hired a driver and met me at the airport in South Bend."

Yawning, Mandy took a seat on the couch, and Ellen joined her. "Sorry. I'm kind of tired."

"Well, you did just fly over the ocean and several states. You'll have to get used to the time change too."

"You're right about that. It took me a week to adapt to Hawaii time, and now I'm back here and will need to readjust." Mandy yawned again, although she wasn't sure it was only the trip making her tired. All the extra work she'd been doing to help Ken and his mother was enough to exhaust anyone. They all worked on the farm from sunup to sunset. And now she had much to do here, which would also be tiring.

Mandy looked around. "The place looks nice. You're doing a great job keeping it spotless."

"You know me. I like to make sure everything is in its place." Ellen smiled.

"You've always been more organized than me." Mandy lifted her hands and let them fall. "I'm sorry to put you through all this, Ellen. Having the Realtor come by and having to make sure everything looks good so she can show the B&B to potential buyers can't be easy."

"It's okay. I'm doing it for my best friend, so don't give it another thought." Ellen gave Mandy another hug. "I'm so happy to see you."

"Same here."

"Sadie suggested the two of us plan another cruise to Hawaii so we can visit you on Kauai." Ellen stared down at her hands, resting in her lap. "I'm not sure when that would be, though. She has her job at the hardware store, and I'm working here right now, so it would be hard for either of us to take a trip anytime soon."

"I understand." Mandy reached over and clasped Ellen's hand. "You're my best friend, and no matter how many miles separate us, I'll never forget you. We must keep in touch through letters and phone calls. It will help us know how to pray for each other."

"If I'm still working here, or someplace else where there's a computer, we could email each other."

"True. I hadn't thought of that. Now aren't you glad Ken taught us both some basic computer skills?"

"Jah, but I'm not sure I'll ever get really good at it. I'm still leery of pushing a wrong key." Ellen glanced toward the window. "Did you hear a horse whinny outside?"

Mandy tipped her head. "I think so."

✳

Ezra could almost hear his knees knock together as he stood on the front porch of the Pleasant View Bed-and-Breakfast. Whenever he was in the same room with Ellen, he felt like a schoolboy with a crush on the teacher. Only Ellen wasn't his teacher. She was his boss's daughter, and a beautiful woman two years older than him. Every time he looked at her pretty blue eyes or shiny golden blond hair peeking out from under her kapp, his mouth went dry. Ezra was certain Ellen didn't realize his interest in her went beyond friendship, nor did Ellen's father. Ezra certainly would never have admitted it to anyone either. He'd be embarrassed if Ellen knew how he felt, and even more so if he asked to court her, and she turned him down.

He'd known Ellen since they were in school together, but because she was two years older, he'd never imagined them being anything but casual friends. *It's best I admire her from a distance and not let on for now, at least. If Ellen ever gives an indication of liking me, though, I might take the chance.*

Ezra remembered how one day when they were youngsters playing in the schoolyard, he'd gotten a splinter in his thumb and Ellen had removed it. Back then, they saw each other in church, but other than school and church, they'd never made contact. When Ezra became older and saw Ellen at a young people's event, he'd watch her and wish he had the nerve to talk to Ellen or ask her out. But he was too scared to approach the young woman and face rejection.

Pulling his shoulders back and drawing in a breath, Ezra knocked on the door. A few seconds later, Ellen answered.

He took a step to one side, and then two back, bumping the porch railing. "Oops." His cheeks warmed. *She must think I'm a klutz.*

"Guder owed." Ellen smiled. "What brings you by here this evening, Ezra?"

He lifted the paper sack in his hand. "I ate supper at your folks' house, and since your mamm knew I'd be comin' this way to go home, she asked if I'd stop in and give you this." Ezra handed her the sack.

"Let me guess. Mom made something for dinner with red sauce in it."

Ellen looked at Ezra with a sly grin.

"Why, yes. Earlier, when your mamm invited me to stay for dinner, she asked what I liked." Ezra's cheeks grew warm. "I told her stuffed peppers was one of my favorites, but how did you know there was red sauce?"

"Because you have a smudge of it on your face." Ellen pointed to her own face to show him where it was on his.

"Oh, oh." Ezra licked a finger and went over the spot. "Did I get it?"

"Jah, good enough. And don't worry about it," Ellen added. "When that happens to my daed, he always says, 'I'm saving it for later.' Now let's see what Mom has for me."

Ezra watched Ellen peek into the bag while he absentmindedly rubbed his face again.

"Yum. Mom sent me some chocolate whoopie pies. These will be nice to share with Mandy."

"Will you be sending them to her in Hawaii?"

Ellen shook her head. "Mandy's here now. She came back to get her and Ken's personal things, because they're staying in Hawaii for good."

"Your daed mentioned that." Ezra turned sideways and gestured to the FOR SALE sign out front. "What are you gonna do once this place is sold?"

Ellen shrugged. "I'm not sure. It all depends on who buys it and whether they want me to continue working here."

Since Ellen hadn't invited him inside, Ezra figured it was time to go. "Guess I'll be seein' you, Ellen. Maybe at the next young people's singing."

She'd barely said goodbye, when Ezra leaped off the porch and raced for his carriage. "If Ellen had any interest in me at all, she'd have invited me in to taste one of those whoopie pies," he mumbled, releasing his horse from the hitching rail. Most B&Bs in the area didn't have a designated place for visiting horse and buggies, but this one did, which made it nice for Ezra or any other Amish person who might come by.

As Ezra climbed into his buggy and headed for home, he had a little talk with himself. It wasn't the whoopie pies he wanted, for Nora Lambright had served some of those after supper this evening. The truth was, he'd hoped Ellen might invite him in so he could spend a little more time with her. *Of course*, Ezra reminded himself, *I'd have probably tripped over my own tongue trying to make a sensible conversation.*

He snapped the reins. "Giddy-up there, Harley. Let's get home. My mamm's probably wonderin' why I missed supper tonight."

As Ezra headed down the road, he grimaced. *I can't believe I showed up with red sauce on my face. How embarrassing.*

✳

"Who was at the door?" Mandy asked when Ellen returned to the living room.

"It was Ezra Bontrager. He had supper at my folks' place this evening, and my mamm asked him to drop off some chocolate whoopie pies for me on his way home." Ellen held up the paper sack. "In a little while, let's each have one with a cup of lavender tea." Ellen placed the sack on the coffee table and took a seat beside Mandy again.

"Isn't Ezra good friends with Sadie's brother?" Mandy asked.

"Jah, he and Saul have been hanging out with each other since eighth grade. And Ezra still works at my daed's shoe store."

Mandy nodded. "I've seen him there when I've gone to buy shoes. He's kind of quiet, but always polite." She pulled a throw pillow away from her back and scooched into the couch. "How old is Ezra anyway?"

"He's a couple years younger than the both of us, remember?"

"That's right. . . . I'm surprised he isn't courting someone by now. Ezra isn't too hard to look at, and he's earning himself a fair living." Mandy turned toward Ellen. "He could make a nice young woman a good catch."

"So what do you think you'll go through first?" Ellen quickly changed the subject.

"I haven't decided yet. I'll make some decisions in the morning." Mandy pointed to the sack of whoopie pies. "I'm ready for some of those now. Should I go to the kitchen and fix us some tea?"

"No, that's okay. Please stay here and rest. I'll be back soon with the tea and some napkins." Ellen hurried from the room.

Mandy leaned against the sofa cushions and closed her eyes. Even though it'd be hard to leave this home again, her place was in Hawaii with Ken. For the next two weeks, she would concentrate on packing up all their belongings, knowing after that, she'd return to her loving husband.

CHAPTER 7

I can't believe I've been here a whole week already. There's so much to do yet." Mandy rubbed her forehead and groaned. "I don't know about you, but I'm exhausted."

"It has been a job, but between me and your family you've had plenty of help." Ellen gestured to the boxes on the floor in front of where they knelt. "We've emptied all of the closets, gone through the garage, and made a place for anything left over your folks could put in a yard sale or give away to family or friends."

"Yes, and what a relief. I'm glad all the furniture is staying with the B&B." Mandy closed another box and marked on the outside what it contained. "I never realized how much work it would be to go through everything and make a decision as to what to keep and what to give away." Her shoulders sagged.

Ellen wished Mandy didn't have to return to Hawaii, and that she and her husband would come back to stay. But under the circumstances, their choice was for the best.

Ellen stared down at the boxes. *This is difficult, letting go of a good friend. But I need to be supportive and strong. Mandy is relying on me.*

Mandy gestured to the open box, full of Ken's clothing. "Since the Realtor is bringing someone by at noon, I'd better close this up. We need to be out of here before they show up."

Ellen nodded. "I'm glad Sadie and Barbara are free today and can meet us for lunch. It's been a long time since the four of us got together for a meal and a nice visit."

"You're right." Mandy smiled. "I'm looking forward to it."

*

Shipshewana, Indiana

Even with the clouds hanging low and snow in the forecast, Ellen looked forward to being with her friends. Drawing in the aromas of cooking meats and deep fried foods as she and Mandy entered the Fireside Café in Yoder's Shopping Center, she realized how hungry she was.

"Sadie and Barbara are over there." Ellen pointed to one of the tables. "I wonder if they've ordered already."

"Let's go see." Mandy followed as Ellen led the way.

A busy waitress heading toward the kitchen with a tray full of dirty plates, stepped between the two girls, nearly running into Mandy. The woman's eyes widened as she stopped in her tracks. "Pardon me, miss."

"It's okay." Mandy spoke pleasantly.

As they approached the table, Barbara and Sadie stood up and hugged Mandy.

Ellen's heart clenched when she saw tears gather in her friends' eyes. She struggled not to cry too. Today might be the last time they'd be together for some time. Surely, none of them would be going to Hawaii anytime soon, so they'd probably not meet as a group again until Mandy was able to make another trip to the mainland.

"Have you two placed your orders yet? I'm famished." Ellen hoped to lighten the mood.

Sadie shook her head. "We wanted to wait till you and Mandy got here. That way they'd bring all our food out together. Oh, and by the way—everyone's lunch is my treat today." She pointed her finger at Mandy. "And no arguments, please."

Mandy gave a small laugh. "Have I ever won an argument with you?"

"Well, maybe once." The flecks of green in Sadie's hazel-colored eyes became more pronounced when she chuckled and poked Mandy's arm.

Mandy snickered in response.

"Shall we take turns ordering, or should we all go up to the counter at once?" Barbara pushed a small piece of her nearly black hair back under her white head covering.

"Here's how we're going to do this." Sadie pulled a notebook and pen from her black-and-white quilted purse. "You can all write down what you want, and then I'll go place our orders. It only makes sense, since I'm the one who'll be paying."

Sadie waited until everyone wrote down their requests, then she headed for the counter.

Mandy took a seat beside Barbara, while Ellen sat across from them.

"Where's your cute little girl today?" Mandy asked. "I was hoping I'd get to see her."

"I left Mary Jane with Gideon's mamm. She's cutting another tooth and is kind of fussy, so I figured it'd be best not to bring her along." Barbara's blue eyes brightened as she told how her one-year-old girl had learned to walk. "She never tried to crawl. She just pulled herself up at the coffee table one day and took a few steps."

Mandy laughed. "I'm looking forward to being a mother someday."

"Parenting is a lot of work," Barbara said. "But the rewards are many, and I wouldn't trade motherhood for anything."

Ellen couldn't help but notice the look of longing on Mandy's face. She and Ken had been married over two years. No doubt she'd hoped to be pregnant by now. Well, at least Mandy had found a good man. It didn't take a genius to see that she and Ken were deeply in love.

Ellen tugged on her lower lip as she shuffled her feet under the table. *I wonder if I'll ever fall in love and get married. I'd like to find my soul mate, raise a family, and grow old together. But maybe it's not meant to be. I might end up like my aunt Ruth, in her sixties and still single.*

Sadie returned to the table and sat beside Ellen. "This feels like old times, doesn't it, ladies?"

They nodded.

"How are things in Hawaii, Mandy?" Barbara asked.

"The weather was beautiful when I left Kauai a week ago, but Ken, his mother, and I have been so busy since his dad passed away that we've barely had time to notice. I can't imagine how the two of them are managing while I'm gone."

"What about Ken's brother?" Sadie asked. "Wasn't he helping his dad with the chicken farm while you and Ken lived in Middlebury?"

"Yes, he was, but after Charles died, Dan didn't want to work there anymore." Mandy fiddled with her purse straps. "A few days before I left Kauai, Dan and his wife moved to California, where her parents live. Fortunately, they were renting, not buying a house."

Barbara's dark eyebrows furrowed. "He left his mother when she was in need? I can't imagine anyone doing such a thing."

"His actions might seem strange, but Dan took his dad's death pretty hard. In fact, he could barely function for the first several weeks. He and his wife talked it through and decided the best way for him to deal with everything was to leave the island—at least for a time." Mandy pursed her lips. "It was hard on his mother to see them go, but Vickie seemed to understand. And she appreciates having Ken and me there to help with the farm."

Sadie's shoulders drooped as she heaved a heavy sigh. "Hawaii is so beautiful. When we were all there, enjoying our vacation, it felt like I'd had a taste of paradise."

"It's always seemed that way to me," Mandy agreed. "But losing Ken's father dampened our spirits. To tell the truth, we haven't had time to do much of anything fun since it happened."

"Losing a loved one is always hard." Barbara clasped Mandy's hand. "I'll remember to pray for you, Ken, and his mother."

Mandy smiled. "Thank you."

A waitress came with their food, and the conversation turned to other things. Ellen felt thankful for this opportunity to be with her friends, but she couldn't help wondering how things were going at the bed-and-breakfast. Would the people who looked at it make an offer?

✳

Middlebury

Sunday morning dawned with a beautiful sunrise. Most of the snow in the area had melted, and a taste of spring was in the air. It put Ellen in a cheerful mood as she and Mandy headed down the road with her horse and buggy toward Gideon Eash's parents' house, where church would be held.

Seeing a FOR SALE sign as they went past a house took Ellen's thoughts in a different direction. The Realtor had called Mandy last evening, saying the couple who looked at the bed-and-breakfast realized they weren't ready to take on the commitment of running a business that would tie them down. Ellen wondered why they'd even bothered to look at the place if they understood all the work involved. It seemed like a waste of the agent's time, and the news had dampened Mandy's spirits. Selling the B&B would help her and Ken financially, and be one less thing to worry about as they focused on running Ken's father's business on Kauai.

Once more, Ellen wished she had enough money to buy their home. But apparently, it was not meant to be.

Fortunately, they hosted no guests right now, so she hadn't fixed the usual continental breakfast she prepared on Sundays when guests occupied rooms.

Ellen glanced at Mandy, sitting beside her in the front of the buggy with a faraway look in her eyes. "May I ask what's going through your mind right now?" Ellen took one hand off the reins and touched her friend's arm.

"Oh, reminiscing a bit." Mandy looked over at Ellen and smiled. "In some ways it seems like a long time ago that I drove a horse and buggy. In other ways, it feels like only yesterday when I sat in the driver's seat, guiding my horse down the road."

"Do you ever regret not joining the Amish church?" It was a question that had been on Ellen's mind for some time, but she'd never had the nerve to ask before.

"Sometimes, but I couldn't join the church and marry Ken, so I don't regret that. He's everything I've ever wanted in a husband, and I love him so much." Mandy spoke in a quiet voice.

Ellen nodded. "When you and I were stranded on Kauai, every time Ken came around, it was obvious that you two had fallen for each other." She relaxed her grip on the reins a bit, allowing her horse to pick up speed as they drew closer to the Eashes' place. "At first it upset me, because I was afraid if you two established a permanent relationship it would mean you'd become English and probably stay in Hawaii. But then, Ken chose to move here. So by the time you two got married, I'd accepted things and felt confident that even though we weren't both Amish, we could still remain friends."

Mandy's eyes glistened with tears. "And friends we shall always be. Our bond is as strong as if we were sisters."

Ellen couldn't argue with that. Ever since she and Mandy were children, they'd gotten along. As they grew into adulthood, their relationship had become even stronger. The distance between Hawaii and Indiana could never change that.

CHAPTER 8

Lihue
Kauai County, Hawaii

s Mandy's plane pulled up to the gate a little after three o'clock Tuesday afternoon, the FASTEN SEATBELT sign shut off. Passengers began assembling their belongings, whether from the overhead bins or under the seats in front of them. After retrieving her bag from the upper bin, Mandy remained in the aisle seat she had in coach. If she'd had the money for first-class seating, she would have been one of the first people off the plane. But that was okay. She was just glad to be home.

Mandy saw the flight attendant waiting by the door as a mobile bridge attached itself to the plane. She could hardly wait to see Ken. But the passengers ahead dillydallied down the aisle like slow cattle.

As she exited the security gate, Mandy heard a familiar voice call out to her. Her heart swelled and tears clogged her throat when she spotted Ken waiting. Mandy had missed her husband during the two weeks she spent in Indiana, but it didn't hit her how much until now. He looked so handsome in his blue-and-white Hawaiian-print shirt and navy blue shorts. Ken's skin had darkened in the two weeks she'd been gone, making his blond hair stand out even more.

"It's so good to have you home. I've missed you like crazy." He wrapped his arms around Mandy in a welcoming hug.

"I've missed you too." She stood on tiptoe and gave him a kiss, not even caring if they had an audience. *If I had joined the Amish church when my friends did, I would never display this much affection in public—even greeting my husband after an absence.* She glanced around. Several other couples were hugging and kissing. To them, she and Ken didn't look out of place or appear too forward.

They walked hand-in-hand to the baggage claim. As much as Mandy missed her family, being with her husband again was a reminder that here in Kauai was the place she needed to be. Whether in Hawaii or back in Indiana, when she was with Ken, it felt like home again.

In the baggage area, her husband picked off a suitcase from the conveyer belt. "I think this is your bag." Ken rolled the case up to Mandy.

"Nope, my bag is bigger and has a long scratch down the front." She giggled.

He slapped his forehead. "Oops, that's right. I'll go back and get the right one."

"Hang on. I'll go with you." Mandy smiled up at him.

"Well it's been a couple of weeks since I've seen the suitcase." He gave her a silly grin. "Anyway this bag is black and looks like all the rest."

Ken returned the case back on the moving belt, and soon after, a man came up and grabbed the bag. "I was wondering where my suitcase was." The man looked over his shoulder at Ken, as he darted off toward the car rental shuttles.

Mandy scanned the luggage and spotted her bag. "There it is Ken— next to that tan suitcase."

He grabbed the bag and rolled it over to her. "Now we have the right one."

Mandy unzipped the outer pocket. "Here's proof—my navy blue umbrella."

"If you hadn't caught my mistake, we could've taken the wrong suitcase home."

"That poor man would not have been happy." Mandy clutched Ken's arm as they headed for the parking lot.

"It was hard to be back in Middlebury again without you. Seeing our business for the last time and moving away from Indiana permanently was difficult too." Mandy let go of Ken's arm and clasped his hand.

"I figured it would be difficult. Wish I could've been there with you." He tenderly squeezed her fingers. "I appreciate all the hard work you did and that you hung in there until it was finished." His gentle voice was soothing to her soul.

"It would be nice to be able to be in two places at once."

"Yeah." Ken's blond hair blew in the breeze. "Sometime in the future we'll plan a trip to Indiana."

"I hope so. We both work hard, and it would be fun to go there for a relaxing vacation next time."

"By then the B&B will belong to someone else, and maybe we'll have our own house here. Mom's been good about letting us stay with her, but she needs her space—and so do we."

"I can't wait to pick out a permanent home together, but it can wait. There's plenty of room at your mom's house, so at least we aren't crowding each other." Mandy stepped aside while Ken opened the door of their camo rig and put her suitcase inside.

"Are you hungry? Should we stop somewhere for a bite to eat before we go home?" Ken asked.

Her heart skipped a beat when she looked into the depth of his eyes. "That would be nice. I didn't have much to eat on the plane, and the few snacks I brought along didn't fill me enough." She gripped his hand tightly. It felt warm and comforting. "A late lunch sounds great."

"Okay. Let's stop at the Lemongrass Grill in Kapaa. While we eat, you can fill me in on everything that's been going on in Middlebury."

Mandy smiled. "I will. And you can catch me up on everything that's been happening here during my absence."

✳

Kapaa

Mandy stared at the menu their hostess handed them. So many mouthwatering choices. She enjoyed coming to this Pan-Asian eatery with pagoda-inspired décor.

Mandy had a favorite she'd ordered before, but today she might try something different. The server brought them ice water and asked what they'd like to drink. They both ordered iced tea with lemon, but since they weren't certain what they wanted to eat yet, the middle-aged waitress said she'd return in a couple of minutes.

"Would you like an appetizer, Mandy?" Ken asked. "We could share some lobster ravioli, if that sounds appealing."

Mandy licked her lips. "Sounds good."

When the waitress returned, she placed the iced teas by their napkins. Ken put in their appetizer order, and also the guava barbecued ribs for his entrée. Mandy ordered shrimp scampi—one of her favorite island meals.

While they waited for their food, Mandy filled Ken in on how things went with her family, as well as at the B&B. "Someone came to look at it while I was there, but they weren't interested in buying our business."

"The right buyer will come along." Ken leaned closer to Mandy and whispered, "I said this before, but it bears repeating. I missed you so much, and I'm glad the Lord brought you safely back to me. I can't imagine my life without you."

Sitting beside Ken, Mandy rested her head on his shoulder. "I feel the same way about you."

When their waitress brought the appetizer, Ken and Mandy bowed their heads for silent prayer. While Ken often prayed out loud, they sometimes prayed silently for their meals. Ken called it "praying Amish," since that's the way Mandy had grown up saying her prayers.

After their prayer ended and they'd begun eating the lobster ravioli, Ken told Mandy how things went on the farm. "The chickens are laying well right now." He blotted his mouth with the dinner napkin. "We've been keeping our regular stores supplied, as well as the Palm's Bed-and-Breakfast."

Mandy paused from eating to sip her water. "How have Luana and Makaio been doing since I've been gone?"

"As far as I know they're getting along well. My mom went over the other day with some eggs, and when she came back she said Luana's daughter, Aliana, is expecting another baby."

"I'm sure the Palus must be excited about having a second grandchild." Mandy smiled. She hoped it didn't seem forced. It was difficult not to be envious, when she wanted a baby so bad. But maybe there was a reason she hadn't gotten pregnant yet. With all the things at the organic farm keeping her busy, it was probably best that she wasn't expecting a baby right now. Someday, though, when the time was right, Mandy hoped she and Ken would become parents.

*

Middlebury

It was almost eight thirty in the evening when the doorbell rang. Ellen went to answer it, figuring the guests who had reserved two rooms were probably on the porch. Gwen Adams had called over an hour ago, saying their plane had gotten in late and they were waiting to pick up a rental car.

Ellen opened the door. A woman and a man with two teenage girls waited, each holding a suitcase.

"Hello. I'm Lew Adams." The man reached out his hand. "Glad we finally made it."

Ellen shook hands with the family. "Welcome to the Pleasant View Bed-and-Breakfast. Please, come in and I'll show you to your rooms."

When the family entered the living room, Mr. Adams looked around, as though studying every detail. "I noticed a FOR SALE sign out front," he said. "Would you mind telling me the reason you're selling the place?"

His wife nudged his arm. "I can't believe you asked that question, Lew. It's none of our business why this home is being sold."

His lips quivered slightly as his nose creased. "I want to know a few details. Figured you would too, since. . ." He stopped talking and turned to face Ellen. "How much are you asking for the business?"

"Actually, this home is not mine. I'm managing it for the owners who have moved to Kauai, Hawaii. You would need to contact their Realtor for details on the price." Ellen opened the drawer of the end table near the couch and took out one of Polly's business cards. "Here's her contact information."

"Hmm. . ." Mr. Adams studied the business card. "We're thinking of relocating to this area, and Gwen has often talked about owning a bed-and-breakfast." He looked at his wife. "What do you think, dear? Wouldn't it be nice to own a place like this?"

Before Gwen could respond, one of the girls spoke up. "I don't wanna live in a B&B, Dad. We'd have no privacy. Besides, what kind of cute guys live in this small town anyway?"

"Really, Susan, you're only concerned about your love life? Dad's idea sounds like fun to me," her sister commented. "In fact, it'd be a new adventure."

Susan rolled her eyes. "You would say that, Jill. You're eager to move out of Chicago and start over somewhere else." She sighed, then took her cell phone from her purse. "I'd miss all of my friends, school, and all the cool places to shop for the trendiest styles. Oh, and you have no idea how much work would be involved if Mom and Dad bought a bed-and-breakfast."

Jill folded her arms, squinting as she stood almost nose-to-nose with her sister. "How do you know about B&Bs and how much work is involved in running one? And why do you have to throw cold water on everything, Susan?"

"I don't, but you—"

Their father stepped between them. "We don't need to talk about this tonight. In the morning, though, I would appreciate the opportunity to walk through the whole house. If I like what I see, I may get in touch with the real estate agent for more details."

Ellen sucked in her breath. *If these people should decide to buy Ken and Mandy's B&B, I could be out of a job, because with two teenage girls, I doubt they'd need me to work here anymore.*

Chapter 9

By the middle of May, Lew and Gwen Adams had moved into the bed-and-breakfast as its new owners, and Ellen was out of a job. The couple's daughters would be helping their parents during the hours they weren't in school. Ellen had graciously offered to explain how she'd been running things in Mandy and Ken's absence, but Mrs. Adams stated she had her own way of doing things and would figure it out.

A week ago, Ellen had moved back to her parents' house, but she still hadn't found another job. She'd driven by the bed-and-breakfast yesterday on her way to the grocery store in Shipshewana. The spacious home looked pretty much the same on the outside, but she had a hunch the inside may have changed.

Ellen saw new potted plants near the front flower bed, and more along the driveway. She wondered how much other vegetation the owners would add.

During the time the Adamses had stayed at the B&B, Gwen made it obvious that she was contemplating things she would change if she lived there. She never mentioned anything specific, but a few times Ellen caught her standing in the living room or dining room, looking around as though deep in thought.

Everyone does things differently, Ellen reminded herself as she put her head covering in place. *I need to stop pining for what obviously wasn't meant to be and move forward with my life.*

Right now, her immediate need was to go outside and get her horse and buggy ready for the trip to the Blue Gate Restaurant, where she would meet Sadie for breakfast. Since Saturdays were Sadie's day off, this was a good time for them to get together.

✳

Shipshewana

"I'm not sure what you're having, but the breakfast buffet is what I'm leaning toward." Sadie looked across the table at Ellen and grinned.

"It would probably be good, but I'm not all that hungry this morning." Ellen glanced out the window, then back again. "I may have a bowl of oatmeal."

"Is that all? Don't you want to order some toast to go with it?"

Ellen shook her head, feeling a little put out with her friend's mothering.

"Are you still depressed about losing your job at the B&B?"

"Jah. I probably shouldn't panic, because it's only been a week, but I haven't found anything yet."

"Well, not to worry. I may have the answer for you." Sadie leaned forward, resting her elbows on the table. "A part-time position at the hardware store has opened up. They'll be interviewing people today and Monday. If you're interested in working there, that is."

Ellen's lips pressed together as she thought about her options. Working at a hardware store was not at the top of her list, but no jobs were available at any of the bed-and-breakfasts or hotels in the area.

"I'll give it some thought, Sadie, but I probably won't put in my application today."

"How come?"

"I promised to run several errands for my mamm, and then I need to get home and help her and my younger sister do some gardening."

"Okay, but I'd make sure to go first thing Monday morning. You don't want to miss the opportunity for a job."

Once again, Ellen felt like Sadie was being too pushy. She most likely meant well, so Ellen made no comment.

Their waitress came, and Sadie chose the buffet, along with her drink. Ellen chose a beverage, and was about to order oatmeal, but changed her mind. "Guess I'll have the buffet too. The line has gone down some. I hope there's still a good variety left."

Their waitress smiled. "It has been busy since we opened this morning, but don't worry. There's plenty of food waiting for you."

Ellen and Sadie got up and headed for the buffet. When they returned to the table, they offered silent prayers.

"Have you heard anything from Mandy lately?" Sadie picked up a piece of bacon.

"Not since last week when I called to inform her that the new owners had moved into the bed-and-breakfast." Ellen took a drink of water and swallowed hard. Thinking about how difficult it had been to leave a job she'd enjoyed made her stomach knot up.

✳

Middlebury

"I can't wait to pick your sisters up at the train station in Elkhart Monday morning."

Ellen heard the excitement in her mother's voice. Ruby, who was twenty, and Darla, seventeen, had been working at a restaurant in Sarasota, Florida, all winter and were finally coming home. Normally the girls returned to Indiana in April, but this year they'd chosen to stay an extra month. Ellen couldn't blame them. The weather in Florida, similar to Hawaii, was beautiful this time of the year. If it hadn't been for her job at the B&B, Ellen might have tried to get a job for the winter in Sarasota too. At least Darla and Ruby hadn't had to deal with snow during the winter.

The girls would return to their jobs as waitresses at the Amish-style restaurant in Middlebury, where they would work until late fall.

I'm sure when I see my sisters they'll be sporting nice tans from all that Florida sunshine. They will probably look healthy compared to my pale face. Ellen filled a pot with water, set it on the burner, and lit the propane stove. She watched her mother grab the bread-and-butter pickles from the refrigerator. Mom liked to can them in the summer, and the family ate the delicious pickles year-round.

"I'll need to bring up some more *bickels* from the basement, since this is the last jar upstairs," Mom commented.

"I can get you some when I'm done peeling the potatoes." Ellen placed another peeled spud on the cutting board, quartered it, and tossed the pieces in a bowl with the others.

"No hurry, I'll get them after we eat dinner." Mom arranged the pickle slices on a glass tray. "Will you be free to go with us to pick up your sisters?"

Ellen was on the verge of saying she couldn't go because she'd be applying for a job at the hardware store Monday morning. But the interview could wait until Monday afternoon. Darla and Ruby would expect everyone in the family to greet them when they stepped off the train, and Ellen wouldn't let her sisters down.

Usually, the girls went to and from Florida on the Pioneer Trails bus. But they wanted to try something different and come home on the train this time.

Perhaps my sisters would like to go to Hawaii with me sometime, Ellen thought as she grabbed another potato. *If they like Sarasota, I'm sure they'd fall in love with the Hawaiian Islands. Maybe by the time we're all ready to go, Lenore will be old enough to join us.*

Ellen figured returning to Hawaii was a silly dream, but it was fun to have a goal, even if it never came about.

Mom put the jar of pickles away and checked on the meat simmering in a pan on the stove.

"Something smells good in here, ladies. What's for supper?" Ellen's father sniffed the air as he entered the kitchen.

"Lemon chicken and mashed potatoes." Mom pointed to some glass jars on the counter. "And canned green beans from last year."

"I got the recipe for the chicken when I was on Kauai with Mandy," Ellen interjected.

"Sounds real tasty." He jiggled his bushy eyebrows. "How soon till we eat?"

"The chicken's almost done, and Ellen has the potatoes boiling on the stove. All I need to do yet is open two jars of beans and get them heated." Mom smiled. "Lenore's in the dining room setting the table, so by the time you get washed up we should be ready to eat."

"All right then. I'll see you at the table." Grinning widely, Dad sashayed out of the room. He was in an exceptionally good mood this evening. Perhaps it had been a profitable day at the store.

"The table is set. What else can I help with?" Lenore came in and stood next to Mom.

"You can put the lemon chicken on a platter and cover it with foil to keep warm." Mom pointed to the spare tongs on the counter.

A short time later, supper was on the table. Everyone was about to sit down when someone knocked on the front door.

"I'll get it." Lenore hurried out of the room. When she returned, Ezra was with her.

"Sorry for the interruption." Tugging the brim of his hat, Ezra handed Dad his lunchbox. "You left the store without this." He shifted from one foot to the other. "Figured you might want to have it come Monday morning."

"Danki, Ezra." Dad pointed to an empty chair at the table. "If you haven't eaten yet, why don't you join us?"

Ezra gave his shirt collar a tug. "Well, I. . ."

"Come on, son. I bet you're *hungerich*."

"I can't deny my hunger, but I don't wanna barge in."

"There's always room for one more at our table," Mom spoke up. "If your mamm's not expecting you for supper, we'd be happy to have you join us."

"My folks went out to eat this evening, so I'm on my own. Figured I'd make a sandwich when I got home, but what your havin' smells a lot better than a hunk of bologna between two slices of bread."

"Come on, then, you can take the seat over there beside Ellen."

Ezra rubbed the back of his neck. "Jah, okay." A splotch of pink erupted on his cheeks as he made his way over and sat down awkwardly. For some reason, Ezra seemed a bit nervous this evening.

Lenore looked over at Ellen and rolled her brown eyes, but at least she didn't say anything. Ellen could almost imagine what her little sister might be thinking.

After everyone prayed, Mom picked up the first plate of food to pass around the table.

Ezra looked at Dad. "Your *fraa. . . Sie is en gudi Koch*."

"You're right, Ezra. My wife's a real good cook." Dad motioned to Ellen. "And so is my oldest dochder, who cooked the chicken. Ellen will make a fine fraa for some lucky fellow someday."

Ellen's face heated. She wished she could make herself disappear. What was her outspoken father trying to do—get Ezra to become interested in her?

She squirmed in her chair as Ezra's dark eyes darted from side to side. *How embarrassing. I'll bet poor Ezra wishes he'd gone home and fixed a cold sandwich.*

Ellen glanced at her father, sitting at the head of the table with a smug-looking smile on his bearded face. *I hope Dad's not trying to play matchmaker. If so, he's barking up the wrong tree, for Ezra and I have nothing in common.*

CHAPTER 10

*M*onday morning Ellen awoke with a headache. The pain in her forehead was almost intolerable—like the car horn she'd heard blaring the other day across the street from the Blue Gate Restaurant. Even so, she wouldn't let it stop her from applying for a job at the hardware store or going to Elkhart to greet her sisters' train.

When Ellen stepped into the kitchen, Dad handed her a slip of paper. "When I went to the phone shack to check for messages, I found one for you. Wrote it down to make sure I got it right."

Ellen grimaced as she silently read the note.

"What's wrong?" Mom moved across the room and placed her hand on Ellen's shoulder. "You look *umgerennt*."

"The message is from Sadie. It seems the part-time position she told me about has been filled." Using the tips of her fingers, Ellen made tiny circles across her forehead. "Guess I'll have to keep on looking."

Dad poured a cup of coffee and handed it to Ellen. "If we had more work at the shoe store right now you could help out there, but for the past few weeks there's only been enough to keep Ezra and me busy."

Ellen shook her head. "It's okay, Dad. I'm sure something will open up for me soon." She handed the cup back to him. "Did you forget that I don't care much for *kaffi*? I usually drink *tee*."

"Oh, you're right." Dad reached under his hat and scratched his head. *"Ich bin allfatt am eppes vergesse."*

"You're not always forgetting something, Nathan." Mom chuckled, giving his arm a tap. "Only certain things you can't remember."

He nodded. "It's what happens when a person gets old. Sometimes I feel like *en aldi schachdel*."

Lenore poked her head into the kitchen. "You're not an old and worn-out cow, *Daadi*."

"*Jah*, I am. See here—I have the *runsele* to prove it." With a deep laugh, he touched the wrinkles on his forehead.

Ellen couldn't help smiling. Dad could be such a character at times. She felt fortunate to have good parents. They both tried to keep a positive attitude, even during difficult times.

I should try to be more cheerful. As Ellen reached for the aspirin bottle and took some pills for her headache, she reflected on Proverbs 17:22: *"A merry heart doeth good like a medicine; but a broken spirit drieth the bones."* If she didn't find a job soon, she would need to quote the verse often to remind herself to think positively and look for things to laugh about.

✳

Elkhart, Indiana

A wisp of Darla's dark hair blew in the breeze as she and Ruby stepped off the train with their satchels in hand.

Ellen let Mom, Dad, and Lenore greet the girls before she gave them big hugs. "Welcome home, Sisters. You're both so tan. How was your trip?"

"It was good. I enjoyed riding on the train more than the bus." Ruby's blue eyes twinkled. "Think I might travel the same way when I return to Sarasota this winter."

"Same here." Darla pushed a few hairs hanging loose back under her kapp. "I'm glad we'll have a few days off before we start working at the restaurant in Middlebury again. I want to spend a little time with some of my friends and get caught up on my rest."

Ruby slipped her arm around Ellen's waist. "You look *mied*. Have you been working too hard at the bed-and-breakfast?"

Ellen shook her head. "I'm not managing the place anymore. When you and Mom talked on the phone the last time, didn't she tell you the B&B sold?"

"*Jah*, but I figured you'd keep working there with the new owners."

"No, they have two teenage daughters who'll be helping them, so I'm currently unemployed."

"Oh, Ellen, I'm sorry." Darla's sympathetic tone conveyed how much she cared.

"I'll check at the restaurant and see if they might be hiring." Ruby gave Ellen's shoulder a pat. "It would be nice if you could work there too."

Ellen shrugged. "We'll have to see how it goes." Truthfully, she didn't want to work as a waitress, but then she shouldn't be picky—especially now.

"Come on, girls, let's get your luggage," Dad said. "You can continue your conversation on the way home."

They moved over to the section of the train where their luggage had been stowed, and watched as it was removed and placed on the ground. Dad waited for some folks ahead of him to get their suitcases.

Ellen watched a mother and her young daughter grab their matching flowered bags. As they walked away, she noticed how cute the little girl's tiny case was.

Dad stepped forward and picked both girls' suitcases up at the same time. Groaning, he quickly set them back down. "Oh, boy—my hernia's bothering me again."

"Again?" Mom's eyes narrowed. "How long has this been going on, Nathan? And why haven't you mentioned anything about having a hernia before?"

Scrunching his face, he placed both hands against his abdomen. "It's been bothering me awhile but never hurt this bad before." He looked over at Ruby. "It might be better if you girls get your own luggage to the van."

"Of course, Dad. You need to take it easy."

Darla and Ruby picked up their suitcases and followed Mom and Dad across the parking lot. Ellen and Lenore walked behind.

When they got to the van, Mom followed Dad around to the door and opened it for him. "Now, take your time getting in, Nathan. I'm right here to lean on."

"Danki, Nora, but I can do this myself." It was all Dad could do to get in the passenger's seat up front. Roy Steffy, their driver, got out and put Darla and Ruby's suitcases in the back of the van, while Ellen, her three sisters, and Mom took seats in the middle of the vehicle.

"Did something happen to you, Nathan?" Roy closed the driver's door and started the van.

"It's my hernia acting up. I shouldn't have picked up both suitcases at the same time."

"Yep, a hernia can sure be a nuisance, especially if it worsens over time." Roy glanced at him, then pulled the vehicle out of the parking lot.

"I think you should see the doctor." Mom tapped Dad's shoulder.

"Don't worry. I'm sure I'll be fine once we get home."

"I hope so, but if it doesn't quit hurting, I hope you'll—"

"Okay, Nora, whatever you say."

Mom looked over at Ellen and rolled her eyes.

Reduced to an annoying dull ache, Ellen's headache was almost forgotten. She was concerned about her father, who never complained and rarely got sick. From the way Mom sat, with lips compressed and hands clasped tightly together in her lap, Ellen was certain she was still worried about Dad. No doubt she'd be calling the doctor tomorrow morning, and Dad would have no choice but to go to the appointment.

Ellen bit her lip as they drove over the Elkhart River. She hadn't seen her father in this shape before and wondered if it was serious. Perhaps the doctor would suggest surgery to repair the hernia. If so, how long would her father be out of commission?

✷

Middlebury

Ezra brought his lunch to work and decided to eat it outside in the shade, since the store was quiet. He watched the neighbor's little dog come over, wagging its tail. *If Nathan doesn't show up soon, and it gets busy in the store, I hope I'll manage okay.* He gave the pup some chips and patted its head. "Thanks for keeping me company during my break, little guy."

When a buggy came by, Ezra looked to see if it was Nathan, but the rig kept going. *I wonder what is keeping my boss. Usually you can set a pocket watch to his punctuality.*

Ezra ate his lunch and went back to the store. He'd finished washing up when he looked out the window and saw a car pull in. An elderly

English man got out and headed for the store with a pair of old boots.

"Good afternoon," Ezra said when the man placed the boots on the counter.

"Hello, young man. I need these repaired. Do ya do that sort of thing here?" The man squinted through his glasses.

"Sorry, but we only sell new shoes." Ezra reached into his pocket, pulled out a hanky, and wiped his damp forehead. "But a couple of shops in Elkhart repair shoes, as well as a few in surrounding towns. Maybe one of them can help you out."

"Okay then, I'll look them up." The man turned around, and was almost out the door, when he stopped. "If I can't get these fixed, I'll probably be back to look at what you have here in this store." He gave a wave and closed the door.

Ezra glanced at the battery-operated clock, across from the counter where he stood. It was one o'clock. Nathan should have been here by now, even if he'd stayed at the house to have lunch after picking Darla and Ruby up at the train station.

Fortunately, not too many customers had stopped by during the morning hours. But even with the ones who had come to shop, Ezra kept busy—either running back and forth between the store and the shed where they kept a surplus of shoes or waiting on customers. He was glad he didn't have to work by himself at the store every day. A business like this was too much for one person to run.

Some days when lots of customers came in, Ezra wished Nathan would hire another employee. With three people working in the store, it would take some pressure off Ezra so he'd feel free to ask for a day off. As it was, he had to run all his errands in the late afternoon or every other Saturday, when the shoe store was closed. If he had to schedule a doctor or dentist appointment, that was even more difficult. None of the doctors in the area were open on Saturday, and some didn't even work on Fridays. So Ezra's only alternative was to ask for time off when he had a medical appointment.

The front door opened, and an Amish family with six children entered the store. Ezra had seen them before, but they didn't live nearby, and he didn't know their names.

Oh, boy. His cheeks felt a flush of heat. *What I could use right now is a helper.* Ezra rubbed his forehead. *If they all want shoes, I'm in big trouble.*

"May I help you?" he asked, stepping out from behind the counter.

The man nodded. "I need a new pair of work boots." He gestured to the woman standing close to his side. "And my *fraa* and most of our *kinner* need shoes to wear for chores and gardening."

"Okay, I'll see what I can find."

Ezra was busy helping the man's wife choose a pair of shoes, when Ellen entered the store. "When you have a minute, I need to talk to you." Her pinched expression portrayed worry as she moved closer to Ezra.

"Sure, I'll be with you in a few minutes." Ezra finished up and then excused himself, saying he'd be back to fit the woman's children for shoes.

He motioned for Ellen to join him behind the counter. "What is it?"

Tugging on the strings of her head covering, Ellen spoke quietly. "My *daed* hurt himself when he tried to pick up my sister's suitcases at the train station this morning. He admitted to Mom that he has a hernia, and when we got home he hurt so bad he had to lie down."

Ezra's forehead wrinkled. "Sorry to hear it."

"Needless to say, he won't be able to work this afternoon, so he wants you to be in charge." Taking a deep breath, Ellen continued. "Mom will be calling the doctor to see how soon we can get him in."

"Oh, boy. Sure hope I can manage things on my own." Ezra's head filled with fuzzy thoughts.

Ellen touched his arm briefly, before pulling her hand aside. "I can see business is heavy right now. Would you like me to stay and help out till closing time?"

He nodded, feeling a sudden release of tension. "*Danki*, Ellen. You showed up at just the right time."

CHAPTER 11

"How are you feeling?" Ellen asked when her father came into the kitchen Tuesday morning.

"I'm doin' all right." Holding his hand against his stomach, he moved slowly across the room and took the coffee pot from the stove.

"Are you still in pain?" Ellen sat at the table, sipping a cup of hot tea.

"Some. But it doesn't hurt too much, as long as I don't pick up anything heavy or move the wrong way." With a groan he couldn't conceal, he lowered himself into a chair at the table.

"Where's Mom? Is she still in bed?"

He shook his head. "She got up before me, dressed, and headed outside. Said something about checking for phone messages."

"I bet she went to the phone shack to make you a doctor's appointment," Ruby spoke up from across the room, where she was thumbing through the calendar pages.

"Actually, Mom called the doctor's office yesterday to see about getting an appointment," Ellen said. Annoyance flitted across Dad's face. "Since they didn't call back yesterday, she's hoping to hear something this morning."

Dad's brows furrowed. "Don't need a doctor to tell me what's wrong. I don't have time to go either. Ezra can't run the store by himself." He lifted his gaze toward the clock. "That young man is used to me being there to run things and answer any questions he might have."

"Ezra will have to get through the day without you, because your health comes first," Ellen was quick to respond.

"Better not put the buggy before the horse, Dad." Ruby shook her head. "Maybe what you're dealing with isn't a hernia at all."

His lips compressed. "Jah, it is. I had a hernia once, before you were

70

born, and I'm almost 100 percent sure it's happened again. But this time it involves another place on my *bauch*."

"Where on your stomach, Daadi?" Lenore asked when she came into the kitchen.

Dad touched a spot above his waist. "It not only hurts, but if I pulled up my shirt, you'd see the protrusion."

"No need for that." Ruby held up her hand and made a face. "Stuff like that makes me squeamish."

Dad snickered. "I was only kidding. Wouldn't wanna scare you girls."

Mom entered the kitchen through the back door and slipped off her shoes. "Good news! Dr. McGrath can see you at eleven o'clock this morning. The office left a message, so I called to confirm the appointment."

Dad frowned, shuffling his feet under the table. "That won't work, Nora. Did ya forget I'll be working at the store?"

"It's the only time he can see you today, and we're lucky you got an appointment so soon." Mom moved across the room and placed her hands on his shoulders. "They had a cancellation, and I told them we'd take it."

"Okay, okay." Dad looked at Ellen. "Would you mind filling in for me today? Ezra will be expecting me to show up." He released a heavy sigh. "He'll need to know what's going on."

"Well, I . . ."

"Ezra will be in charge, so you shouldn't have a lot to do."

Ellen gave a nod. "Okay, Dad. I'll head over to the store as soon as I've had breakfast."

✳

Ezra looked at the clock on the wall near the counter. *Nathan should have been here thirty minutes ago. I wonder what's keeping him this morning.* It wasn't like his boss to be late for work. *Could Nathan still be hurting?*

Another fifteen minutes went by, and Ezra began to pace. So far no customers had shown up, which was good. Things could be hectic if several people showed up and he was the only one here.

What am I thinking? Ezra smacked his forehead with the palm of his hand. *I should be worried about my boss, not about being here by myself.*

He glanced out the front window and saw Ellen pedaling in on her bike. *Oh, boy. I bet her being here means he's not coming again today.* Ezra hoped Ellen would listen to his requests and not try to do things her own way. *She's a little stubborn but one of the prettiest young women in Middlebury. Ellen's golden blond hair and sparkling blue eyes bring out the beauty on her heart-shaped face.*

Ezra waited at the counter, tapping his boot against the wooden floor. *Maybe I have a chance to win her since we'll be working together again.*

When Ellen entered the shop, she walked up to Ezra with furrowed brows. "My daed's seeing the doctor today, so you're in charge again, and I'm here to take his place."

Ezra turned and looked at the clock again. "Then how come you're late? This is your daed's shop. Don't ya know what time it opens for business?" The thought of having Ellen here to help out again made his stomach tighten. And with her standing so close, Ezra felt like his knees might buckle.

"When I got up this morning I didn't know Dad wouldn't be working today, or that he would ask me to fill in for him again." Her forehead creased. "It took a while to get here." She reached into her purse and pulled out a slip of paper. "Here's a list Dad made out for you. Want me to read it?"

Ezra clenched his teeth. "No, thanks. I can read it myself." He stepped behind the counter and took a seat on the wooden stool. He and Ellen were off to a bad start. At this rate, he'd never get her to like him.

✳

Ellen's face tightened. *Why is Ezra so testy with me? I'd better find something to do. If nothing else, I can sweep the floors and do some cleaning.*

Ellen started in the direction of the back room, where cleaning supplies were kept, but stopped walking and turned around when Ezra called out to her.

"Say, where ya goin'?"

"To get the broom so I can sweep the floors."

He shook his head. "That's not necessary. I'd rather you put some of the new shoes we got in last week on the shelves."

"Okay, I'll do it after I'm done sweeping."

Ezra stepped out from behind the counter, planting his feet in a wide stance. "Thought I was supposed to be in charge today. Isn't that what you said before?"

"Jah, he did, but. . ."

"Then I'd appreciate it if you do as I say."

A rush of adrenaline tingled through Ellen's body. She couldn't believe Ezra's bossy attitude. Who did he think he was, talking to her that way? After all, this was Dad's store, not his. Besides, it wasn't as if she'd never worked here before. During her early teens, Ellen had spent the summer months helping Dad in the shoe store, so she understood a thing or two about the business. By rights she should be the one in charge. But then, she wasn't a full-time employee, and Ezra had worked here for the past few years.

Ezra tapped his foot, never losing eye contact with Ellen. "If you don't want to stock the shelves, guess I'll have to do 'em myself."

Holding her hands behind her back, while gripping her wrists, Ellen said, "I'll put the shoes out."

Ellen had never seen this side of Ezra. She was sure he didn't use an overbearing, almost haughty attitude with Dad, because her father would never put up with that. In all the times she'd spoken to Ezra, he'd never acted so bullish. Maybe the power of being in charge had gone to his head.

Ellen found several shoe boxes stacked inside the storage room and bent down to gather up a few. *Should I say anything to Dad about Ezra's attitude, or just let it go? I don't want Ezra to lose his job, but he shouldn't have talked to me that way.*

✳

Lihue

The piercing sound of his alarm going off jolted Rob Smith out of bed. He peered at the clock on the nightstand by his bed and grimaced: 6:00 a.m. It was too early to be getting out of bed. But if he wanted time to eat and take a dip in the ocean before heading out to look for some odd jobs, he had no choice but to rise at the crack of dawn.

Rubbing his short-cropped hair, Rob glanced across the room, where his buddy, Taavi Kumar, lay on a similar bunk. The young Hawaiian native hadn't moved a muscle. It was apparent the alarm hadn't woken him.

Soon after Rob arrived on Kauai, a little over a year ago, he'd met the island native when they'd been surfing on a beach in Kapaa. When Taavi heard that Rob had no job or place to stay, he'd invited him to share his tiny rental, stating that Rob could begin paying half the rent when he found a permanent job. It may have seemed strange to some people that someone would befriend, and even welcome, a total stranger into their home, but Rob had heard the people of Kauai were considered some of the friendliest folks in the Hawaiian Islands. Taavi's sunny disposition was proof that the rumor must be true, for he had the spirit of Aloha.

While the conditions weren't ideal, since the place only had one bedroom, it was a far cry from sleeping in the dense forest, or under a palm tree near a secluded beach.

Rob shuffled his way to the small kitchen and opened the refrigerator. His stomach growled as he scanned the shelves and spied a slice of pizza still in the box from their supper last night. It wasn't something most people might eat for breakfast, but Rob grabbed it anyway and took a bite. Hot pizza or cold, he didn't care, since it was one of his favorite foods.

After he finished the slice, Rob looked out the window. The dawn moved slowly as it filled the sky, and the morning tide rose and covered the beach. *Looks like it's gonna be a good day for that dip in the ocean.* He looked down at his tan chest and arms.

Rob noticed the bottle of sun protector sitting on the counter. Shaking his head, he muttered, "I'll bet Taavi put it there, but I'm not using that stuff anymore." Because his skin had turned three shades darker since arriving on the island, Rob no longer felt the need to use sun tan lotion. Even Taavi, a natural-born Hawaiian, put a barrier of lotion on his exposed skin before they went surfing.

Rob respected Taavi, but stubborn as he was, Rob wanted to prove he didn't need sunscreen anymore.

Taavi had become a good friend and recently let Rob know that a bellhop position might open up in another month or so at the hotel where he worked as a gardener. It wasn't Rob's idea of a perfect job, and he didn't want to do that for the rest of his life. But if the job panned out, it would be better than panhandling or doing odd jobs whenever he could find them. The money Rob made now, although small, helped Taavi pay the rent and put some food on the table. Since Rob didn't have a lot of other expenses, it was adequate—at least for now. But if a better job more to his liking came along, he'd take it, no questions asked.

CHAPTER 12

Middlebury

*a*fter putting the OPEN sign in the store window Wednesday morning, Ezra saw Ellen approaching. Unable to take his eyes off her, he stood in the open doorway, watching as she parked her bike. Ellen's golden hair, peeking out from under her head covering, looked shinier than ever in the morning sunlight.

Ezra's mouth felt so dry he could barely swallow. *Wish I had the nerve to ask her out.* He shook his head. *But what would be the point when she might say no?*

Ezra thought about yesterday and how he'd acted around Ellen. *Was I a little bit tough on her?* He rubbed his temples. *In time, I hope she'll realize I'm a nice fella. My mamm tells me that all the time.*

"How's your daed?" Ezra asked when Ellen stepped onto the porch. "What did he find out at the doctor's yesterday?"

She lifted her hands and let them fall to her sides. "Dad will be having surgery next Monday to repair both hernias."

"Both?" Ezra's eyebrows lifted.

"Turns out he has two hernias. Who knows how long he's been hurting. Until Monday when we picked Darla and Ruby up at the train station, he'd never said anything about being in pain." She shook her head slowly. "Dad wasn't happy when the doctor recommended he take it easy for several weeks following surgery."

"So he won't be able to work at the store for a while?"

"Right." Ellen stepped inside. "Which means I'll be working here until he's well enough to take over his duties."

Ezra turned and followed her into the store. The notion of working with Ellen for several weeks made his heart pound. *Sure hope I can do this without letting on to Ellen how I feel about her. If she gets any idea of it but doesn't feel the same toward me, she might leave me to deal with customers on my own.*

✳

Kapaa

Mandy had spent a good portion of the morning helping Ken clean out dusty, smelly chicken houses—certainly not one of her favorite chores, but it needed to be done on schedule. When she looked down at her arms and saw a layer of brown dust, she grimaced. "I can't wait to take a shower and get rid of this filth and putrid odor."

"I hear you." Ken wrinkled his nose. "I'm not fond of smelling like poultry either."

Other than caring for her flowers and the organic vegetable garden, Ken's mother didn't do much outside with the chickens. She did, however, take care of the financial end of the business and kept a good record of things. They all had jobs to do, and no one took time off.

This evening, rather than cooking a meal at home, the three of them would attend their church's mid-week potluck supper, followed by Bible study. Mandy looked forward to the fellowship, as well as studying God's Word with other believers.

✳

Middlebury

Ellen stepped into the outside storage shed and clicked on the battery-operated light. She inhaled deeply. The weather was typical of late spring—growing warmer but still less humid, making it nice to be outside. Unfortunately, it was stuffy in the shed. On top of that, as the day had worn on, her tension increased. Ezra seemed to be throwing his weight around, even more so than the previous day. *Does he think he has the right to tell me what to do?*

Unlike yesterday, they'd been busy with customers most of the day, which was good for business, but not good for Ellen. While Ezra waited on customers in the store, he kept her running back and forth to the storage shed to get shoes that weren't in the store. At least the little jaunts to the shed gave her some time away from Ezra.

Their most recent customer, John Schrock, couldn't decide what style of black shoe he wanted. Once he'd made a selection, the size wasn't in the store, which had brought her out to the storage shed. It was close to quitting time, and Ellen hoped it would be her last trip out for the day.

She gathered four boxes of the correct shoe size and started for the door. The top one almost toppled off, but she caught it in time, balancing the box with her chin.

When Ellen entered the store and discovered John wasn't there, her frustration mounted. "What happened to John?" She placed the boxes on the counter, which Ezra sat behind, looking like he owned the place. "I thought he wanted to try on more shoes."

Ezra shrugged. "He changed his mind and bought the first pair he tried on, which were close to his size."

Ellen heaved a sigh, gesturing to the boxes she'd brought in. "Guess I'd better put these on a shelf in the men's section."

"That won't work, Ellen."

She tipped her head. "How come?"

"The shelves are full with the new shoes you put out yesterday, so there isn't room for more boxes."

"But you sold several pair of shoes today."

"True, but not in the sizes you have here." Ezra nodded toward the shoe boxes.

Refusing to look at him, Ellen scooped them up and headed across the room. She almost made it to the door, when the top box slipped. In the process of trying to right it, she lost her grip, and all four boxes landed on the floor.

"Always trouble somewhere," Ellen muttered, going down on her knees to gather up all the shoes that had fallen out.

"Here, let me help you with those." Ezra knelt beside her. He reached out at the same time as Ellen. Her cheeks warmed when he grabbed her hand instead of the shoes.

"Oops! Sorry, I didn't mean to do that." Ezra's ears flamed as he quickly withdrew his hand.

Avoiding his gaze, Ellen grabbed the rest of the shoes as quickly as possible and put them in the boxes. In the shed, she would make sure each pair was in its correct box. Right now, she just wanted to get outside as quickly as possible.

✳

Kapaa

"Looks like we may be in for some rain," Ken's mother commented from the back seat of Ken's SUV.

As huge raindrops slowly splattered on the windshield, Mandy glanced out the front window, and up at the sky. Dark, massive clouds billowed in off the ocean, while palm trees swayed in the heavy wind. Rain was typical for Kauai, but they hadn't had any moisture for the past five days, so the forthcoming storm was a good thing.

"Here we are." Ken pulled into the parking lot and turned off the ignition. "Don't know about the rest of you, but I'm hungry as a shark going after its prey."

Mandy looked over at him and rolled her eyes. "I can't believe you compared yourself to a shark."

He poked her arm playfully. "Didn't say I was a shark—just hungry enough to eat like one."

She snickered. "Okay, whatever." When Mandy opened the car door the rain fell harder. "We'd better hurry inside with our food before we're drenched."

Ken carried the box with their casserole dish and deviled eggs, while Mandy and Ken's mother hurried alongside. When they entered the fellowship hall, they were greeted by Luana and Makaio.

"Aloha!" Luana pulled Mandy into a big hug, as Ken and Makaio headed to the kitchen with their food containers. "So glad you could come tonight. I can only imagine how busy you've all been at the farm." She greeted Ken's mother with a hug too. "How are you, Vickie?"

Vickie's chin trembled. "I miss Charles so much, but thanks to my son and his sweet wife, I'm getting along okay." She slipped her arm around Mandy's waist. "I don't know what I'd do without them."

Mandy teared up. While it might seem to some that she'd made a sacrifice by moving here, she realized it was a privilege.

"Come, let's find a table," Ken called from across the room. "A little birdie told me Luana made my favorite ambrosia salad."

With hands on her hips, Luana looked over at Makaio and frowned. "Did you tell him? It was supposed to be a surprise."

Makaio winked at his wife. "What can I say? Hunger makes me do crazy things."

Mandy giggled and linked arms with Luana and Vickie. "Guess we'd better not keep our hungry men waiting."

✳

Middlebury

Unable to sleep, Ellen crept down the stairs and into the kitchen. She'd no more than lit one of the gasoline lights when Lenore entered the room.

Ellen jumped. "For goodness' sake, Sister, you scared me. What are you doing up in the middle of the night?"

Lenore gave a sheepish grin. "Couldn't sleep, so I came down to find something to eat."

"Maybe we can share the last piece of Mom's apple pie. It would go well with a glass of cold milk."

Lenore nodded. "Sounds good. I'll get the glasses and plates while you fetch the pie and milk."

Ellen bit back a chuckle. "Aren't you the bossy one?"

Lenore dropped her gaze. "Sorry."

"It's okay. I bet you could tell Ezra Bontrager a thing or two." Ellen opened the refrigerator and took out the milk.

"What do you mean?"

"Oh, nothing. I was thinking out loud." Ellen pulled out the pie pan and placed it on the table beside the milk.

Lenore set the glasses and plates down, then opened the silverware drawer. "Don't think we can eat the pie without these." She held up two forks.

Ellen laughed. "Guess we could, but it'd be messy."

They ate their snack in silence, until Lenore posed a question. "How do you like workin' at Dad's store?"

"It's okay, I guess." *But I'd like it better if I was in charge.*

"You're lucky. I wish Dad had asked me to work there."

"Hmm. . ." An idea popped into Ellen's head. "You're out of school now, so if it's okay with our folks, why don't you go with me tomorrow and I can show you what to do."

Lenore's eyes brightened. "Sure hope they say yes. It'd be fun workin' in Dad's store."

Ellen ate a piece of pie, savoring the juicy, cinnamon-flavored apples. *If things go right, and Lenore catches on fast, maybe she can take over for me at the store, and I'll be free to look for another job. No more dealing with Ezra telling me what to do. He can deal with my feisty sister.*

CHAPTER 13

By the first Saturday of June, Ellen felt very thankful for her sister's presence at the store. Lenore's work not only lightened the load, but Ezra's bossiness toward Ellen had lessened a bit as well, since he now had two helpers to tell what to do. Ellen wished this was a job she liked more, but for Dad's sake she would work without complaint—even though dealing with Ezra at times still felt like having a burr under her saddle.

"Where shall I put this pair of *schuh*? I don't see a box for them." Lenore bumped Ellen's arm, halting her thoughts.

Ellen took the black sneakers from her sister and looked inside to check the size. "Did you look on the shelf for size nine in women's shoes? Sometimes people put the empty box on the shelf but set the shoes someplace else."

Lenore squinted her blue eyes. "You want me to go through every box on the shelf?"

"Jah." Ellen pointed in the right direction. "As soon as you find it, I'd appreciate some help opening several boxes in the back room."

"Okay." Lenore smiled. "I like workin' here in the store. Don't you?"

"It's all right, but I'm hoping to find another job after Dad comes back."

"If you quit working here, do you think Dad will let me keep helping?"

"Maybe. That's why I'm training you the best I can—so you can fill my shoes." She snickered.

"Good one, Ellen." Lenore grinned. "When I get paid I'd like to go shopping. Maybe we could go together."

"That would be nice, and we could stop for ice cream afterward." Ellen glanced out the window and saw a minivan pull into their lot. Things had been busy today, with a steady stream of customers.

Lenore headed down the women's aisle, and Ellen turned toward the front door as an English couple with three children entered the store. Since Ezra was behind the counter, waiting on a customer, Ellen greeted the couple. "May I help you?"

The woman, who wore her brown hair in a long braid, nodded. "My girls and I need new shoes." She gestured to the man and small boy. "They may want to try on a few pairs too."

Ellen smiled. "I'd be happy to assist." She directed the man to the men's and boys' section, then led the woman and her daughters to the women's department.

Ezra came out from behind the counter. "Lenore, when you get done with whatever you're doing, could you help Ellen?" he called.

Ellen looked back at Ezra. *There he goes again—telling us what to do.*

"Okay, I'll put these away and be right back to help." Lenore rushed off.

Ezra's bossiness didn't seem to bother Ellen's sister. If it did, she never let on. *Perhaps I'm just too sensitive.*

"Is this your store?" The woman looked at Ellen with a curious expression.

She shook her head. "My father owns it."

"Oh, I see. I didn't realize until we came in that it's an Amish shoe store." The woman reached into her purse and withdrew a small camera. "Mind if I take a few pictures? This is our first time visiting Amish country, and I want to take some photos to share with my friends in Chicago."

"It's okay to take pictures of the shoes, but please, no photos of those who work here."

The woman's shoulders rose as she gave a huff. "Okay, if that's what you'd prefer."

Ellen didn't have a chance to explain, for the woman grabbed her daughters' hands and hurried down the first aisle.

Lenore came back and stood by her sister. "How can I help?"

"Depending on what our customers want, I may need you to run out to the shed for more shoes." Ellen glanced over her shoulder and saw Ezra talking to the man and his boy. A few seconds later, they started down one of the aisles.

Heading down the aisle of women's shoes, she and Lenore were almost run over by the young girls, each waving a pair of shoes in their hands. Before Ellen could say anything, the girls zipped past them and raced toward the front of the store. Thinking their mother would go after her daughters, Ellen paused.

"Where's their mom?" Lenore whispered.

Glancing around, Ellen shrugged. Then, hearing some giggling in the next aisle, she hurried to see what was so funny. The girls both wore shoes several sizes too big for them and stood posed as their mother snapped a picture.

The youngest girl pointed to her feet. "I want these shoes."

"Me too." Her sister eyed Lenore, when she stepped up to her.

Ellen looked at the children's mother. "Would you like me to measure the girls' feet? Then I can check and see if we have their sizes in stock."

"Yes, please do."

"I'll get the shoes for you, once we know their sizes," Lenore said.

Ellen asked the children to take a seat on the bench at the end of the aisle. While she measured the girls' feet, their mother took a few more pictures. Ellen hoped she wasn't in any of them. Most people didn't come into the store with a camera. *Why do they feel the need to take pictures? Is our business so different from an English shoe store?*

✳

Ezra had been talking to the English man who'd come into the store with his family, but he didn't seem interested in buying shoes. The young boy had gone outside a few minutes ago, and the father followed.

Ezra looked out the window. Father and son sat side-by-side on the bench. He felt a twinge of envy. *Sure hope I have a son someday. Of course I'll first need a fraa.*

Turning, he glanced at Ellen. He'd noticed that she seemed to be avoiding him. She spent most of her time training Lenore to restock when deliveries were made, wait on customers, run the battery-operated cash register, and sort through boxes of shoes. At this rate, he'd never get a relationship started with her. If he could only get up the nerve to ask Ellen out without fear of rejection. And it didn't help that he kept saying the wrong things whenever he talked with her.

Ezra returned to his seat behind the counter. *I wonder if Ellen is expecting her sister to take over for her when Nathan returns to the store. I haven't been very pleasant to Ellen since she started helping out while her daed had surgery and recovers. Maybe I'd better change my ways and quit telling her what to do.*

He shifted on the wooden stool. *Wish there was something I could say to make things better. Would it help if I told Ellen I was sorry?*

✳

Nora stepped out of the kitchen and stood watching Nathan sitting in his favorite chair, staring out the window with a wistful expression. Her husband was bored, no doubt wishing he could go back to work at the shoe store. It was difficult to hold him down, and she'd be glad when the doctor said Nathan could return to work. All he'd talked about since he got out of the hospital was the store—wondering how things were going, if Ezra and Ellen were managing okay without him, and if Lenore was fitting in well.

Nora sighed. Having her husband down like this was testing their marriage. He'd become irritable and snapped at her for the littlest things. She had considered talking to their bishop or one of the other ministers about it. Instead, she'd confided in her mother when she came by earlier. Mom was in the kitchen now, fixing coffee.

Nora stepped forward and placed her hand on her husband's shoulder. "Do you need anything, Nathan?"

He shook his head, never taking his gaze off the window.

"Are you feeling all right?"

"I'm fine."

"If you're hurting, I'll bring you one of the pain pills the doctor prescribed."

"Said I'm fine. I don't like taking those pills. And if I need one, I'll get it myself."

Nora stepped back, feeling like she'd been punched. "Okay, I'll be in the kitchen with Mom if you need me." She crept down the hall, stopping in the bathroom for a tissue. She blotted her eyes and blew her nose.

Nathan doesn't appreciate anything I do. It's like he's become a different person. Doesn't he realize how much I care about him?

Nora paused to reflect on what her mother had said earlier this morning. *"Be patient, kind, and supportive, for this too shall pass."*

Mom also explained how some people can change when pain racks their body. She'd said, "Nathan doesn't intend to be nasty. He's upset, not only because he hurts, but because his normal routine has been interrupted. Remember, the husband is the head of the household—the main breadwinner for his family. When he can't do what he normally does, it's difficult to see his family doing everything for him. I'm sure when he's feeling himself again, he will most likely apologize and say how grateful he is to have you by his side."

Looking at herself in the bathroom mirror, Nora took a deep breath. "Mom is right," she said to herself quietly. "I must show Nathan how much I love him and, at the same time, try not to overwhelm him with too much attention."

Nora pulled out a clean washcloth from storage and dampened it with cool running water. After applying the refreshing cloth to her face, she felt more relaxed.

Leaning against the bathroom counter, Nora closed her eyes. *Lord, help me be an understanding wife. Show me when to speak and when to keep quiet. Please help my husband to heal quickly so he can return to his store and things will be better between us.*

CHAPTER 14

Kapaa

By the end of June, Mandy and Ken had established a routine that allowed them to complete things well and in a timely manner.

On this beautiful Monday morning, Mandy's stress seemed to melt away as she sat on the lanai with Ken and Vickie, drinking guava juice and listening to a Hawaiian music CD.

"You should get out your ukulele and play something for us," Vickie said.

Mandy's toes curled in her flip-flops. "I haven't practiced in a while, and I'm not that good. Now, Makaio—he's mastered the art of ukulele playing."

"You're being modest, Mandy." Ken nudged her arm. "You played a lot when we lived in Indiana, and everyone who heard you enjoyed your playing."

Mandy smiled. "Guess I'll have to get it out again soon."

The doorbell rang.

"I'll see who it is." Vickie rose from her chair. A short time later she came back with Taavi and a tall, nice-looking young man with dark brown, cropped hair. Mandy didn't recognize him and wondered if Ken knew who he was.

"This is my friend Rob Smith." Taavi gestured to the young man. "He's been on the island about a year, and is staying at my place right now." Taavi introduced Mandy and Ken.

Ken got up and held out his hand. "It's nice to meet you, Rob."

"Same here." Rob shook Mandy's hand as well. He looked back at Ken.

"Taavi says you two have been friends a long time."

Ken nodded. "We struck up a friendship soon after my folks moved to the island."

"How long ago was that?"

"I was ten at the time. Of course, when I met Mandy and we fell in love, I moved to her hometown in Indiana. We lived there a little over two years." Ken dropped his gaze. "We came here a few months ago when my dad had a heart attack. After his death, Mandy and I decided to stay and help my mom run Dad's organic chicken farm."

"I see." Rob shifted his weight and looked over at Taavi. "You about ready to go?"

Taavi shook his head. "We just got here, and we haven't told Ken what we came for yet."

Ken gestured to the vacant chairs on the lanai. "Take a seat, and tell me what's up."

"If either of you would like a glass of juice, please help yourself." Vickie pointed to paper cups and a pitcher of guava juice on the glass-top table.

"Thanks, Mrs. Williams." Taavi took a cup and poured himself some juice, but Rob shook his head.

Mandy couldn't help noticing how Taavi's friend kept rubbing his hand over the top of his pale blue shorts. Was he nervous about something or just anxious to go?

After Taavi emptied his cup, he leaned closer to Ken and tapped his shoulder. "The reason we stopped by is to invite you to join us on the beach. Because of the offshore winds, the waves are just right for surfing this morning. So how 'bout? Can't be a better time for hittin' the waves."

"Sounds like fun, but I shouldn't be out on the water when there's work to be done here. In fact, I've taken a long enough break."

Taavi flapped his hand. "Aw, come on. When was the last time you got out your board and rode a few waves?"

Ken shrugged. "It's been a while."

"The last time you went surfing was before you moved to Indiana," Ken's mother interjected.

Mandy reached over and clasped Ken's hand. "We've done all our morning chores, so I think you should go. You've been working hard and deserve some down time."

Vickie's head moved up and down. "Your wife is right, Son. We can manage for a few hours without you. Please go with Taavi and Rob and have a good time."

Ken lifted both hands in defeat. "Okay, I can see I'm outnumbered here."

Mandy smiled. She was glad he'd given in and agreed to go. Maybe tomorrow, or some other day soon, she'd take time off and go looking for shells, the way she and Ellen used to do during their time together on Kauai.

✳

Middlebury

"It's good to have you back in the store." Ellen stood behind the stool where her father sat at the counter and placed her hands on his shoulders.

He reached back and patted one of her hands. "It's good to be back, but are you sure you don't want to keep working here? We're busy enough for three workers, and I can let Lenore go."

Ellen stepped around so she could see his face. "Lenore enjoys helping in the store, and there's no need for both of us to continue working here. Besides, I heard a job might be opening at one of the hotels nearby, so I'd like to apply for that."

"No problem." Dad smiled. "You should be happy doin' whatever you want." He glanced at Ezra, as he fitted one of their church members for new shoes. "Don't know what I would have done during my recuperation if you and Ezra hadn't taken over here. That young man is a hard worker. He seems to enjoy working with shoes."

Ellen nodded. *He also enjoyed telling me what to do.* She glanced at the clock. "It's almost closing time. Would you mind if I leave a little early? I have a few errands to run and want to get to the stores before they close."

Dad shook his head. "No problem, Daughter. Go on ahead. Lenore can ride home with me."

"Danki, Dad. I'll see you both at supper."

✳

Ezra finished helping his customer about the same time Ellen left the store. He had heard most of the conversation she'd shared with her dad about quitting the store and finding another job. *Shoulda figured it was coming,* he told himself. It didn't take a genius to see Ellen wasn't happy working here. No doubt she'd been happier at Mandy and Ken's bed-and-breakfast. He remembered Ellen saying how she enjoyed managing the B&B and that there was no other place she'd rather work.

Ezra reached around and rubbed a knot in his lower back. *It's probably my fault she's leaving. No doubt I drove her away.*

He felt like giving himself a swift kick in the pants. *Guess I have no idea how to win a young woman's heart—especially Ellen's. Maybe I'll never establish a relationship with her or any other woman. I could end up being a lonely bachelor all my life.*

Ezra glanced at Lenore as she swept past him with a broom. *She'll probably be married and starting a family before I find a woman who's interested in me.*

Ezra knew he was giving in to self-pity, but he couldn't help it. He'd botched things up with Ellen and might never get another chance.

Of course, Ezra reasoned as he headed down the men's aisle to put a pair of shoes back on the shelf, *I might see Ellen at the next young people's singing. Maybe I'll get up the nerve to offer her a ride home afterward.* Other times when the chance came, he chickened out. At the last singing a few weeks ago, he'd tried to approach Ellen, but her friend, Sadie, came along and invited Ellen to ride home with her and her brother, Saul.

"Maybe it was for the best," Ezra muttered under his breath. "She might have said no, anyways."

✳

Kapaa

Ken enjoyed the gentle rolling of the ocean waves. It felt good to be back on his board. He'd almost forgotten the pleasure he felt when the only thing between him and the powerful ocean was the board beneath his feet.

Ken lay on his stomach and paddled with his hands. *I've sure missed this. Wish I had more free days to be on the water.*

He and Taavi had taken some waves together, while Rob stuck to himself. Ken didn't ask why Taavi's friend seemed so standoffish. He figured either Rob was aloof, or took some time to warm up to someone new. Besides, for the moment Ken felt an overwhelming sense of freedom. Surfing gave him a few hours away from never-ending chores, as well as the stress of missing Dad.

Ken felt one with nature as he cut through the water, gliding with no effort on his board with each wave. With the wind and spray on his face, he had a sense of flying.

After a few practice runs on smaller waves, it didn't take Ken long to regain his balance. Feeling more confident, he watched in anticipation, hoping some bigger waves would form.

Taavi had chosen a wave to take. Ken watched as his friend stood up, then disappeared on the other side of the wave. A few seconds later, Taavi reappeared, the power of the wave surging him forward until it took him a few feet from shore. Taavi then stood in waist-deep water, holding his board and waving at Ken.

"My turn now." Ken watched as the ocean swelled. He lowered himself on the board, then paddled as the swell grew bigger. Finally, he stood to ride the wave that had formed. It was his biggest one yet today.

"This is great!" he shouted, feeling weightless as the energy beneath his board moved him forward.

Skimming along the surface, Ken felt like he was part of the ocean. After riding the wave out the whole way, he waded over to Taavi, who stood waiting for him on the beach.

"Good one, Ken! Looks like ya got your surfing legs back."

"Man that felt great." Ken couldn't help smiling. "The waves are getting bigger. Are you ready to tackle another one?"

"Naw. Think I'll sit this one out." Taavi looked toward Rob, sitting on a towel. "I need to hydrate. After I get some liquid in me, I'll join you."

"Sounds good." Ken didn't waste any time returning to the deeper depths. He paddled out past where the waves were breaking and sat on his board. It was peaceful out here where the water bobbed his board up and down. Ken shielded his eyes and looked toward the beach. Taavi sat beside Rob.

Swaying and rocking with the motion of the sea, he remained seated on his board, glancing back and waiting for the next wave to form.

It feels so right, being out here again. The one thing missing is Mandy, waving to me from the beach.

Seagulls flew overhead squawking, and farther out in the ocean, Ken saw a cruise liner slowly meandering along the horizon. *A ship is what first brought Mandy over the Pacific to this island, and then eventually to me.*

Looking over his shoulder, Ken saw the formation of another wave. As the ocean stirred, he took one more glance toward the beach. He couldn't hear them, but Rob and Taavi were waving their arms and pointing at something.

They're right! This is gonna be a big wave.

He lay down on his board and waited. *Sure wish Mandy was here to see this.*

✳

Mandy groaned and clutched her stomach. She hadn't felt well all morning. She'd had some mint tea earlier, but it did nothing to settle her stomach. She'd gone to her room to lie down, while Vickie did some business paperwork.

Mandy lay on the bed, staring at the ceiling and listening to the zebra dove's distinctive sound through the open window. The soft breeze moved the curtains, as the gentle smell of plumeria drifted through the room. In some ways she wished she'd gone to the beach to watch Ken and the others surf. But then, feeling this nauseous, it wouldn't have been much fun.

Mandy's thoughts turned toward home. Mom had called yesterday, telling Mandy she'd be having surgery on her heel, due to plantar fasciitis that hadn't responded to more conservative treatment. She wouldn't be able to walk for a while, allowing time for healing. Mandy wished she could be there to help out, but Mom said she'd have plenty of help from other family members and friends like Ellen's mother, Nora.

Mandy thought of Ellen and wondered what she was doing right now. It would be late afternoon in Middlebury. Her friend might be helping her mother with supper or doing some chores.

Mandy remembered the first time she and Ken had been on the beach together, watching Taavi surf. It was thrilling yet frightening to observe the way Taavi kept his balance on the board and rode the high waves. Ken liked to surf too, and she'd been equally enthralled watching him. Surfing in the ocean, where danger could lurk, was not for the faint of heart. Even though Mandy had learned to swim, she'd never wanted to surf. She couldn't imagine being out where your feet didn't touch the bottom.

Another wave of nausea coursed through Mandy's stomach. She drew in a slow, deep breath and let it out, hoping to squelch the unpleasant feeling.

She placed both hands on her stomach and closed her eyes. *I wonder if I could be pregnant. Wouldn't it be something if I was carrying Ken's child?* The only problem was Ken needed her to help with the chickens, and if she were expecting a baby and continued to feel ill, she might not be up to helping. Perhaps Vickie would hire someone to assist Ken.

As the nausea settled down, Mandy relaxed. *Maybe if I sleep awhile, I'll feel better when I wake up.*

Mandy was close to drifting off when her cell phone rang. She reached over to the nightstand to pick it up. "Hello."

"Mandy, it's Taavi. Something horrible has happened."

"What's wrong, Taavi? You sound really upset."

"It. . .it's Ken—he was attacked by a shark. The ambulance came, and they're taking him to the hospital. You and Mrs. Williams had better get there right away. I hate to say this, Mandy, but it doesn't look good."

CHAPTER 15

Lihue

*P*acing the floor, Mandy shivered and rubbed her hands over her bare arms. *I wish Ken hadn't gone surfing with Taavi and his friend this morning.* The waiting room offered no privacy. Several others crowded the room, waiting for news about their loved ones having surgery.

Mandy crumpled the tissue she held so tight that the veins on top of her hand stood out. *If my husband dies, I'll blame myself for encouraging him to go surfing.*

Vickie sat stone faced, staring straight ahead. *Since she urged Ken to join his friends, I wonder if she's also blaming herself. Poor Vickie. She's still trying to deal with her husband's death, and now one of her sons has been critically injured. If Ken doesn't make it, his mother will be devastated, and so will I.*

Tension grew as time passed. It was hard to think clearly. Mandy wanted to be with her husband—see for herself if he was alive. But several doctors and nurses were working on him, so Mandy, Vickie, Taavi, and Rob had been ushered into this room to await the verdict.

Dear Lord, she prayed, *please don't let my husband die.* She placed both hands on her stomach as a wave of nausea hit. *What if I'm pregnant and never get the chance to tell Ken he's going to be a father?* One negative thought followed another.

As soon as they'd arrived at the hospital, Vickie had called Ken's brother in California to let him know what happened, Mandy phoned Luana and Makaio. They assured her they'd be praying and would notify their pastor, who would put it on the church prayer chain. Luana said she and Makaio would come to the hospital soon.

Mandy called her folks to tell them what had happened to Ken and left a message. She wished they could be here right now, but with Mom's foot surgery, travel was out of the question.

She'd also called Ellen and left a message, asking for prayer. *The more people praying for Ken, the better.*

She looked at Taavi, sitting with his head down and hands pressed against his forehead. "Taavi, would you please tell us with precise detail how the shark attack occurred?" When they'd first gotten to the hospital, Ken's friend had been so shook up that his account of things had been sketchy.

Vickie leaned in to listen, her eyes glistening with tears. "Yes, please explain what happened to my son."

Taavi lifted his head and looked at them with a grim twist to his mouth. He sat several seconds, before beginning to speak.

"I'd gone back to the beach after riding some waves with Ken. Rob sat on a towel by our cooler. While we enjoyed a breather, we took turns watching Ken through the binoculars. You could see it written all over his face—he was in his glory, having fun anticipating the bigger waves." Taavi paused before continuing. "Then I saw it—a large fin, cutting through the water in Ken's direction."

Vickie's tears spilled, and Mandy's vision blurred as she reached for her mother-in-law's hand. She almost felt faint visualizing the scene.

"Taavi and I were waving our arms, trying to get Ken's attention," Rob interjected. "I'm guessing he thought we were pointing at the big wave that started forming behind him."

Taavi spoke again. "Then just as he lay down on his board and started paddling, I saw the fin once more, right next to Ken's board. But before we could call out to him, the shark attacked. The water all around Ken turned red." He paused and gulped in some air. "Rob and I grabbed our boards, while Ken fought hard. When we reached him, the shark was gone."

Rob's head moved slowly up and down. "I've never seen so much blood in all my life."

Mandy felt bile rising in her throat, and she swallowed hard to push it down. She couldn't imagine what Ken must have gone through.

"By the time we got him to shore, someone had called 911, and people swarmed around, offering assistance," Rob interjected. "One man who applied a tourniquet to your husband's arm said he had survived a shark attack once himself."

"You risked your own lives to bring my husband to shore. I'm at a loss for words." Mandy shuddered. The ocean wasn't safe. Neither Ken nor his friends should have been out surfing today. What was supposed to be a fun day had turned into a tragedy.

"Mandy and I are grateful to you." Vickie dabbed her eyes with a tissue.

A doctor entered the room, bringing Mandy and Vickie to their feet. "Mrs. Williams?"

"I'm Ken's mother." Vickie motioned to Mandy. "And this is his wife."

Mandy stepped forward. "How's my husband? Is he going to be okay?"

His brows knit together. "Ken suffered severe lacerations and might lose his left arm. The shark bit his side and left leg too."

"But my son will be okay, right?" Vickie's voice sounded shaky.

"We're doing all we can, but our biggest concern is infection. We'll be taking him into surgery soon, but depending on the extent of his injuries, he may be faced with more surgeries in the days ahead." The doctor hesitated a moment, as if weighing his words. "If you're a believer, it wouldn't hurt to send up some prayers."

"We're both Christians," Vickie was quick to say. "And we believe in the power of prayer."

He nodded.

Soon after the doctor left, Luana and Makaio arrived and hurried over to hug Vickie and Mandy. As Luana gently patted her back, Mandy began to sob. "What if Ken doesn't make it? What if. . ."

"He's on the prayer chain, Mandy." Luana's voice was soothing. "Many prayers will be said on Ken's behalf. We must have faith and trust that God's will is done."

"Ken is young and strong," Makaio put in. "I believe he will make it. And I don't want you or Vickie to worry about anything. I'll go over to the farm and take care of things this evening."

"Don't worry about that." Taavi jumped up. "Rob and I will go. One or both of us will make sure the chickens are fed and watered for as long as you need our help."

"That means a lot to me." Vickie looked at Taavi and Rob. "Thank you for rescuing my son. Who knows what could have happened if you hadn't gone out to him."

Mandy dried her eyes on the tissue Luana gave her. She moved close to Vickie and gave her a hug. "God knows how much we both need Ken, so we have to believe He will answer our prayers."

Vickie nodded. " 'For we walk by faith, not by sight,'" she quoted from 2 Corinthians 5:7.

"Yes," Luana agreed, "And we must keep the faith."

$$*$$

Middlebury

"Did you or Dad check for phone messages yet?" Ellen asked her mother as they finished doing the breakfast dishes Tuesday morning.

Mom shook her head. "I haven't been out, and your daed was in a hurry when he and Lenore left for work this morning, so I doubt he took the time to check either."

"That's right. There's a sale going on at the store right now. No wonder he wanted to leave early." Ellen picked up another dish to dry. "Bet they'll be busy from the minute the store opens till closing time."

"Did you ask if your help was needed today?"

Ellen shook her head. "I didn't think about the sale until now. Guess I could drop by and see if Dad would like my help."

Mom smiled. "Good idea."

Ellen finished drying the last of the dishes and put them away. "I'm going out to the phone shack to check for messages. When I come back inside I'll get ready and head to the shoe store."

"Danki, Ellen. I hope it doesn't mess up any plans you've made for today."

"Not really. The only thing I'd wanted to do was stop by the restaurant and say hi to Darla and Ruby. Since they're both working the breakfast shift today I thought maybe I could visit with them during their break."

"Are you hoping there might be an opening at the restaurant?" Mom asked.

"No. I'm going to wait and see what happens with the hotel position that's supposed to open soon."

"You miss your job at the B&B, don't you?"

"Jah, but I miss Mandy more. It's not the same with her living so far away." Ellen moved toward the back door. "I'm heading outside now, Mom. Be back soon."

Ellen's flip-flops snapped across the graveled driveway as she made her way to the phone shack. Her nose twitched at the charred scent left over from their barbecue pit, where they'd roasted marshmallows the previous night. It was fun to spend time with her family gathered around the fire, singing and enjoying their toasted marshmallows spread between graham crackers and pieces of chocolate. Someday when Ellen had a family of her own, she hoped there would be many evenings of fun, food, and fellowship. For her and many others in their Amish community God came first and family second. Ellen's dad often said, "Put the two together and you have the key to satisfaction and happiness."

Ellen tipped her head back and looked up when a beautiful cardinal swooped past, landing in a nearby tree. It reminded her of the red-crested cardinals she'd seen in Hawaii, but only their heads were red.

Ellen's thoughts went to Mandy. She hadn't heard from her in a few days. No doubt, she and Ken were keeping busy.

Ellen reached the phone shack and stepped inside. The light on the answering machine blinked, so she pushed PLAY to hear their messages.

"Ellen, it. . .it's Mandy. Something horrible has happened." Ellen heard sniffling. "Ken was attacked by a shark while surfing." Another few seconds of silence. "Oh, Ellen, he lost so much blood. I don't know anything definite yet, but it's bad, and I'm worried that Ken may lose his arm. He could even die if—" Mandy's voice broke on a sob. "Please pray, Ellen. I've left a message with my folks, and could you ask others to pray too? I'll call again, when I know more."

Ellen sat in stunned silence, barely able to take it all in. Her fingers touched her parted lips as tears pricked the back of her eyes. *Poor Mandy. I wish I could be with her to offer support. And Ken—what he went through must have been terrible.* Ellen couldn't fathom the terror he must have felt. Just the idea of being on the ocean's surface, not knowing what creature might lurk beneath, sent a tremor of fear through her body.

Why can't I be with her? I'll ask the church leaders if they will give permission for me to fly to Kauai so I can go right away.

CHAPTER 16

Lihue

*M*andy yawned and stretched her arms out to the sides. Her body ached from sleeping in a half-sitting position all night. She glanced over at Vickie. The poor woman hadn't slept much either. How could they get any restful sleep slouched in hospital chairs next to Ken's bed?

The doctor had said the surgery went well, but due to extensive wounds, it was too soon to predict if Ken was out of the woods. Their first goal had been to stop the bleeding and stitch and reattach what they could with Ken's arm and leg wounds. The physician added that Ken needed to rest and stay immobile to let the stitches and staples heal the torn tissue. Another surgery would happen soon.

A lump formed in Mandy's throat as she stared at her husband's motionless form. He'd drifted in and out a few times, but hadn't fully regained consciousness. She longed to speak to Ken—tell him she was here and that everything would be all right. She'd never felt as helpless as she did now.

Ken's mother needed support as much as Mandy. Losing her husband was reason enough for her not being able to cope, but now she was confronted with this situation. Mandy hoped she and her mother-in-law would get enough rest to keep up the ongoing vigil.

In addition to worrying about possible infection setting in, Mandy was concerned that Ken might not be able to use his arm as he once had.

Mandy closed her eyes. *Dear God, please bring us through this uncertain time in our life.*

Mandy's cell phone vibrated, and she pulled it out of her skirt pocket.

Realizing it was from Ellen, she rose from her chair and tiptoed out of the room to answer the call.

✳

Middlebury

"How is Ken doing, Mandy?" Ellen twisted her head covering ties around her fingers. She'd been praying and hoping Ken would get the best care available.

"He's out of surgery and in his room, but it's too soon to tell if his arm or leg will fully heal." Mandy's voice sounded far away—as though she were talking in a box. "Oh, Ellen, I'm so scared. I wish we hadn't come back to Hawaii. If we'd stayed in Middlebury, the shark attack wouldn't have happened."

Ellen could almost feel her friend's pain. She wished she could reach through the phone and hug Mandy.

"I'm going to see our ministers today and ask for permission to fly so I can come to Kauai and be with you."

"You'd really come all that way?"

"Of course. You're my best friend, Mandy. Since your mother can't make the trip, I want to be there to offer the support you need."

"It would mean so much to me if you were here."

Ellen shifted on her chair inside the phone shack. "I talked to my folks about this, and they're okay with me going. Dad said in some cases our ministers have allowed a person to fly when a friend or relative is faced with a crisis."

"Can you afford a plane ticket? I'm sure it won't be cheap—especially if you're planning to leave soon."

"Please let me worry about everything. You have enough to be concerned with right now. I'll call you back once I know for sure that I'm coming." Ellen struggled not to cry. "We're all praying here, Mandy. And if everything goes well, I'll see you soon."

"Thank you, Ellen. You have no idea how much this means to me."

"I'm certain if I were faced with a similar situation, you'd be there for me."

"Yes, I would."

"All right then. Talk to you soon."

When Ellen hung up, she remained in the phone shack. *Heavenly Father, please be with Mandy, Ken, and his mother. Give Mandy and Vickie patience and courage to deal with everything they must face. And when I approach the ministers in our church district, I ask that they would be in one accord and grant me permission to fly.*

Ellen drew a quick breath. *If the ministers give their consent, please give me the courage to get on the plane that will take me to Kauai.*

✳

Lihue

Ken groaned, and Vickie woke up with a start. Her heart pounded as she watched her son's head thrash about. "Shark! Shark!" It was unbearable for Vickie to hear Ken's panicked words.

She jumped up and stood by his bed, speaking in a soft tone and offering reassurance that he was safe. But Ken continued to moan, and then he cried, "Help! Somebody, help me, please!"

Although he was heavily sedated, Ken seemed to be reliving the attack. Vickie picked up his hand and caressed it gently, hoping it would bring her son comfort in his restless state. The attack must have been a horrible experience, and now Ken was living through the emotional anguish of the event all over again.

With a sense of urgency, she released his hand and pushed the CALL button. A few minutes later, a middle-age nurse entered the room. Before she could say a word, Vickie stood up. "My son is in pain. Will you please give him something?"

The nurse shook her head. "It's not time yet. We don't want to overmedicate."

Vickie's nails pushed into the palms of her hands. It was all she could do to keep from screaming. "Didn't you hear what I said? Ken is in pain. He's been groaning and thrashing about."

The nurse checked Ken's vitals. For the moment, at least, he'd stopped groaning. "According to the doctor's orders, the patient will receive more pain medicine through his IV in thirty minutes." She looked at Vickie and offered a sympathetic smile. "Is there anything I can bring you—a cup of coffee or some tea?"

"No thanks." Vickie returned to her chair. The only thing she wanted was the assurance that her son would be okay. Ken loved to surf. Would he ever go in the water again?

She waited until the nurse left, then took her cell phone from her purse. Despite having told her eldest son about Ken's situation, Vickie hadn't heard whether Dan would be coming or not. *Surely he must realize how much I need him right now. If he were as concerned about his brother as he said when I told him what happened, he would have booked the first flight to Kauai.*

Although Dan didn't like hospitals, surely he'd want to be here when his brother was in need—not to mention offer his mother support. The boys were not close growing up, but Vickie had hoped they'd find some common ground as they matured. One son wanted to be inside most of the time, reading or on the computer. The other boy could have lived on the beach.

Vickie's fingers clenched around the phone. *It's too bad Ken isn't more like Dan—then he wouldn't have gone surfing.*

Vickie leaned back in the chair and closed her eyes. *Poor Mandy. Except for me, she has no one to be with her during this time. I should be more reassuring, but right now I can barely hold my head above water.*

She dialed Dan's number. He answered on the second ring. "Hi, Mom, I'm glad you called. I was about to phone you."

"Oh?" Vickie felt a ray of hope. Maybe Dan would be coming after all.

"I'd planned to catch a flight out this morning, but my wife got sick. Don't know if it's the flu or what, I wouldn't feel right about leaving her."

"What about her folks? Can't one of them stay with Rita?"

"No, it should be me."

Vickie rubbed her forehead. "Maybe once she feels better, you can come."

"We'll see." Dan paused. "How's Ken? Is he gonna be okay?"

"I hope so, but it's too soon to tell."

"Well, please keep me informed."

"Yes, of course." Vickie wondered if her son heard the regret in her tone. She understood Dan's need to be with his wife, but she needed his support right now.

A few minutes after Vickie hung up, Mandy entered the room. "I just talked to my friend, Ellen. She is going to speak to the church leaders and ask for permission to fly here."

"That's nice. I'm sure you'll appreciate her support." Vickie bit the inside of her cheek. *I wish my oldest son cared enough to come and support me.*

CHAPTER 17

Over the Pacific Ocean

Leaning into her neck pillow, Ellen tried to relax. With nothing except white puffy clouds to view out the window, all she could think about was the fact that she was on an airplane, bound for Hawaii. At times she'd have a tight grip on the armrest, like now, as the plane hit some turbulence.

She remembered when the plane left Seattle, looking out the window, she could see majestic Mount Rainier. It was breathtaking. They didn't have anything like that back home in Indiana. What a beautiful view for the folks in Washington State to appreciate.

When the plane hit another bump, she shifted in her seat and looked away from the window. *It's best not to think about it. Focus on something else, like the flight attendant suggested earlier.*

She removed the airline magazine from the seat pouch in front of her. Mandy had flown a couple of times and was probably used to it by now. For Ellen, though, this was a new experience—one she wasn't going to forget.

Ellen thumbed through the magazine, then returned it to the pouch. Reaching under the seat in front of her, she lifted her tote bag and withdrew a journal. The last entry she'd posted had been yesterday when she'd flown from South Bend, Indiana, to Chicago, then on to Seattle, where she'd spent the night at a hotel near the airport. Both flights had been fairly smooth.

Another bump caused Ellen's stomach to feel queasy. She hoped she wouldn't get sick, like she had on the cruise ship to the Hawaiian Islands a couple of years ago.

Ellen opened her journal and began to write, while nibbling on a handful of pretzels. The time for this trip was about five and a half hours. She figured they were almost halfway there.

Her nerves heightened when the flight attendant announced that the pilot was going around a storm causing some of the turbulence. The passengers were instructed to keep their seat belts buckled.

Ellen glanced out the window and saw a flash of lightning in the distance. In an effort to focus on something else, she flipped back in her journal to the day she'd heard Mandy's message about Ken's shark attack. She had met with the ministers of her church district that evening and gotten permission to fly, since it was an emergency situation to help a friend. While not all Amish districts would have allowed such a thing, she was glad hers did, because another trip by train, and then on a ship, would have taken too long.

Once the decision had been made for Ellen to make the trip to Kauai, she'd hired one of their drivers to take her to a travel agency in Goshen. Mandy's parents had given Ellen the money for her ticket, since Mandy's mother was unable to travel and appreciated Ellen's willingness to go in her place.

Ellen was glad her own parents hadn't tried to dissuade her from making the trip. Mom and Dad understood her need to be with Mandy during this difficult time. Ellen's friends, Sadie and Barbara, had also been encouraging, saying they wished they could join her.

Ellen had made up her mind that she would remain on Kauai for as long as her friend needed her. Since she had no job to go back to and had purchased a one-way ticket, there was no reason to hurry home. Once Ken recuperated sufficiently, she'd purchase a ticket home.

✳

Middlebury

"You okay, Nathan?" Ezra stepped up to the counter where his boss sat staring at a pair of men's shoes a customer had decided not to purchase.

Nathan looked up at him and blinked. "I'm fine. Just sitting here, thinking is all." He put the shoes inside the box and peered out the window as a buggy drove by.

Ezra was tempted to ask what his boss was thinking about but didn't want to appear nosey. He figured Nathan might be mulling over something related to his shoe store. Or he could be wondering how Ellen was doing. With her flying on a plane for a long distance, Ellen's parents were bound to be concerned.

Ezra gestured to the shoebox. "Want me to put that back on the shelf for you?"

Nathan shook his head. "That's okay. I'll take care of it. I need to stretch my legs anyway." He stepped out from behind the counter and pulled out his pocket watch. "I bet Ellen's almost to Oahu by now. She'll change planes there, and should arrive on Kauai sometime after three o'clock, Hawaii time."

Ezra's lips pressed together as he lowered his head. Apparently he wasn't the only one thinking about Ellen. *Why did she have to take off for Hawaii?* Ezra kept his thoughts to himself. He understood that she wanted to help, but there must be other people Mandy could call on.

Ezra shook his head. *I'm being selfish. I want Ellen here so I can see her and keep trying to work up the nerve to ask her out.*

He headed toward the storage room to see if Lenore had finished unloading the boxes of shoes that had come in earlier. Ellen's sister was young and a bit immature, but she always did as she was told.

When Ezra entered the storage room, he was surprised to see Lenore on the floor with her head bowed and eyes closed. He wondered if she might be asking God to give Ellen a safe journey.

He didn't want to interrupt, so he stood still. He couldn't get over how much Lenore resembled Ellen in appearance. But the sisters' personalities were nothing alike. Ellen seemed more serious and wanted everything to be just so. Lenore, on the other hand, tended to be carefree and a bit disorganized.

Ezra slipped out of the room. *I need to get busy and quit letting my thoughts wander all over the place.*

✻

Lihue

Ellen's face broke into a wide smile when she approached the baggage claim area and saw Luana and Makaio waiting for her.

Luana opened her arms with a welcoming smile. "Aloha, Ellen!"

Tears welled in Ellen's eyes as she stepped into the sweet woman's embrace. "Aloha! It's so good to see you both again."

"It's good to see you as well." Makaio greeted Ellen with a warm hug. "So glad you could return to the Garden Island. Your *ohana* welcomes you back."

Ellen sniffed and swiped at her tears. Seeing Makaio and Luana again was like coming home to family. During the months she and Mandy had stayed with the Palus, Ellen had felt like part of their ohana.

"Which one is yours?" Makaio asked as people's luggage began moving along the conveyor belt.

"It's that one." Ellen pointed to a black suitcase with a green strap around the middle.

As though it weighed no more than a feather, Makaio swooped it right up. "Any more?"

Ellen shook her head. "I packed light and got everything I'll need in one suitcase." She lifted her tote bag. "My purse is in here, along with my journal and some snack food."

Luana slipped her arm around Ellen's waist and gave her a tender squeeze. "We have a room ready for you at the B&B, and it's yours, rent free, for as long as you decide to stay."

"Thank you." Ellen teared up again. "I never thought I'd be coming back to Kauai—certainly not under such unsettling circumstances. How is Ken doing?" she asked as they headed for the parking lot.

"Not well, I'm afraid." Luana's forehead wrinkled. "It's been three days since his surgery, and he's still pretty much out of it. I don't believe he's been able to talk to Mandy and give her the details of the shark attack." Luana paused. "I can hardly think about what happened to Ken. It must have been dreadful. From what Mandy told us, the doctor felt the surgery went as well as could be expected. They're keeping him sedated, but his prognosis. . . Well, it's too soon to tell."

"There's still a chance he could lose his arm," Makaio interjected.

Ellen's chest tightened. "Poor Mandy. I can only imagine how hard this must be for her. Ken's mother too. I'm anxious to see them."

"If you're not too tired, we can go by the hospital now." Makaio opened the trunk and put Ellen's luggage inside.

"I'm fine. I slept some on the plane." Despite the sleep she had, Ellen was exhausted from the long trip, not to mention the time change. But there was no way she could go to bed tonight without first seeing Mandy.

Chapter 18

You look like you're about to cave in," Vickie whispered to Mandy. "Why don't you go out for some fresh air and a snack? I will stay by Ken's bedside, and when you come back I'll take a breather."

"Okay." Mandy leaned close to the bed and kissed her husband's hot forehead. He'd been running a fever for the past three days, and it had not abated.

Clutching her purse in one hand, Mandy left the room. As she approached the nurse's station, she spotted Ellen coming down the hall with Luana. Mandy quickened her footsteps. It was all she could do to keep from running full speed ahead to greet her friend. And if she hadn't been in a hospital, that's exactly what she would have done.

"Oh, Ellen, it's so good to see you." Choking back tears, Mandy enveloped her friend in a hug. "I can't thank you enough for coming." She pulled back to gaze at her friend's smiling face.

"It's good to see you too. I'm glad I was given permission to come." Ellen looked over at Luana. "I'm also thankful to Luana and Makaio for giving me a room at the B&B while I'm here."

"We're happy to do it, Ellen." Luana touched the yellow plumeria flower nestled close to her left ear.

"Where is Makaio?" Mandy asked, looking past Luana.

"He's hunting for a place to park the car." Luana shook her head. "I've never seen so many vehicles in the hospital parking lot. It's almost full."

Mandy clasped Ellen's hand. "Let's sit in the waiting room until Makaio gets here. Then we can all go to the cafeteria to visit and get something to eat." She glanced at the clock behind the nurse's station. "It is almost suppertime. I'm sure you must be hungry."

Ellen nodded. "But I'm more anxious to hear how Ken is doing."

"I'll wait for Makaio near the hospital's front door, so he knows where you are." Luana gestured to the waiting room on this floor. "You two go ahead. Makaio and I will join you when he gets here. If Ken's mother is here, maybe she'd like to have supper with us too."

Mandy nodded. "Vickie's with Ken. We've been taking turns sitting by his bedside, so she probably won't eat till I go back to the room."

Luana gave Mandy's shoulder a pat. "When Makaio was in the hospital with a broken leg a few years ago, I didn't want to leave his side either. Of course," she quickly added, "his injuries weren't nearly as serious as Ken's."

Mandy breathed slowly in and out, as a wave of nausea coursed through her stomach. If she was pregnant, why did her nausea occur at odd times of the day?

"I'm off." Luana smiled, then headed down the hall.

When they entered the waiting room, Mandy felt relief that no one else was there. It would be easier to talk.

"You look tired," Ellen commented after they'd both taken a seat. "What can I do for you, Mandy?"

Mandy clasped her hand. "Right now, just knowing you're here is enough."

"How is Ken doing?" Ellen asked.

"He's running a fever and has been in and out of consciousness, but is never coherent enough to make conversation." Mandy sniffed. "Ken mumbles a lot and sometimes yells out." She shuddered. "Oh, Ellen, it must have been awful for him, being in that water and under attack. Taavi and Rob have told us what they saw from the beach and when they rescued Ken, but we won't know the whole story until he's able to talk."

Ellen squeezed Mandy's fingers. "I'm so sorry you, Ken, and Vickie are going through this. I keep asking myself why things like this happen."

"I'm trying to keep the faith and believe God will heal my husband, but my fear gets in the way, making it hard to hope for the best."

"It would be hard for anyone in a similar situation. It might help to focus on Psalm 31:24—'Be of good courage, and he shall strengthen your heart, all ye that hope in the Lord.'"

Mandy tipped her head back and closed her eyes. *Thank You, Lord, for bringing Ellen here and for the reminder of Your Word.*

✳

Kapaa

Ellen rolled over in bed, squinting against the sun's rays peeking through the partially open plantation shutters. She felt disoriented until she became fully awake and realized she'd spent last night in a cozy room at the Palms Bed-and-Breakfast. After leaving the hospital last evening, Ellen had visited with Luana and Makaio for a while. Then, unable to keep her eyes open, she'd retired to her room and fallen into a deep sleep.

Ellen lay in the same bedroom with the twin beds she and Mandy had used the last time they'd stayed. The place looked the same, with the pretty Hawaiian quilts covering the beds. The paintings of palms, beautiful scenery, and flowers still hung on the walls.

Ellen smiled, remembering the mornings she and Mandy woke up and talked about home and their families. Then they'd clamber out of bed and hurry to the kitchen to help Luana make breakfast for the guests.

She tipped her head, hearing voices coming from the kitchen. No doubt, Luana had begun fixing breakfast.

Ellen rose from the comfortable mattress and padded across the cool tile floor to the window. Opening the shutter slats a bit more, she gazed at the beautiful flowers in Luana's garden. The rich orange-red color of the hibiscus called to her, as did the lovely off-white plumeria. While the flowers at home in Mom's garden were lovely, none took her breath away like the tropical flowers found on the Hawaiian Islands.

The tantalizing aroma of food drew Ellen's attention away from the pleasant scene. *I must hurry and get dressed so I can help Luana.*

✳

A short time later, Ellen found Luana at the stove, frying sausage and eggs, while Makaio sat at the kitchen table, reading the newspaper.

Luana turned from the stove, and Makaio looked up from his paper. "Aloha. *Pehea 'oe?*" they asked.

"Hello. I'm doing well." Ellen was glad she still remembered some of the Hawaiian words Makaio and Luana had taught her and Mandy.

Luana pointed to the pitcher of pineapple juice on the table. "Please, help yourself. The eggs and sausage will be ready in a few minutes."

Ellen poured herself a glass of juice and took a sip, letting it roll around on her tongue before swallowing. This was no store-bought juice. Luana had obviously squeezed it from a fresh pineapple. "Is there anything I can do to help?"

Luana shook her head. "Not this morning, at least."

"There's something you can help me with." Makaio glanced at his wife, then back at Ellen.

"What would you like me to do?" she asked.

"You can have a talk with my *wahine* and convince her to fix Spam for breakfast every day." He winked at Ellen. "Luana knows it's my favorite breakfast meat, yet she fixes it so seldom."

Luana puffed out her cheeks, while wrinkling her nose. "You know that's not true, Husband. You're such a big tease."

"Just wanted to see if I could get a reaction." He chuckled and pointed at her. "And see there. . .it worked."

Luana lifted her gaze to the ceiling. "Look what I have to put up with, Ellen. When you find the man of your dreams, I hope for your sake he's not such a jokester."

Makaio held up his hand. "Ha! You like my teasing, and you know it, Luana."

Ellen laughed. "Some things certainly haven't changed around here. You two are so much fun."

" 'A merry heart doeth good like a medicine,'" Luana quoted Proverbs 17:22.

" 'But a broken spirit drieth the bones.'" Makaio finished the verse.

"It's good to laugh." Ellen sighed. "Especially when we're faced with unpleasant things."

"You mean, like Ken's shark attack?" Makaio questioned.

She nodded. "I'm eager to go back to the hospital and find out how he's doing today."

"And we shall—right after breakfast." Luana set the platter of eggs and sausage on the table.

"Do you have time to go? I could always call a taxi to take me to the hospital."

Luana took a seat and motioned for Ellen to do the same. "We don't have any B&B guests scheduled today, so I have plenty of time on my hands."

Ellen smiled. She appreciated this couple's humor, hospitality, and generosity. If anyone could make a person feel loved, it was Makaio and Luana Palu.

✳

"Those chickens sure produce a lot of eggs," Rob commented as he and Taavi headed down the road in Taavi's Jeep with several boxes of well-packed eggs, as well as a cooler full of fresh chicken. They'd dropped a dozen eggs off at a widow's house and were now heading for a bed-and-breakfast also on the list.

Taavi and Rob had gotten up early this morning and stopped by the organic chicken farm to see what Vickie wanted done. It was Rob's first time at the farm, and he'd been curious what the place looked like. The Williamses' home was large, and so were the chicken houses.

After Vickie gave them a list of places to deliver eggs and chicken, she'd asked Rob if he wanted a full-time job, saying it could be some time before her son was able to work again. Since Rob was currently unemployed, he'd jumped at the chance. Most of the work would be done there at the farm, and he'd pretty much be on his own. It would be better than having a job where he had to deal with finicky folks, like the people he'd served when he worked at a restaurant several months ago. That wasn't the kind of work he enjoyed. Rob would much rather be outside, where he could soak up the sun and be surrounded by nature.

"Whatcha thinkin' about?" Taavi nudged Rob's arm.

"Not much. Just glad I have a full-time job."

"Yeah. I was glad when Vickie asked you to work full-time. I don't mind helping out when I can, but with my job at the hotel and the odd hours I work, I may not be available to help at the farm that much."

"No problem. I'm sure I can handle things on my own."

"Maybe, but both Mandy and Ken were working there before, so—"

"Hey, who's that?" Rob pointed to a young woman dressed in plain clothes, sitting on the front porch of a stately looking home. A sign above the door read: The Palms Bed-and-Breakfast.

Taavi leaned against the steering wheel and squinted. "Well, what do you know? I think that's Ellen Lambright, from Middlebury, Indiana. Sure never expected to see her here again."

As Taavi pulled his rig onto the driveway, Rob kept staring at the woman. Even from this distance he could see she was pretty. "Is she Amish?" he asked, turning to face Taavi.

"Yeah." Taavi turned off the engine and set the brake. "I'm surprised you knew that, though."

Rob gave an undignified huff. "Come on, Taavi. Who doesn't know about the Amish? I've seen some of those Amish reality shows."

Taavi tipped his head. "Do you think they're real? I mean, I doubt they're portraying the Amish correctly."

Rob shrugged his shoulders. "Who knows? Ya can't believe half of what you see on TV these days." He hopped out of the Jeep and went around back to grab the cooler. "Guess we'd better take the chicken and eggs inside so we can be on our way. According to the list Vickie gave us, we've still got several stops to make."

"We can't just drop them off and leave right away. At least not here; it would be rude," Taavi explained. "We won't stay long, but these folks are great people. I'll introduce you to Ellen too."

Rob remained silent. The last thing he needed was any distractions.

CHAPTER 19

Carrying a box of chicken, Rob followed Taavi up the back stairs and onto the lanai, where several lounge chairs had been placed. Too bad he didn't know these people. It would be a nice place to relax and unwind. The house had a small view of the water. Not that the cramped rental he and Taavi shared was unbearable. It just didn't offer all the pleasing comforts this place had.

Taavi shifted the box of eggs in his hands and knocked on the door. He seemed to be careful to avoid the elaborate seashell wreathe decorating the door.

A few seconds later, a tall Hawaiian man appeared. "Aloha, Taavi!" He grinned. "Bet ya brought us some eggs and chicken."

"Sure did." Taavi stepped inside, and Rob followed. After they'd set their boxes on the kitchen table, Taavi turned to Rob. "This is Makaio Palu. He and his wife, Luana, are the owners of the B&B. Makaio, this is my friend and roommate, Rob Smith."

Rob shook hands with Makaio. "It's nice to meet you." He thought this fellow seemed friendly and engaging right off the bat, in his tropical shirt with his shark tooth necklace.

Makaio's handshake was hearty. "Good to meet you too."

"Vickie Williams hired Rob to work at the farm, so you'll probably be seeing a lot of him in the days to come. At least till Ken's able to work again." Taavi's words were optimistic, but not his tone.

"We'll look forward to getting acquainted with you." Makaio glanced toward an open door, leading to a hallway. "My better half is on the phone right now, but she should be coming into the kitchen shortly to do some baking. If you have a few minutes to spare, please wait. I'm sure she'd like to meet you."

Rob glanced at Taavi. "What do you say? Do we need to go now or did you want to hang out for a while?"

"We do have a few more deliveries to make, and I have to be at work soon, so. . ."

Taavi's sentence was cut off when a dark-haired, pleasant-looking woman appeared, along with the fair-skinned Amish woman Rob had seen on the front porch.

Taavi made the introductions, pointing out that Luana was Makaio's wife, and Ellen Lambright, a friend of Mandy's, was staying with them.

The Amish woman gave Rob a shy smile, then put the eggs and chicken in the refrigerator.

"Would either of you like a glass of juice?" Luana asked. "I have fresh pineapple and orange this morning."

"Orange sounds good to me." Taavi looked at Rob. "How 'bout you?"

"No thanks, I'm good." Rob glanced at Ellen when she joined them again. "Is this your first time to the island?" From what Taavi said earlier, Rob already knew it wasn't, but he didn't want Ellen to know they'd been talking about her.

"Actually, my friend Mandy and I were here a couple of years ago." She took a seat at the table. "We didn't make it back to the cruise ship on time, and it left without us. Makaio and Luana graciously took us in. Due to unforeseen circumstances, we ended up staying here a few months."

"That must have been kinda scary."

"It was at first, seeing the ship leaving without us and not knowing what awaited Mandy and me." Ellen smiled. "Makaio and Luana were very gracious to help us out in our time of need."

Luana stepped up to Ellen and placed a hand on her shoulder. "They were both a big help to us—especially when Makaio fell from a ladder and broke his leg. We thanked God for sending them to us at exactly the right time."

These folks must be religious. Rob shifted uneasily. *Think it might be time for me to go.* He turned to Taavi. "If you're finished with your juice, I think we ought to hit the road."

"You're right. We should be on our way." Taavi put his juice glass in the sink. "Thanks for the drink. It was nice seeing all of you."

"Yeah, same here." Rob followed Taavi across the room, but when he reached the door, he looked over his shoulder at Ellen. Her vivid blue eyes matched the color of her plain blue dress. It was hard not to stare. *I bet she's spiritual too.*

With a farewell wave, Rob hurried out the door.

✳

Lihue

The minute Ellen saw Mandy in the hallway outside Ken's room, she knew something was wrong. Mandy's face looked puffy, and her eyes were wet and dull.

Ellen clasped Mandy's hand. "Is Ken worse?"

Mandy pressed a fist against her chest. "He's fighting an infection, and when the doctor came in this morning he said Ken may end up losing his arm, despite the surgery." She blinked, pulling in a quick breath. "They are still dealing with his other wounds. The doctor said the swelling and fever need to go down before they can do more surgery."

"Oh, Mandy, I'm so sorry." Ellen rubbed her friend's back. "We need to pray harder for Ken."

"I've been praying." Mandy's chin trembled as she looked upward. "I've done nothing but pray since I was notified of the shark attack. I don't understand why God isn't answering my prayers."

As her friend's shoulders began to shake, Ellen reached out and pulled Mandy into her arms. They stood like that as Mandy released heart-wrenching sobs.

Ellen waited until the tears subsided. Remembering the hospital's chapel down the hall, she guided Mandy in that direction.

When they entered the small room, Ellen was relieved that no one else was there. At the moment, she was at a loss for words. But maybe sitting with Mandy in the chapel would help her find the right words to give Mandy some encouragement and much-needed hope. *How can I explain why one person's prayer is answered and another's isn't? But then,* she reasoned, *all prayers are answered. Some, just not the way we would like.*

After they'd taken a seat on one of the benches, Ellen took Mandy's hand. "One of our church's ministers preached an inspiring sermon a few months ago. He said, 'When we pray, God will answer in one of three ways. Yes. No. Wait.' Maybe God is asking you to wait. Sometimes when a person has to wait for an answer to prayer, they grow in their faith."

Mandy slowly nodded. "Your minister was right, but I'm just struggling right now. Ken and I have only been married a couple of years, and we've never faced anything so traumatic."

"With God's help, you'll get through it."

"Thank you, Ellen. I don't know what I'd do without you right now." Mandy swiped at the tears on her cheeks. "So who brought you to the hospital today?"

"Luana dropped me off. She has some errands to run but said she'd come up when she's done."

"Vickie's in with Ken now." Mandy twisted a piece of her shoulder-length hair around one finger. "I was getting ready to go to the cafeteria for lunch when you arrived. Will you join me?"

Ellen nodded. "Of course. We can talk more while we eat."

✳

Mandy stared at the untouched tuna salad on her plate. When she'd ordered the item for lunch, it had appealed to her, but now, as a wave of nausea hit, she could barely look at the salad.

"What's wrong?" Ellen pushed her chair in closer to the table. "Aren't you hungry?" Mandy placed both hands on her stomach. "I've been feeling queasy for several days, and I missed my monthly." Her voice lowered. "I think I might be pregnant."

"Have you seen a doctor or done a home-pregnancy test?" Ellen spoke in a tone of concern.

Mandy shook her head.

"Does Ken know what you suspect?"

"No. I wasn't going to say anything till I knew for sure." Mandy groaned. "Now, with his accident, I can't say anything until he's better."

"I understand, but. . ."

"You're the only person I've told, so please don't mention it to Vickie, or anyone else."

"Of course not. It's your place to share the news."

"If there is any news. It might be all the stress I'm under playing havoc with my hormones."

"Could be, but you won't know unless you take a pregnancy test." Ellen flicked back her narrow head covering ties.

"You're right. I'll pick one up soon." Mandy took a sip of water. After she set the glass down, she breathed deeply through her nose. It seemed to help some.

"What can I do to help out while I'm here?" Ellen asked. "Coming up to the hospital isn't enough."

Mandy took a small bite of salad. "It is enough, and I appreciate the support, but if you'd like to do more, we could use some help at the farm with the chickens."

Ellen's brows lowered a bit. "Didn't Vickie hire someone to help out? I met him at Luana and Makaio's this morning when he and Taavi delivered eggs and chicken."

"Yes, Rob is working there, but he's taking Ken's place. Before the accident, both Ken and I were caring for the chickens." Mandy dropped her gaze. "Now that I'm at the hospital most of the time and not feeling well, I can't do much at the farm."

Ellen leaned closer. "Would you like me to take over for you? Since my folks have raised chickens—although on a smaller scale—I can probably figure out what to do."

Tears welled behind Mandy's eyes. "You wouldn't mind?"

"Not at all. I can start by helping with this evening's chores. After Luana gets here and has visited with you and Vickie for a while, I'll ask her to take me back to the B&B so I can change into my everyday dress, and then I'll head over to the organic farm."

✳

Kapaa

Rob heard the gate to the chicken enclosure open, and he turned to see who'd come in. He was surprised to see the Amish woman he'd met at the bed-and-breakfast. "Can I help you with something?"

"I'm here to help."

"Huh?" Rob rubbed one side of his temple.

"I saw Mandy earlier, and when I asked if there was something I could do to help, she mentioned taking her place out here."

Rob's eyes narrowed. "You mean working with the chickens?"

"Yes."

"In those clothes?" He pointed to her brown dress, and then the matching scarf on her head.

"These are not my good clothes. It's what I would wear if I were at home doing chores."

Rob's forehead wrinkled. "This is a dirty job. You should wear a pair of jeans and some work boots, not a dress."

"I'd never put jeans on, but I'd wear boots if I had some." Ellen pursed her lips. "I'll bet there's a pair of Mandy's in the chicken house I can borrow."

Rob lifted his hands in defeat. This woman clearly had a mind of her own.

"Come on, then—follow me and I'll show you where the chickens go during the night."

"I know where it is, because I've been here before." Ellen folded her arms. "Ken gave Mandy and me a tour of the place when we were staying with Luana and Makaio a few years ago."

Rob tapped his foot impatiently. "But have you ever worked here?"

"No, but then you haven't worked here very long, either."

"True, but I've had a little experience with chickens."

"Oh? Where did you learn about raising chickens?"

"From my grandparents."

"Oh. Do they live here on the island?"

"Nope. I've only lived here a short time myself." Rob started walking. "Now let's get busy and get the chicken house cleaned."

Coming up to the chicken house, Ellen spotted a pair of rubber boots. "Those are Mandy's work shoes. I'll use them."

Rob paused to watch Ellen switch from her shoes to Mandy's boots.

"There, that's better, don't you think?" She looked up at him and smiled.

Rob nodded and followed her into the chicken house. *Sure hope she doesn't talk my ear off while we're cleaning the place. The last thing I need is to listen to a bunch of idle chatter or be asked a bunch of questions I'd rather not answer.*

CHAPTER 20

*T*wo days had passed since Mandy mentioned to Ellen that she might be pregnant. As she drove home from the hospital to get some rest, she decided to find out. Mandy couldn't even think how she would be able to take care of a baby too. Her mind swirled with continuous questions, but she needed to keep her focus on the road.

Mandy slipped on her sunglasses. The stress had brought on a headache.

As she drove on, Mandy barely noticed the fresh smell of salty air reaching her nostrils. Even the fragrant flowers blooming along the way didn't faze her. Her senses were on hold. All focus was on Ken and finding out if they were in the family way.

At the light, Mandy had time to take a refreshing drink from the water she'd purchased in the vending machine on her way out of the hospital. Her heart clenched. *Will he be happy if I am pregnant? What if he can't hold the baby because of his arm? What if he doesn't get better and the Lord chooses to take him from me?*

"Please, Lord, don't take my husband. If I'm carrying our child, this baby needs his daddy," Mandy whimpered out loud.

When the light turned green, she focused on the road. *I'm giving in to negative thoughts again. Why can't I pray, believing?* So much for the pep talk Ellen had given her two days ago. Mandy's thoughts bounced like a rubber ball, and her emotions were all over the place. *I should think positive thoughts.* Mandy willed herself to seek them out—something as simple as being thankful it was Ken's left arm that was injured, and not his right. *At least my husband won't have to learn to write with his other hand. And Ken is still here. He's a fighter. He just has to make it.* Mandy swiped at tears running down her cheeks.

Except for the chapel in the hospital, Mandy hadn't been to church since Ken's accident. Could that be why she felt so disconnected from God? It took all her energy to go to the hospital each day, sometimes spending the night. Surely the Lord, as well as everyone at church, understood her reasons for not being in church these days.

Mandy was glad when the pharmacy came into view. At least now she had something else to think about. She pulled Ken's rig into a parking space, shut the engine off, and got out.

Unfamiliar with where the pregnancy tests were located, once inside, Mandy sought a clerk for directions.

In addition to the test kit, she purchased a few items they were running low on. These days Mandy spent most of her time at the hospital, so there wasn't much time for running errands.

Moving down the last aisle, she grabbed a travel-size toothpaste and brush kit. She could easily store it in her purse, which made it convenient for the overnight stays at the hospital.

Mandy paid for her items and hurried from the store. She was eager to get home and take the test. One way or the other, she needed to know.

✳

Middlebury

Nora pulled back on her horse's reins and guided the mare up to the Freys' hitching rail. She'd come to pay a call on Mandy's mother, Miriam. *I wonder how my friend is coping with her daughter being so far away and needing support.*

Nora set the brake and sat for a moment. *It's one thing to send my daughter to help out, but at least she'll be coming home. Don't know what I'd do if Ellen ever decided to move away—or worse yet, leave the Amish faith.*

Nora got out of the buggy and secured her horse. Then she reached into the buggy to make sure things were secure in the box of food she'd brought from home. Since Miriam was still recuperating from foot surgery, friends and neighbors had been bringing in meals to help out. Today was Nora's turn. In addition to preparing supper for Miriam, Isaac, and their three boys who still lived at home, Nora was eager to find out how Mandy's husband was doing.

Walking up to the house, she noticed the pristine flowerbeds. Despite Miriam being laid up for a while, her family had been pitching in to keep things watered and weeded. Of course, most Amish helped one another when there was a need. Nora liked the ways of their church, and how their ministers fed them spiritually. She was happy to be a part of it.

When Nora stepped onto the porch, the front door opened, and fourteen-year-old Melvin greeted her. "Come in. My mamm said you'd be comin' today."

Nora smiled in response. "Are you taking good care of her?"

"Jah, she's resting inside."

"That's good. Lots of rest is good for her right now." Nora took a step, then stopped. "Oh, there's a cardboard box in my buggy. Would you mind taking it into the kitchen?"

"Sure, no problem. Mom's in the living room. If you wanna visit her, I'll put the box on the kitchen table." Melvin leaped off the porch before Nora could say thank you.

She entered the living room and found Miriam on the couch, her foot encased in a special boot-like apparatus and propped on a stool. "How are you doing?" Nora took a seat beside her friend. "Are you able to put any weight on your *fuuss*?"

"Jah, but I still have to wear this cumbersome boot and use my *gricke*." She gestured to the crutches leaning beside her against the sofa.

"I bet you'll be glad when your foot has healed and you can get back to doing everything you did before the surgery."

"I'm counting the days." Miriam frowned. "It's hard to sit in one spot and look out the window when I want to do things in the garden." She repositioned her booted foot. "I've never been one to sit around."

"Just give it some time. You'll get better before you know it."

"How are things at your place?" Miriam asked.

"I painted the bathroom yesterday but need to put things back in place later on today."

"You're a busy gal, for sure."

Nora smoothed her dress. "I brought everything to make supper for your family. But is there anything else I can do for you while I'm here?"

"I can't think of anything right now. Sadie and her mamm came by yesterday and did the laundry. They also picked produce from my garden." Miriam shifted her leg again on the stool. "The day before that, the bishop's wife and two other ladies from our district came over and did some cleaning. And lots of folks have brought in food."

"It's nice to be a part of a caring community."

"That's for sure. One of our English neighbors said she knows many people who aren't fortunate to have good friends and neighbors."

Nora's forehead wrinkled. "I can't imagine how that would be. The friendships we've established in this community are tried and true."

Miriam reached over and patted Nora's arm. "Jah, and they even reach all the way to Hawaii. I can't tell you how much I appreciate your daughter going there to be with Mandy. It's meant a lot to her and me as well. It's hard to be away from family—especially when there's a need."

Nora nodded. "I miss Ellen, but she's where she needs to be right now."

✳

Kapaa

Ellen headed for the house. She and Rob had worked up quite a thirst, and she'd told him she would get them something cold to drink.

She looked down at Mandy's boots and noticed how dirty they were. She would clean them later, but for now she just removed the boots before going inside.

When Ellen entered the kitchen, she heard muffled sobs coming from the adjoining room.

She stepped into the dining room, where she found Mandy at the table with her head down and hands up to her face. Her sobs tore at Ellen's heart.

"What's wrong?" She placed her hands on Mandy's trembling shoulders. "Has Ken's condition worsened?"

Mandy lifted her head and took a deep breath. "I took a home-pregnancy test. It was positive."

Ellen pulled out the chair next to her friend and sat. "Congratulations! Aren't you excited?"

"I am, but with Ken still in serious condition, this news is bittersweet." Mandy pulled a tissue from her skirt pocket and blew her nose. "I can't even tell him he's going to become a father."

"Maybe not now, but when he gets better." Ellen rubbed her friend's shoulder.

Mandy's gaze lowered. "You mean, if he gets better. What if Ken loses his arm, or his leg never heals properly and he can't work again? What if—"

"There you are, Ellen. What's takin' so long with the water?" Rob marched up to her with hands on his hips. "I'm dyin' of thirst. What happened—did ya decide you've had enough work for the day and quit on me?"

Ellen ground her teeth together. *Doesn't Rob see how upset Mandy is?* She was tempted to give him a piece of her mind, but she didn't want to upset Mandy any further. *I quit working for Dad because Ezra was so bossy, and now I'm stuck dealing with Rob. Seems I may have gone from a hot kettle into the fire pit.*

CHAPTER 21

Seeing Ellen's face tighten, Rob realized he'd spoken too harshly. He pulled off his baseball hat and laid it on the nearby counter. *Boy, I'm sure not being careful about my tone. Think I'd better lighten up.* He glanced at Mandy and noticed her red face and tear-stained cheeks. "Are you okay? Is your husband worse?"

She sat, seeming to collect her thoughts. "He's the same as before." Mandy rose from her chair. "Excuse me. There are some things I need to do." She glanced at Ellen, then fled the room.

Ellen stood too. "I'll get your water, Rob." She headed for the kitchen and he followed.

"That's okay. I'll get it, Ellen." Rob made a beeline for the refrigerator, took out two bottles of water, and handed one to Ellen. "Sorry for speaking in a harsh tone to you when I first came in."

Ellen took a drink of water before she spoke. "I appreciate your apology."

"I shouldn't have been so demanding."

She nodded.

Rob wondered if she was still upset. Her eyes avoided his as she fiddled with the ties to her cap, looking everywhere but at him. He opened his bottle and drank all of it, then took a seat at the table. "Mind if I ask you something?"

"Not at all." Ellen looked at him.

"How long are you planning to stay on the island?"

Ellen pulled out a chair and sat across from him. "I'll be here for as long as Mandy needs me."

"Is everything okay with her today? When I saw her in the dining room, it seemed like she may have been crying."

"Mandy's going through a rough time. A lot of people are praying for her and Ken, so I'm trusting God that everything will work out."

He fingered the checkered tablecloth. "Do you believe in the power of prayer?"

"Yes. Don't you?"

No. God let me down when I needed Him the most. Rob kept his thoughts to himself. Pushing the chair aside, he stood. "I've had enough of a break. How about you? Are you ready to get back to work, or would you rather stay inside for a while where it's cooler?"

"I'm ready too."

"Okay, great." Rob raced for the door and held it open for her.

Ellen offered him the sweetest smile. "Thank you, Rob."

✳

Mandy lay on her bed, staring at the slow-turning ceiling fan. Learning that she was expecting a baby should have been a most joyous occasion, and she felt guilty for not being more excited.

What will Ken say when I tell him he's going to be a daddy? I'm sure Vickie and my folks will be glad to hear this news.

Mandy touched her stomach. It was amazing to think a new life was growing mere inches from where her hand rested. *Ken and I will become parents in less than nine months.* She rolled onto her side. *Why did I encourage him to go surfing with his friends?* Mandy had twisted and turned that horrible day into so many different scenarios. But going over and over it didn't change what had happened.

Mandy had looked forward to the day she would surprise Ken with the news that they were expecting their first child. It would have been so special—just the two of them, alone and uninterrupted. Mandy's dream never included her husband lying in a hospital bed before learning he was going to be a father.

So many decisions fell on her now, but she didn't feel up to making any of them. All Mandy wanted to do was sleep. Despite her exhaustion, she couldn't turn off her concerns.

Mandy sat up and lifted her Bible from the nightstand. She turned to Isaiah 41, which she'd marked with a peach-colored ribbon. She read verse 13, which was underlined: *"I the Lord thy God will hold thy right hand, saying unto thee, Fear not; I will help thee."*

She clutched the Bible to her chest. *Help me, Lord, to remain calm and remember Your blessings.*

Mandy got off the bed. She needed to get back to Ken and relieve his mother. First, she would call her parents and leave a message. She wanted to give them an update on Ken and share the news of her pregnancy.

✳

Later that evening as Ellen cleared the supper dishes at the bed-and-breakfast, she thought about Rob and how nice he'd been to her this afternoon. She couldn't get over how he'd apologized for acting bossy—and the pleasant way he'd spoken to her as they worked in the chicken house.

Nothing like Ezra. He was never pleasant to work with. Ellen didn't know why she was comparing Ezra to Rob. There was no chance of a relationship with either of them. Ezra wasn't her type, even though her mother spoke highly of him whenever the opportunity presented itself.

If Mom knew I was interested in Rob, who's English, she'd say I should nip it in the bud.

Well, Mom need not worry. There's no chance of me developing a relationship with Rob either. When I leave Kauai, Rob will go on with his life, and I'll return to mine in Middlebury. Ellen had to admit she felt drawn to Rob, even though she didn't know much about him.

Determined to concentrate on the job at hand, she grabbed a spoon and put the leftover green beans in a plastic container.

Ellen glanced at Luana, busy loading the dishwasher. *I wish I could tell her about Mandy's pregnancy. But it's not my place to say anything. Mandy will share the news when she feels ready.* Ellen put the beans in the refrigerator. Mandy hadn't even told Ken yet, which was sad, because her husband should have been the first to know. Ellen could only imagine what it felt like to be in her friend's position.

"You've been quiet this evening. Even the jokes Makaio told at the supper table didn't make you laugh," Luana mentioned when Ellen handed her a few more dirty dishes. "Are you tired from putting in a hard day at the farm?"

"Not too much. It was a pretty easy day. I'm just worried about Mandy and Ken." Ellen wet the dishrag and began wiping the kitchen table.

"We're all concerned, but worry won't change a thing." Luana folded her hands. "Remember the remedy for worry?"

Ellen nodded. "Prayer."

"Exactly."

"I've been sending up lots of prayers since Ken became injured, but sometimes worry creeps in."

"How well I know. I've had plenty of things to worry about over the years. But fretting never changed any of my circumstances. All it did was stress me out."

"I felt that way when Mandy and Ken moved to Kauai and I was left to run their B&B. At first I thought it was only temporary. But when they decided to sell, my stress level increased."

Ellen finished wiping the table and put the dishrag on the drying rack. "I enjoyed my responsibilities at the B&B and wanted to buy their business. But of course I didn't have enough money for even a small down payment."

Luana tipped her head. "Does Mandy know you wanted to buy it?"

"No. I saw no point in telling her, since I couldn't afford it. I'm just glad for Mandy and Ken's sake that it sold right away. At least they don't have to worry about mortgage payments anymore. They probably didn't get much from the equity they'd built up in the two years they owned the B&B, but whatever they made should help pay some of Ken's hospital bills."

Luana poured detergent into the proper receptacle and closed the dishwasher door. "I hope they don't have to use any of it. They're going to need money for their future. Who knows—if Vickie should decide to sell the farm, Ken and Mandy might want to buy a house of their own."

"Do you think they would move back to Middlebury?"

"Unless Vickie were willing to move to the mainland, I doubt they would leave her." Luana pursed her lips. "If that brother of Ken's had stayed here instead of running off to California because he couldn't deal with his dad's death, Vickie would have all the help and support she needs." She shook her head. "I doubt Ken will be back to work anytime soon."

*

When Vickie entered the house, she found Mandy on the couch, holding her cell phone. She turned to face Vickie with raised brows. "I'm surprised to see you. I assumed you wouldn't come home until I returned to the hospital."

"Ken's asleep, so I decided to get a few things done here before I go back."

"I thought we were taking turns." Mandy placed the cell phone in her lap.

"That was the plan, but the nurse gave Ken a pretty strong sedative, so there's no point in either of us being there right now." Vickie studied her daughter-in-law's pale face and red-rimmed eyes. "We both need a good night's sleep in our own beds tonight. Do you agree?"

"It would be nice, but. . ." Mandy's voice trailed off.

Vickie took a seat beside Mandy. "Is something other than Ken's situation bothering you?"

Mandy gave a slow nod. "I have some news."

"Oh? Is it about the farm?"

"It's about me. I took a home-pregnancy test earlier today. It was positive."

Vickie sat several seconds, letting her daughter-in-law's words sink in. Then she pulled Mandy into a tight hug. "That's wonderful! We needed some good news." She dabbed at the tears trickling down her cheeks. "Have you told your folks?"

"I called a few minutes ago and left them a message."

"Ken's going to be so excited about this when he wakes up and you share the good news." Vickie leaned in closer.

Mandy shook her head. "I'm not going to burden him with this right now."

"Burden him? What do you mean?" Vickie bit down on her bottom lip. "Knowing he's going to be a father will give my son a reason to get well."

"You heard the doctor say Ken has a long recovery ahead. I don't need him worrying about me." Mandy clasped Vickie's arm. "Please don't say anything to Ken about my pregnancy. I should be the one to tell him, but not till I feel he's ready."

"You're right, it is your place to give Ken the news, but I hope you won't wait too long." Vickie didn't understand Mandy's reasoning, but she would keep quiet and let Mandy do the telling.

CHAPTER 22

Lihue

$\mathcal{M}$andy sat beside Ken's bed, looking at the book about Hawaiian customs she'd purchased in the hospital gift shop. If Kauai was to be her permanent home, she wanted to know everything about its origin, the ways of the people, and anything that might be of interest. If her parents or any of her friends or extended family in Indiana ever came to visit, she would share her knowledge of the island with them.

Mandy longed to be with her family, although it did help to have Ellen with her.

Sighing, she set the book aside and placed both hands against her stomach. *I wonder if Mom and Dad will come when the baby is born. It would be wonderful to see them. Since it wouldn't be considered an emergency, they wouldn't fly, but maybe they'd come by boat.*

She glanced over at Vickie, dozing in her chair. *At least Ken's mother will be here to see her new grandchild when it's born.*

"Mandy. . ."

She jerked her head in Ken's direction, pleased to see his eyes were open. She leaned close to his bed and clasped his right hand.

"Wh–where am I?"

"You're in the hospital."

"What day is it?"

"July eighth. You've been here for thirteen days." Mandy squeezed his fingers. "Do you remember what happened?"

"Yeah. It was a shark that got me, but everything's kinda fuzzy." Ken moved his head from side to side. "How bad am I hurt?"

Before Mandy could respond, Vickie woke up, wide-eyed. "Oh, Ken, it's so good to see you're fully awake." She left her chair and moved closer to the bed, then leaned down to kiss his forehead.

"Hi, Mom."

"How are you feeling, Son? Are you in much pain?"

Ken grimaced. "Yeah." He looked back at Mandy. "How bad are my wounds?"

"There are lacerations on the left side of your body that include your arm, side, and leg." Mandy blinked to keep from shedding tears. She needed to remain strong for Ken's sake. "You've had surgery on your arm, and your leg will be next. It's been a slow process due to an infection that set in."

"Guess I'm in a real mess. Not worth much to anyone right now."

Mandy lifted Ken's uninjured hand and kissed it. "You're worth the world to us. We're so happy you're alive."

"Taavi and Rob told us what they saw from the shore. What do you remember about the attack?" Vickie questioned.

Ken groaned and closed his eyes for a few seconds. "I'm not sure how accurate it is, but this is what I remember: I was on my board, getting ready for a big surge. Then I saw Taavi and Rob waving at me and pointing. I thought they were trying to tell me the huge wave I'd been waiting for was coming. But then I felt a bump against my board." Ken paused, sweat beading on his forehead.

"It's all right if you don't want to talk about it." It was hard for Mandy to see her husband's pained expression.

"It's okay." He took a deep breath. "After the bump, I was knocked into the water. As I swam toward my board, a fin surfaced. Then the shark came toward me." Ken looked at Mandy, his eyes wide with fear. "It was like it happened to someone else when the shark took a bite out of my arm. I felt numb—no pain, as I fought back, kicking and punching at him. Then the shark pulled me under, biting into my side, and shaking me like a rag doll. When I saw blood rising to the surface, I thought for sure I was a goner."

Mandy's throat constricted. She tried to imagine the horror of what Ken went through.

"When I kicked at the shark, its sides felt like cement," he continued.

"It had to be a miracle, because the shark gave up and let go. But in my exhaustion and with the loss of blood, I couldn't even swim. If it hadn't been for Taavi and Rob, I'd have either drowned or bled to death." Ken groaned as his eyes glazed over. "The whole time I kept thinking, 'I'll never see my family again.'"

Vickie put her finger against his lips. "That's enough talk now. You need to rest." She looked at Mandy. "Would you please call a nurse to give Ken something for pain? It's clear he's hurting."

Mandy's hand trembled as she pushed the CALL button. It scared her beyond reason, listening to the horrible ordeal her husband had gone through. How the big beautiful ocean could hold so much terror was beyond comprehension.

When the nurse came and gave Ken something for the pain, Mandy sat in silence and watched him drift off. She couldn't help wondering if he would ever go in the water again. The emotional trauma of what he'd been through would no doubt be with him for a long time.

✳

Kapaa

"I'm glad you suggested we take a break for lunch, 'cause I'm hungry." Rob stepped into the kitchen behind Ellen.

She turned to look at him and smiled. "Some people don't work well on a full stomach, but if I don't eat regular meals, I tend to get shaky."

He lifted his hand toward her, then quickly lowered it. "Do you have diabetes?"

"No, it's nothing like that. I've noticed my blood sugar drops if I don't eat, though I don't have any other symptoms of diabetes. The last time I had blood work done, the results came back within normal limits."

"A friend from when I was in school had juvenile diabetes, and he paid close attention to his diet." Rob opened the refrigerator and took out his and Ellen's lunch sacks.

When they approached the table, Ellen spotted a note from Vickie. She picked up the paper and read it out loud: " 'Ellen and Rob, if you finish your work this afternoon and would like to cool off, feel free to use the pool.'"

Rob pulled out a chair and sat down. "A swim sounds great, but I'd have to go back to Taavi's place and get my swim trunks." He leaned forward, resting his elbows on the table. "What about you, Ellen? Do you have a swimsuit?"

"I do, but it's at the bed-and-breakfast. Guess I can walk over and get it."

"Okay!" Rob slapped his palms together. "After we eat, let's finish up what we were doing, and then we'll get our suits and meet back here."

Ellen smiled. The idea of taking a dip in the pool on this hot day sounded great. And although she would never admit it, so did swimming with Rob.

✳

When Rob returned, wearing his swim trunks under a pair of shorts, he was surprised to see Ellen in the pool. He stood on the deck and tried not to stare. Ellen's backstrokes were graceful, but powerful. She was a strong swimmer, and looked good in her modest, but attractive blue swimsuit.

He removed his shorts and draped them over one of the lounge chairs, then stepped onto the pool ladder. *Sure hope I don't say or do something stupid. Don't know why, but I feel like a schoolboy right now, with a crush on his teacher.*

Once in the water, Rob swam toward the deep end. He'd only made it halfway, when he bumped into Ellen. "Sorry about that. Are you okay?"

"I'm fine." Her face turned pink as she treaded water in front of him. "How about you?"

"No injuries here, but I should have been watching where I was going." Rob figured his face might be red too.

She gave a small laugh and swam in the other direction.

They remained in the pool about an hour, swimming, diving, and splashing each other. Rob couldn't remember when he'd had such a good time or felt so relaxed. He was disappointed when Ellen got out of the pool.

"If you're hungry, come join me for some cookies." Ellen slipped on a terry cloth cover-up, then gestured to a tray sitting on one of the small tables.

Rob hadn't noticed it until now. Of course, her beauty kept him focused, because he hadn't taken his eyes off Ellen since he showed up at the pool. Too bad she was Amish.

He got out of the water and wrapped a towel around his waist. "Where'd the cookies come from?"

"Luana sent them when I went for my swimsuit. They're made with coconut and macadamia nuts." She pointed to a pitcher of iced tea. "I found that in Vickie's refrigerator. Since she told us this morning we should help ourselves to any beverages, I figured it would be all right if I brought out the tea." She poured two glasses and handed one to Rob.

He grinned and took a drink. "Thanks. This hits the spot."

Rob wished the day didn't have to end. He could get used to lounging around the pool—especially with such a pretty companion. Ellen might be Amish, but she was anything but plain.

"You've never said much about your family or mentioned where they live." Ellen picked up a cookie and took a bite.

"They live on the mainland, in the same old house they've lived in for years." Rob lifted his glass and took a drink. The cold tea felt good as it slid down his parched throat. He was on the verge of asking Ellen about her family, when the outside telephone rang. Ellen rose from her seat to answer it.

When she returned to the table, her wrinkled forehead let him know something was wrong. "What's up?"

"That was Mandy. Ken woke up and was able to talk."

"Well, that's good."

"Yes, but the doctor came in and gave them some bad news."

CHAPTER 23

Rob looked at Ellen. "What's the bad news? Has Ken gotten worse?"

With furrowed brows, Ellen nodded. "Even though he's awake and talking, the infection in Ken's arm has gone deeper, and if they don't get it cleared up, he could lose his arm."

"Aren't they giving him antibiotics for that?"

"Yes, but they're going to start him on a stronger one. Also, his leg needs surgery, so Ken's recuperation is a long way off."

"Sorry to hear it." Rob shuffled his bare feet under the table. "I can't imagine what their hospital bills will be like."

"It is a concern, but I believe their needs will be met." She picked up her glass and set it on the tray. "I'd like to go to the hospital to be with Mandy. Would you be able to give me a ride?"

"Sure, if you don't mind riding on the back of my motor scooter. It's not as big and intimidating as a motorcycle, but it'll get us there."

"I have no problem with that. I'll go inside, put the snacks away, and change into my dress."

"Sounds good." Rob set his glass on the tray. "I'll use the pool house to change. As soon as we're ready, we'll be off."

✳

"I only have one helmet, but you're welcome to wear it," Rob said as they approached his motor scooter.

Ellen shook her head. "That's okay. I'll tie my scarf over my white kapp to hold it in place."

"I'm not as worried about your bonnet as I am your safety." Rob looked at Ellen as if he were sizing her up and down. "You sure you're up for this?"

"Of course."

Rob climbed on his bike and turned to Ellen. "Okay now, you need to approach the bike from the left side. Then place your foot on the foot-peg and swing your body over the seat—sorta like you're getting on a horse. You can put your hands on my shoulders for balance if you need it."

Feeling more than a bit awkward, Ellen followed his instructions.

"Now place your other foot on the second foot-peg and sit up straight. Now put your hands around my waist and hang on tight."

Ellen's insides quivered as she placed her hands around Rob's middle. Was the nervousness she felt from anticipation of riding the scooter, or could it be the nearness of him?

Rob looked over his shoulder. "Make sure when I lean that you lean with me. And when I stop for a light, keep your feet on the foot-pegs."

"Okay."

"One more thing. Don't put your head too close to mine or we'll bump heads when the bike slows down."

"I'll do what you said." Ellen never imagined herself on the back of a motor scooter, and with an English fellow, no less.

✳

Lihue

When they arrived at their destination, Rob told Ellen he'd wait for her in the waiting room, while she went to look for Mandy. "I'll just hang around in case you need a ride home. I mean, back to the bed-and-breakfast." He didn't understand why he felt so rattled all of a sudden. All that time with Ellen in the pool this afternoon, and now he struggled to manage a sensible sentence. *Must be the exhilaration of the ride over here.* He had to admit, having her arms wrapped around his waist felt pretty nice.

Ellen smiled. "Okay, I'll be back soon."

When she headed toward the nurses' station, Rob picked up a magazine and took a seat. He couldn't concentrate on the magazine, however. All Rob could think about was Ellen and how much fun he'd had with her today. He hadn't enjoyed the company of a woman that much since. . . He closed the magazine and slapped it on the table. *I can't let my mind go there again. I'm glad Ellen won't be staying on the island indefinitely, so there's no chance of us developing a permanent relationship.*

He moved over to the window and looked out at the cars in the parking lot. *Coming to this island has been good for me. It's helped me feel calm and relaxed—at least till Ellen showed up and messed with my head. Bet anything she doesn't have a clue I've been thinking about her.* Rob tapped his foot. *I wonder what she thinks about me.*

Someone tapped Rob's shoulder, and he whirled around, surprised to see Ellen looking up at him. "You're back already?"

She nodded. "I spoke to Mandy, and she wants me to stay for a while. So either she or Vickie will take me back to the B&B when one of them is ready to go home."

He pulled his fingers through the ends of his thick hair. "Okay, then. Guess I'll see you tomorrow at the farm."

"Tomorrow's Sunday, and I'll be going to church with Luana and Makaio. You're welcome to join us if you like."

"No thanks. Those squawking chickens still need to be fed, so I'll be over at the farm at least part of the day."

"I'll see you Monday morning then."

Was that a look of disappointment I saw on her face? Rob wondered as Ellen walked away. *Did Ellen invite me to church because she thinks I need religion, or could she want to spend time with me?*

✳

Middlebury

"That was one good supper, Nora." Ezra leaned back in his chair and gave his belly a thump. "Stuffed peppers and mashed potatoes are my favorite meal. Danki for inviting me to join your family tonight."

Nora smiled from across the table. "It was nice you could come, and I'm glad you enjoyed the meal." She began collecting the plates. "We could have our desserts outside on the front porch."

"Maybe in a while, after my supper settles." Nathan patted his midsection.

"All right, we can hold off for a while." Nora picked up a few glasses.

"Can I help with the dishes?" Ezra rose from his chair.

She shook her head. "My daughters will take care of that, but it was nice of you to ask."

"Why don't the two of us head out to the living room for a friendly game of checkers?" Nathan suggested. "Unless you're not up to the challenge."

"Dad's a hard one to beat," Lenore spoke up as she cleared a stack of plates from the table.

"I'm pretty good at checkers, so jah, I'll take you on, Nathan." Ezra grinned at Lenore and winked. She was a cute girl—full of spunk.

"When you're done playing, and my daed's food settles, we'll have dessert." Lenore grinned. "We're having peanut butter cream pie."

"Well, I'll be. That's another one of my favorites."

"I know." Lenore's gaze dropped.

Ezra found the blush of pink that spread across the girl's cheeks to be kind of cute, but his thoughts went straight to Ellen, since Lenore resembled her.

Ezra rubbed the back of his neck. He'd wanted to ask about Ellen all evening but was too embarrassed to say anything in front of everyone. If he could get Lenore alone for a few minutes, he might have a chance to make an inquiry.

I could ask Nathan about Ellen, Ezra thought as he took a seat at the card table in the living room. *Maybe if I mention her in a nonchalant way, he won't catch on.*

"Have you done much fishing this month?" Nathan asked as he got the checker game from the bookcase and set it between them.

Ezra took a seat and began helping Nathan set up the game pieces. "Nah. I'd sure like to, but I don't seem to have the time."

"Maybe if we have a slow day at the shoe store, I'll close up early, and we can go fishing together." Ellen's dad placed the empty checker box on the coffee table and took a seat at the card table.

"Sounds good to me." Ezra enjoyed spending time with Ellen's family. He wished she could be here too. "Say Nathan, I've wondered what you've heard from Ellen these days. Is Mandy's husband doing any better?"

"The last we heard, Ken was still struggling with his injuries."

"That's too bad." Ezra pulled out his hanky to blow his nose. *Something in the room must be bothering my allergies.* "Guess Ellen won't be back for a while."

"She plans to stay in Hawaii for as long as Mandy needs her. Could end up to be several more months." Nathan pushed Ezra's checker pieces toward him. "Ready to play?"

"Jah, sure." Ezra's hope of seeing Ellen soon had gone out the window. He wondered if he'd ever get the chance to tell her what was in his heart. And when he got the chance, would she be receptive?

CHAPTER 24

Lihue

*M*andy was almost sick with worry. It had been two weeks since Ken's doctor put him on a stronger antibiotic, and today he was scheduled for another surgery. This time it involved his arm and leg.

She glanced out the window, watching the clouds billowing in the blue sky. Oh, how she wished her husband felt better.

Mandy turned away from the window and began to pace the floor of his hospital room. Was there no end in sight for Ken? *Maybe I'm not praying hard enough, or in the right way. There must be some reason God's allowing us to go through this right now.*

In addition to her husband being faced with a long recovery, the hospital bills were mounting. She'd called her folks an hour ago and left a message, asking them to return her call. *If only they could be here with me right now.*

Vickie had stepped out of the room a few minutes ago to call Dan and give him the latest on Ken. Mandy didn't understand why Ken's brother hadn't come back to Kauai, at least to see Ken and offer his mother support. It wasn't her place to judge, but she thought Dan seemed selfish. Could he have taken his father's death so hard that he couldn't deal with coming home?

Mandy looked outside the window again. A few vehicles whizzed by, with colorful surf boards tied to the roof. *I wonder if the authorities put signs on the beach, warning people of the recent shark attack.* Mandy hated to think of anyone else getting hurt if there were no warning signs posted.

She jumped when her cell phone vibrated. Seeing it was her folk's number, she stepped outside in the hall to take the call. Ken slept, and she didn't want to disturb him.

"Hello."

"Mandy, it's Dad. I heard your message and wanted to call right away."

She swallowed hard and choked back tears. "Oh, Dad, it's so good to hear your voice. Ken will be going in for another surgery soon, so he could use some extra prayer."

"You've got it. I'll spread the word and get those in our church district praying."

"Thank you."

"How are you doing, Mandy? You sound like you're about to cave in."

"I–I'll be all right. I have to be, for my husband's sake." Mandy took a deep breath. She needed to get herself together and stay strong. "How's Mom doing? Is her foot healing okay?"

"Yes, she's staying off it as much as possible and wearing the boot the doctor ordered."

"That's good." Mandy blew her nose on a tissue she'd pulled from her pocket.

"Have the hospital bills started coming in yet?" Dad asked.

"Some. But there will be more in the days ahead."

"Well, try not to fret about it. I've talked to a few people in our area, and everyone wants to help. There's going to be an auction to help raise money for Ken's medical expenses."

"That will help so much. Ken and I have some money in the bank from the sale of our bed-and-breakfast in Middlebury, but with his extended hospital stay that money will be gone in no time."

"Mandy, there's no reason for you to use all your savings when others can help. With a baby on the way you're gonna need money for future expenses."

Mandy's vision blurred. She wished she could reach through the phone and give her dad a hug. His words were a great comfort to her.

Kapaa

"Sure hope I don't have to feed and water chickens the rest of my life." Rob grunted as he filled another container with fresh water. He glanced at Ellen. "Don't get me wrong—I'm grateful for this job. But it's not something I want to do forever."

She set the bag of chicken feed aside and looked up at him. "What would you like to do?"

He shrugged. "I'm not sure. Guess I won't know till I find the perfect job."

"I had what I thought was a perfect job once, but I lost it when new owners took over the bed-and-breakfast Mandy and Ken used to own."

"Did you look for a job at another B&B?" Rob continued to fill the feeders.

"I did, but there weren't any." Ellen sighed. "If I'd had the money I would have bought my friends' business and run the place myself."

He tipped his head. "You liked it that much, huh?"

"Yes."

"Sounds like a lot of work to me." He rinsed off the waterers.

"It is work, but enjoyable—at least it was for me. When I took over for Mandy and Ken after they moved here, I learned firsthand how much responsibility goes with running that type of business." Ellen's forehead wrinkled as she swatted a place on her arm.

"What's wrong? Did you get a mosquito bite?"

"Yes, and they're quite pesky today."

"There are a lot more mosquitoes during the summer months here on Kauai."

She glanced around. "In some ways, being here reminds me of home."

He quirked an eyebrow. "How could Hawaii remind you of your home?"

"It doesn't. I just meant being here and taking care of the chickens. My family has laying hens, although not this many. I'm used to caring for them."

"I see. So, do you like it here on Kauai?"

"Oh, yes. It's a beautiful place."

"Think you could ever live her full-time?"

"No, my family means too much to me." Ellen held a hand against her chest. "My home is in Indiana, and I'm a member of the Amish church, so there's no way I'd ever move to Hawaii for good."

"Oh, I see." Rob finished up with his chore, then leaned against the door frame and folded his arms. "What's it like, being Amish in Middlebury, Indiana? I mean, you dress different than the English, but does your church have special rules?"

"Yes, of course. Our regulations are taken from the *Ordnung*, passed on from our ancestors. But of course, each church district is led by a bishop, two ministers, and a deacon. They guide the congregation in making wise decisions regarding any changes to the rules."

"Hmm. . . Interesting."

Their conversation was interrupted when Taavi showed up. "I just got off the phone with Mandy," he announced. "I called to check on Ken, and she let me know that he's having more surgery today."

Ellen's eyes widened. "Really, I didn't know."

"No one did—not even Mandy till she went to see him this morning." Taavi moved closer to Ellen. "Came by here to see if you wanted a ride to the hospital."

"Yes. Yes, I do. I'll have to change out of my work clothes first." Ellen looked at Rob. "I hope you don't mind me leaving you with all the work here today, but I need to be with my friend."

"Sure, no problem. Go ahead with Taavi. I understand."

She gave him a brief smile, then hurried out the door.

Rob looked after her, slowly shaking his head. *I wonder if Mandy knows what a great friend she has. Wish I had a friend like that—someone who'd do just about anything for me. But the one person who would have. . . Well she's. . .* Rob grabbed the chicken feed and hauled it across the room, bringing a halt to his disconcerting thoughts.

✳

Lihue

Ellen sat quietly beside Mandy in the waiting room. She'd spent lots of hours here since her arrival on Kauai. She could see out the door to the waiting room, as nurses and doctors walked past in a flurry of activity. A few patients came by, pushing their IV poles. Others were in wheelchairs that family members maneuvered down the hall.

Ellen couldn't get over how many people were sick or recovering from some sort of injury. She closed her eyes. *Dear Lord: Too often I take my good health for granted. Thank You for allowing me to get out of bed each morning and for the good health I have. Please keep me strong and healthy, so I can continue to help where I'm needed.*

And most of all, Dear Jesus, please guide the doctors' hands as they perform surgery on Ken. Bring healing to Ken's body, and strength to his wife and mother. Amen.

"I wonder how long Ken will be in surgery."

Ellen opened her eyes and saw Taavi looking over at her, as if expecting an answer. Vickie answered instead.

"It could take several more hours."

Mandy groaned. "It's hard to sit and wait when I don't know how my husband is doing."

"Waiting is always the hard part." Vickie's chin quivered. "I remember how anxious I felt when Charles had his heart attack and I could do nothing but wait and pray while he was in surgery."

Ellen wished something she could say would ease the tension everyone felt. Maybe it would help if they talked about something else. She turned to Vickie and said, "Rob and I got the chickens watered and fed before I came here. This afternoon he will do the other chores on the list you left him."

"Things would be a lot easier if I didn't own that silly farm." Vickie twisted her gold wedding band around her finger. "But it's all I have left to remind me of Charles and the memories we made there together." Her face tightened as she turned toward Mandy. "If you and Ken hadn't stayed to help me after Charles died, my son would not be in surgery right now."

"But you're family, and we wanted to help." Mandy's voice choked.

"We all have a tendency to blame ourselves when tragedy occurs," Ellen spoke up. "But often the people blaming themselves are not the ones responsible." She clasped both women's hands. "While we can't change the past, we can pray about the future. Why don't we do that now?"

They all bowed their heads, and Taavi volunteered to pray out loud.

"Heavenly Father, You know how hard it is for us to wait for news about Ken. He's in Your hands and those of the skilled doctors and nurses. We ask that You heal Ken's injuries and restore his health. In Jesus' name we pray, amen."

Hearing Taavi's heartfelt prayer caused Ellen's throat to clog. Opening her eyes, she saw moisture in Mandy and Vickie's eyes as well.

A few minutes later, a doctor entered the room. "Mrs. Williams?"

Both Mandy and Vickie stood up.

"I'm Ken's wife." Mandy's voice trembled. "And this is his mother."

The doctor nodded. "I wanted you to know that Ken is out of surgery and in the recovery room."

Mandy stepped forward. "How is he? Can his arm be saved?"

"We believe the arm will heal, but it's too soon to know about his leg. It could be six months or longer before the muscle will attach itself and establish blood flow, and with any luck, regenerate a nerve."

Ellen stood and slipped her arm around Mandy's waist. "He will be fine—you'll see. And it won't be luck. It'll be all the prayers going up on Ken's behalf."

"Yes." Vickie nodded. "We are so thankful for the prayers."

Mandy leaned her head on Ellen's shoulder. "I don't know what I would do without your friendship. Thank you for being here with me."

Ellen hugged Mandy and Vickie. "I want to help in any way I can. If there's something specific either of you want done, all you need to do is ask."

CHAPTER 25

*T*he first Tuesday of August, Ellen went with Mandy to see an ob-gyn. While Mandy saw the doctor, Ellen sat in the waiting room. After almost an hour had passed, she wondered what could be taking so long.

I hope everything's all right. Ellen picked up a magazine, then set it down. *Too bad Ken can't be with Mandy this morning instead of me. What a shame he doesn't know about the baby.*

Ellen didn't feel it was fair of Mandy to keep her pregnancy from Ken. He had a right to know he was going to be a father. It would give him something to look forward to. But it was Mandy's decision to make, and she would honor it.

She picked up the magazine again, flipping through the pages of pre-natal information and advertising. Ellen scanned an article about different birthing methods, as well as classes expecting parents should consider.

Instinctively, she rested one hand on her stomach. *I wonder what it would feel like to have a tiny life growing within me. If I never get married, I won't experience the joy of being a parent.*

Ellen set the publication aside, and browsed through a few more magazines. Finally Mandy came out. "How'd it go?" Ellen whispered as they headed for the door.

"I'll tell you about it when we stop for lunch on our way to the farm."

✳

"I'm anxious to get to the hospital and see how Ken is doing," Mandy said as they headed toward the farm in his SUV. "I hope you don't mind if we eat at a fast-food restaurant. There's a place up ahead that makes some tasty fish tacos."

"It's fine with me, but if you'd rather not stop for lunch, we can eat when we get to the farm."

"Maybe that would be better. We can talk in private about everything that's going on." Mandy looked over at Ellen and smiled. "My mother-in-law always has plenty of food in the fridge, so I'm sure we can find something we like."

"Okay. Sounds good."

*

Kapaa

When they reached the Williamses' place, Ellen went to see how Rob was doing, then met Mandy in the kitchen.

"There's a three-bean salad, and you could use some ham slices for a sandwich." Mandy pointed to the refrigerator. "Of course we have plenty of bottled water or juice."

Ellen stepped over to retrieve the food. "Aren't you going to join me?"

"I'm not hungry right now. Maybe I'll grab a bite at the hospital later on."

Ellen closed the refrigerator and placed the bread, ham, and all the fixings on the table. "You need to keep up your strength, Mandy. Remember, you're eating for two now. And you want the baby to be healthy, right?"

"Of course, but the doctor said I'm doing fine. My pregnancy is going well, and I have another appointment set up, so you needn't worry."

"I don't mean to sound bossy. I'm concerned about you."

"I appreciate that, but my biggest concern is for Ken right now." Mandy's forehead wrinkled as she leaned against the counter. "Even though he's been doing okay since his last surgery, Ken's getting antsy waiting for them to make a cast, and then a brace, for his left leg. My poor husband wants to get out of that hospital."

"I don't blame him." Ellen took out a paper plate and a napkin. "Have the doctors said how much longer he will have to remain there?"

"It depends on how much time it takes for him to be fitted and make sure the brace is functional and supporting his leg in order to help with the attachment of the muscle." Mandy clasped her hands together. "I've decided to wait until Ken comes home from the hospital to tell him about the baby. He has enough on his mind right now." She opened the refriger-ator and took out two bottles of water, handing one to Ellen. "If you don't mind, I'm going to head for the hospital right away. I'm sure by now Vickie needs a break, and I am eager to see Ken."

"No problem. I'll eat lunch and then see what Rob needs me to do outside." Ellen gave her friend a big hug. "Everything will be easier once Ken comes home. And don't forget. I'll stay for as long as you need me."

Mandy squeezed Ellen's arm. "Thank you so much. You're a good friend. Oh, and one more thing."

"What's that?"

"You've been working hard since you got here, so why don't you take some time off for yourself?"

"No, that's okay. I don't need to."

"You should see a few sights while you're on the island. Your time on Kauai shouldn't be all work." Mandy stood with her arms crossed.

Ellen dished some of the three-bean salad onto her paper plate. "I didn't come here for a vacation. I came to help out and be a support to you."

"Even so, it could be a long time before you return to Hawaii, so you should have a little fun while you're here." Mandy moved toward the door. "Just think about it, okay?"

"All right. Tell Ken I said hello. Now that he can have other visitors besides his family, I'll come see him soon. Maybe if Luana and Makaio are free, they'll want to join me."

✳

Rob entered the kitchen and found Ellen at the table with her back to him. He had to fight the sudden urge to step up behind her chair and kiss the back of her neck. *What a dumb idea. Ellen would wonder what made me do such a thing. And how could I explain my behavior to her when I can't even justify it myself?*

Rob cleared his throat to announce his presence and was surprised when Ellen didn't turn around. He tried again, a little louder this time.

She jerked her head. "Oh, Rob, I was deep in thought and didn't hear you come in. Would you like me to fix you something to eat?"

"Thanks anyway, but I brought a sack lunch with me today." He opened the refrigerator and returned to the table with a paper sack.

"As soon as you finish eating I'll help you outside with the chickens."

Rob shook his head. "No need. I've been busy all morning, got a lot done, and there's nothing left to do till the chickens are put away this evening."

"Okay. Guess I'll go back to the B&B."

"Say, I have a better idea. Why don't you and I go somewhere for a few hours and do something fun for a change?"

"Where do you want to go?"

"Well, there's Spouting Horn. Have you ever been there?" Rob pulled out his sandwich and chips.

"Just once. It was the day Mandy and I missed the ship. We didn't stay long, so it would be nice to see it again and not be hard-pressed for time." Ellen smiled.

Rob was pleased that she wanted to go. "As soon as I'm done eating, let's grab some bottles of water and head out." He had to admit he too was eager to go.

Ellen picked up her tote bag. "I have some trail mix in here. Should I bring that too?"

"Sure, why not?"

✳

Spouting Horn

When they arrived at their destination, Ellen went to the restroom to check her appearance. Although the ride on Rob's motor scooter exhilarated her, it left her feeling windblown. After removing the scarf she'd tied around her traditional head covering and tucking in a few stray hairs, Ellen returned to the grassy area where Rob waited for her.

She smiled, pointing to the hens and chicks roaming around. It still amazed her how many chickens ran wild on the island. It was one more thing that made Kauai unique. She'd even seen some in the parking lot by the airport the day Makaio and Luana had picked her up.

"Before we go to the overlook, why don't we check out some of the trinkets and souvenirs being sold along the walkway?" Rob suggested.

"Who knows, you might find something you like."

She shrugged. "We'll see."

Many of the vendors sold jewelry, which Ellen had no interest in buying. When they came to a booth selling potholders made by a local woman, she stopped to look at them. "These remind me of the potholders some Amish women make back home," she told Rob. "Only most of ours aren't this colorful."

"Would you like one?" He pushed his sunglasses on top of his head.

"I probably shouldn't spend the money on something I don't really need."

"No problem." Rob reached into his pocket and pulled out his wallet. "I'll get it for you."

"Oh, no, you don't have to do that, Rob."

"I want to."

"Thank you, Rob." She picked up the purchase and placed it in her tote.

"*A'ole pilikia*—You're welcome, no problem." He grinned and took hold of her other hand. "Ready to see the water spout?"

"Oh, yes." Her fingers tingled beneath his grasp. *Does Rob feel it too?*

As they approached the lookout, Ellen's thoughts went to her friend. *This is the spot where Mandy met Ken.* Ellen had often wondered if Ken and Mandy's meeting was a coincidence or God ordained. They seemed to be meant for each other. Mandy had once said that she believed Ken was her soul mate.

Staring out at the ocean, Ellen clasped the handrail in front of her. *Do I have a soul mate somewhere? I hope I discover him before I'm too old for marriage.* Ellen thought about her aunt, Dianna, who hadn't gotten married until she was forty-five. *I certainly wouldn't want to wait that long.*

Unexpectedly, a plume of water shot up from one of the blowholes, causing Ellen to gasp. "Oh, what a magnificent sight! And look over there, Rob." She pointed. "Did you see the rainbow that formed?"

"It is pretty awesome, isn't it?" Rob reached into his pocket and pulled out his cell phone. "I'll wait for the next one to spout and get a picture. But first, let's take a selfie."

Before Ellen could offer a response, Rob pulled her close, held up his phone, and snapped a picture. Then he showed her the photo. "Turned out pretty good, don'tcha think?"

"We Amish don't normally pose for pictures, Rob."

"Sorry about that. If the photo offends you, I'll delete it."

Ellen studied the picture. "Oh, look, the water spouted behind us, and you even captured the rainbow."

"That makes it even more special." He smiled. "If you don't mind, I'd like to keep the photo. It'll help me remember this day after you leave Kauai."

Ellen swallowed hard. She didn't need a photo to remember this day, but how could she say no when he looked at her so sweetly?

CHAPTER 26

Kapaa

$\mathcal{M}$andy glanced at her cell phone to check the time. It was hard to believe it was the middle of August already. She and Ellen had arrived moments ago at the church for supper and Wednesday night Bible study. It was the first one she'd been to since Ken's shark attack. It would be good to fellowship with other believers at their church again, and she was thankful Ellen could join her this evening. It would have been nice if Vickie could have been here too, but she said she had some important paperwork to do.

Since Mandy's nausea had lessened, she had an appetite this evening and anticipated trying out some of the different foods offered at the potluck. She spotted Luana and waved.

"Mandy and Ellen, it's so good to see you." Luana moved across the fellowship hall and gave them both a hug. "Ellen said you might be coming to Bible study tonight." She patted Mandy's back. "How is Ken doing?"

"A little better. There's no more sign of infection, at least." Mandy explained.

"I'm so glad. Will there be any more surgeries ahead for him?" Luana asked.

"The doctors don't know for sure, but we're hoping it won't be necessary." Mandy sighed. "Ken wants to go home."

"That's understandable. This has been quite an ordeal for both of you." Luana stroked Mandy's cheek. "You look tired. I suspect you're not getting enough rest. Are you still spending nights at the hospital?"

"Sometimes, but now that Ken's out of danger, we've been sleeping at home."

Luana glanced across the room. "Let's join up with Makaio. Then we can sit together to eat our meal."

Mandy smiled. "That would be nice. I'd like to hear how things have been going at the B&B."

✳

"I feel bad that I haven't been able to help out at the bed-and-breakfast more," Ellen told Makaio as the four of them found seats at a table.

He shook his head. "We're getting things done, and your help is needed at the Williamses' farm more than at our place."

"That's right," Luana agreed. "You came to Kauai to help Mandy, not us."

"But you're giving me free room and board."

"It's our way of helping out." Luana's expression sobered. "We got some disappointing news yesterday."

"What was it?" Mandy asked.

"Our son-in-law got a job offer on the Big Island, so he and Ailani will most likely be moving. This means we won't get to see little Primrose as often as we like, not to mention their new baby after it's born." Luana's brows furrowed. "If they should decide to move, I'll miss seeing their *keiki*."

Makaio placed his hand on her shoulder. "We'll manage. A flight to the Big Island is less than an hour away."

"True, but it's never easy for us to leave the B&B when it's our busiest season."

"Don't worry. We'll work it out somehow."

Their conversation was interrupted when Pastor Jim came over to their table. Ellen had seen him at the hospital a few times, visiting Ken.

He stood next to Mandy's chair. "I wanted to let you know that a fund has been started to help with Ken's hospital expenses. Please let me or one of the elders know when you receive a bill. Then our church treasurer will write you a check. Although we can't pay for everything, we still want to help."

"Thank you, Pastor." Mandy's gratitude showed by her wide smile.

Ellen felt pleased that both the Amish church back home and Mandy and Ken's church here had offered to help. This kind of giving was Christianity in action.

$$*$$

Middlebury

Nora rolled over in bed, turned on her small flashlight, and looked at the clock near the bed. It was one in the morning, and she couldn't sleep. Ellen had been on her mind most of the day, and even after going to bed. She wasn't used to having her daughter gone so long. The fact that Ellen was so far away bothered Nora. Some Amish families were separated by several miles or lived a few states away, but having a family member living clear across the ocean was not the norm. Of course, Ellen wouldn't be staying there permanently, so it helped to know that much at least.

Nora glanced at Nathan—sleeping like a baby. Not wanting to disturb him, she got up, put on her robe, and slipped out of the room.

When she entered the living room, Nora turned on a battery-operated light, picked up her Bible, and took a seat in the rocker. Some time spent alone with God might help relieve her tension.

She prayed first, then opened her Bible to Isaiah 54. Verse 13 in particular caught her attention: "All thy children shall be taught of the Lord; and great shall be the peace of thy children."

Nora reflected on the words. She and Nathan had taught their daughters to love God and obey His commandments. They'd committed the girls to the Lord at a young age. Nora hoped each of them felt God's peace and would always seek His will.

Nora thought back to over a month ago, when they'd invited Ezra to dinner. Before he'd left to go home, Ezra had asked her for Ellen's address in Hawaii.

I've often wondered if Ezra is interested in our eldest daughter. Nora would keep her thoughts to herself, but maybe the next time she talked with Ellen, she might ask if Ezra had written to her.

Hearing footsteps approach, Nora looked up. She was surprised to see Darla shuffle into the room, the hem of her long robe, brushing the floor.

"Mom, what are you doing up in the middle of the night?" Darla released a noisy yawn.

Nora grinned. "I could ask you the same."

"I heard the squeak of the rocker."

Nora tipped her head. "The sound of this old chair moving woke you, all the way up to your room?"

"Well, at first I got up to get a drink of water. Then when I heard the squeaking noise, I came down to see who was out of bed." Darla took a seat on the couch. "So how come you're up, Mom?"

"Ellen was on my mind, and I couldn't sleep. She's been on Kauai almost two months, and the last time we talked it sounded like she could be staying several more months." Nora's hands fell to her lap as she heaved a heavy sigh. "I miss her and wish she were home."

"Maybe it would help if you called her more often."

"I would if I could catch her. Hawaii time is six hours behind us, so that makes it difficult. Besides, she's often busy at the organic farm or at the hospital offering encouragement to Mandy."

"Any recent word on how Mandy's husband is doing these days?"

"Ken came through his last surgery, but he's still in the hospital. Once he goes home, he won't be able to do any chores around the farm, so Ellen's help there is still needed."

"I thought Ken's mother hired a young man to take care of the chickens."

"She did, but there's too much work for one person. That's why Ellen volunteered to help out." Nora's hands rested on the Bible as she rocked.

Darla brushed some long stray hairs away from her face. "My sister is a good friend. I hope Mandy appreciates the sacrifice Ellen is making for her and Ken."

"I'm sure she does." Nora laid her Bible aside and stood. "I don't know about you, but I'm going back to bed. Before you know it, the old rooster will be crowing, letting us know it's time to get up."

"Okay. *Gut nacht*, Mom. I hope you sleep well." Darla stood and hugged

Nora. "I'll say a prayer for Mandy and Ken. And remember—Ellen's in God's hands. I'm certain my sister will return home as soon as she can."

＊

Thursday morning, Ezra woke up earlier than normal. While he could have gone back to sleep for another hour, he decided to get up and do something he'd been thinking about for several weeks. He couldn't get Ellen off his mind. Last month when he went to dinner at the Lambrights', Ellen's mother had given him her address in Hawaii at his request. It was past time to write her a letter.

It wasn't like Ezra to be so bold, but the longer Ellen had been gone, the more determined he had become to win her heart. He was convinced she was the girl for him, but he was concerned that she might do something foolish and stay in Hawaii.

Ezra went to the open window and lifted it higher. He breathed in the predawn air and looked up at the stars, wondering if they were this bright in Hawaii. In the distance, he heard a dog barking, and the faint hooting of an owl. He enjoyed the peacefulness of a new morning.

Shaking his head, he went to his desk, got out some paper and a pen, and began to write:

> *Dear Ellen,*
>   *I think about you almost every day, and I miss seeing your pretty face at your daed's shoe store. Whenever I see your sister, Lenore, I think of you.*

Ezra dropped the pen and slapped his cheek. *What am I doing? I can't tell Ellen any of that.* He wadded up the paper and tossed it in the trash can. *Guess I'd better start over and be a little more subtle this time:*

> *Dear Ellen,*
>   *I'd like to first offer you an apology for my behavior when I was in charge at your daed's store. I was wrong for acting so bossy, and I hope you'll forgive me. Maybe when you're back*

here, we can start over fresh.

So, how are you doing? Is Mandy's husband getting better? Your daed mentioned that you've been working at an organic chicken farm. Do you have any idea when you might be coming home?

Everything here is going okay. We've been busy at the store the last few weeks. Maybe when you return to Middlebury, you can start working there again.

Take care, and I hope to hear from you soon.

Sincerely,
Ezra Bontrager

Ezra sat back in his chair, locked his fingers together, and held them behind his head. *Looks like a good letter to me. I hope Ellen responds.*

CHAPTER 27

Kapaa

J'm going to step out front to check the mail," Luana told Ellen after they'd finished breakfast.

Ellen smiled. "That's fine. I'll put the dishes in the dishwasher while you're doing that."

Luana brushed the idea away. "Don't bother with those. You need to get ready to work at the farm. I'll take care of the dishes after you're gone."

Ellen knew better than to argue with Luana. She hadn't won a disagreement yet and couldn't change Luana's mind. Even so, whenever Ellen had an opportunity, she did whatever chores she could in Makaio and Luana's home.

As Ellen headed to her room to get her purse, she stopped in the living room to see if anything needed to be straightened. Nothing seemed out of place, so she paused to say good morning to one of their guests and moved on to her room.

When Ellen returned to the kitchen, Luana held a stack of mail. "There's a letter for you on the table, Ellen."

Eager to see who it was from, Ellen picked it up. She was surprised to see the return address was Ezra's. According to the postmark, the letter had been mailed a week ago.

I wonder why Ezra would write to me. And how did he get Luana and Makaio's address?

Ellen took a seat at the table and read the letter.

"What's wrong, Ellen?" Luana asked. "Did you receive bad news?"

"No. It's a letter from the young man who works for my dad."

"Ah, I see. So you have a boyfriend back home you haven't told us about?"

Ellen shook her head. "It's nothing like that. Ezra and I are just friends. I've known him a long time."

"Then why would he write to you?" Luana peered over the top of her reading glasses as she placed the rest of the mail on the table.

"I don't know." Ellen stared at the letter, still in disbelief. "This was a surprise to me."

Luana chuckled. "In my younger days, when a young man wrote a letter to a woman, quite often it meant he had a romantic interest in her."

"Well, it's not that way with Ezra." Ellen reflected on the way he'd acted toward her during the time she'd worked at the shoe store. Never once had Ezra showed any romantic interest in her. It fact, it seemed quite the opposite.

Ellen thought about how she'd gone out to lunch with Rob two days ago. The more time they spent together, the more she enjoyed being with him. He was a lot kinder to her than Ezra had ever been.

✳

"Have you ever done anything like this before?" Rob asked as he and Ellen painted the wooden fence surrounding the Williamses' yard.

"Why do you ask?"

"Just wondered, 'cause from the way you're holding that brush and moving your hand back and forth, it seems like you've had some experience painting."

"I have helped paint some things around my parents' place. How about you, Rob? Have you done much painting before?" Ellen stopped painting and reached up to her face and scratched at a fresh mosquito bite.

"A bit." Rob stared at a smudge of paint near the bite on Ellen's cheek. Pulling a hankie out of his back pocket, he poured liquid from his water bottle onto the cloth. As he reached toward Ellen to wipe the paint off, she pulled her head back.

"Wh—what are you doing?" She gave him a quizzical look, then glanced around, as though worried someone might be watching.

"When you scratched your cheek, you smeared paint on your face." Rob held the dampened hankie up. "May I?"

Ellen didn't resist this time and nodded.

Rob bit back a chuckle as she closed her eyes until he was done.

"Did you get it?" Ellen peeked up at him.

"Yep, it's gone. Good thing the paint washes off with water." Rob's brows furrowed when a movement caught his attention. He looked to the left and spotted a gray-and-black pigeon lying near the fence. "I wonder what's wrong with that grounded bird."

Ellen saw it too. "Is the poor thing hurt, or just scared?" She clambered to her feet, went over to the bird, and then went down on her knees. The pigeon lay still in the grass, as though dazed.

Rob knelt beside her and held the pigeon in his hands. He looked the bird over. Neither of its wings had been broken. "Think it may have plowed into something and is stunned."

Ellen reached over. "Is it okay if I hold it?"

The pigeon didn't struggle when he handed her the bird. Rob wouldn't have struggled either, being held with such tenderness by Ellen. He almost envied the bird.

"Look, it's not afraid and seems like it's used to being handled." She smiled in Rob's direction.

While Ellen talked in a soft tone to the pigeon, Rob noticed a plastic tag around the bird's leg. "This pigeon is banded." He pointed, then touched the bird's foot with the band around it. "I wonder if the pigeon belongs to someone. On occasion, I've seen homing pigeons flying together in a group." Rob ran his hand down the bird's back. "I've heard of people using them around here like a hobby of sorts."

"Is there a way we can find out who the owner is?"

"I'll have to do some checking and see what I can find out." Rob pointed to the band. "I'll write the number and letters down. Maybe that's a clue."

Ellen stroked the pigeon's head just as Rob's hand moved up the bird's back. When their fingers touched, he felt a warm tingle travel all the way up his arm. It was a familiar feeling—one he used to feel whenever he and his girlfriend from back home used to touch. But that was behind him now. He needed to move on. There was no point in dwelling on the past.

Rob concentrated on the pigeon. If there was one thing he didn't need right now, it was a romantic complication—especially with someone like Ellen. It was good she wouldn't be staying on the island indefinitely. *But that shouldn't keep me from enjoying her company while she's here*, Rob told himself.

✳

Mandy arrived home, feeling more lighthearted than usual. She was eager to find Ellen and share some good news.

Mandy put the keys in her purse and set it on the counter. Assuming Ellen must be out back with Rob, she headed in that direction. At least there was a light at the end of the tunnel for Ken.

When Mandy went outside, she spotted Ellen and Rob on their knees with their heads so close, they were almost touching. It appeared as if Rob held Ellen's hand.

Mandy stopped walking and stood, staring. *Has Ellen fallen for Rob? Is the feeling mutual? Should I be concerned?*

Mandy remembered how things had been between her and Ken when they'd first met. It hadn't taken them long to realize they wanted to be together, but there'd been a problem. Ken was English, and she'd been raised Amish.

But that was different, she told herself. *I was not a member of the Amish church, and Ellen is. I hope she's not getting serious about Rob. The last thing Ellen's Mom and Dad need is for her to leave the church and marry an English man or move to Hawaii, so far from home.*

Mandy was reminded once again, that her own parents lived thousands of miles away. She couldn't help wondering if she would ever see her home in Indiana again.

"Hey, Mandy, come see what we found," Rob called. When he and Ellen stood up at the same time, Mandy realized her friend held a pigeon.

"What's going on?" she asked, joining them by the fence.

"We found an injured pigeon," Ellen responded. "Its wings don't appear to be broken, so we're thinking it may have hit a window and is only stunned."

"This bird is banded, so I'm going to try to find out who it belongs to," Rob explained.

Ellen lifted the bird so Mandy could see its leg. "We think this is a homing pigeon."

Mandy smiled, relieved that Ellen and Rob hadn't been holding hands after all. Even when they were children, Ellen had had a soft spot for injured animals, so it was no surprise that she was concerned and wanted to find the pigeon's owner.

"I'm going to put the bird someplace where it's safe from any predators and see if it stays there or flies off." Rob took the fowl from Ellen and headed toward the chicken house.

Mandy stepped up to Ellen. "I have some good news about Ken."

"Oh? What is it?"

"Today the doctor said that if things go well with the cast for Ken's leg, he might be able to come home within the next few days.

Ellen gave Mandy a hug. "That is good news—jah, an answer to prayer."

Mandy nodded. "But once he comes home, it'll take many weeks for him to recover, and he might never be able to walk without a limp or certain restrictions."

"You'll need to take one day at a time. And remember, I'm here for as long as you need me."

"Thank you. It's a comfort to know that."

Ellen pointed to the chickens running around in their fenced-in yard. "It will be some time before either you or Ken can work here again, and I'm more than willing to help out for as long as necessary."

Mandy appreciated her friend's offer, but she couldn't help wondering if at least part of Ellen's willingness to remain here longer had something to do with Rob.

CHAPTER 28

Wailua, Hawaii

As Ellen hung on to Rob's waist, she felt his muscles through the T-shirt he wore. A sense of exhilaration came over her as they sped down the road on his motor scooter toward their destination. She was ready for some casual fun with Rob, away from the repetitious organic chicken farm and all the hard work.

Ellen thought about the letter she'd received from Ezra. She'd sent him a response the next day. It still surprised her that he'd sent the letter. Could Luana have been right when she'd said when a guy sent a letter to a girl, it meant he was interested in her? Ellen didn't get that impression from anything Ezra wrote.

As they sat at the stoplight, Ellen tightened her scarf. "Are we almost there, Rob?"

"Our turn is at the next light, and it's coming up in a couple of miles." Rob glanced back to look at her.

Before long, he sped down a hill and into a dirt parking lot. Rob found a spot to park the scooter near some other vehicles. Then they headed toward a thatched hut to inquire about the kayak rentals. After Rob paid, he suggested they watch a few people go out ahead of them. "It'll give you a better understanding of what to expect."

"That's a good idea." Ellen stood next to Rob, watching as a man and woman came down from the hut to pick out lifejackets. They each found a vest, adjusted the dangling straps, and clipped them on.

"The water looks inviting," Ellen commented.

Rob nodded. "It's a nice way to cool off on a warm day like this."

The couple walked onto the dock. The man climbed in first. When he was settled in his seat, the attendant and his helper held the kayak with a firm grasp against the dock, while the woman stepped in.

"That looks easy enough." Ellen smiled at Rob. "I don't think I'll have a problem getting in when it's our turn."

Soon the other couple left the dock. Ellen enjoyed watching them use their paddles at the same time. They took a few tries to get in sync and moved with smooth strokes along the water. In no time they were heading out to the main part of the river and had started on their trip.

"Are you ready to see some nice scenery?" Rob asked.

"Sure, and it will be good to get some exercise like those people ahead of us are doing."

Ellen and Rob put on their life vests and waited for the attendant to bring the kayak around. Once it was close enough, Rob climbed in. Then Ellen did the same.

"The Fern Grotto tour boats have the right of way on the river," the young man who'd brought the kayak to them stated. "So stay close to the edge of the river when you encounter them."

"No problem. We'll be sure to watch out," Rob replied.

Ellen sat still, eager to start the trip.

When the attendant asked if they were ready for a push off from the dock, Rob and Ellen responded with nods.

Once they were free and floating along, Rob suggested Ellen paddle on the right, and he'd take over the left. They moved along at a nice pace. It seemed a bit intimidating at first, but once Ellen got the hang of things, she found it fun to paddle the kayak.

"There are quite a few people out here today." Ellen pointed to the boats ahead of them.

"I bet a lot of them are tourists." Rob turned his head to look at her. "I'll try to take some pictures of whatever you'd like on my cell phone—just let me know. I'm sure Vickie wouldn't mind if I download the photos to her computer and print them for you."

"Thanks. It would be nice to have a few pictures to show my friends and family back home." Ellen slowed her paddling.

Despite the warmth of the day, the tree branches hanging over the water in places created some nice places to get a reprieve from the heat.

Rob looked over the side of the kayak. "Look how crystal clear the water is, Ellen."

She couldn't agree more. "The scenery is beautiful from this view on the river."

Rob rested the paddle he held. "Yep. We couldn't experience this kind of view on my scooter, that's for sure."

Ellen nodded. She almost felt guilty for having such a good time, when poor Mandy had been going through so much with Ken. But when she'd told her friend about this trip Rob had planned for them, Mandy had encouraged Ellen to go, saying she deserved to have some fun.

Ellen's thoughts turned to the injured bird they'd found the other day. "I'm glad you were able to track down the owner of the pigeon."

"Yeah, it was pretty easy after I found the website of a local pigeon club. When I emailed the man in charge, he was able to tell me who the bird belonged to by the identification number on the tag. After I called the owner, he came right away to get his bird. He was grateful and explained that he lived three miles away. So the pigeon almost made it home by itself."

As they paddled along, Ellen smelled a wonderful fragrance. "Where is that nice aroma coming from?"

Rob pointed to a group of light yellow flowers growing above the river bank. "I'm almost sure those are from the plumeria plants. They have a pleasant odor."

Traveling farther up the river, Ellen noticed some fish jumping. They reached a place where they could beach their kayak and walk along a path. Rob said the trail led to a waterfall, but they'd have to wade through waist-high river water first, in order to get to the falls. Deciding against that option, they walked farther up the river before turning around.

As they paddled toward the Fern Grotto, Ellen saw the tour boat come up behind them.

"Here comes the big boat; we'd better get out of their way." Rob helped Ellen direct the kayak closer to the water's edge.

"There's a large group of people on that boat." Ellen paddled more to keep them from drifting outward.

The tour boat moved fast through the water and passed them by. Ripples of small waves reached their kayak, causing them to bob up and down in the water.

As they traveled on, the river got narrower and shallower. For a few seconds, Ellen imagined being back home on their pond, floating in an inner tube, like she and her sisters had done when they were young girls. She was glad she was here, though, and wished the day never had to end. It was fun spending time with Rob.

"Would you like to pull over along here and drink some of the water we brought?" he asked.

"I could use a break, and rehydrating is a good idea." Ellen followed his lead, paddling their way to the bank.

Once close enough, Rob grabbed a root and held on to it to keep them snubbed close.

They got out their waters and drank, while resting along the bank. Ellen watched another couple from the other direction and waved.

"This was a good idea. I'm glad we could come here today." Rob took a long drink and wiped his mouth on his shirtsleeve.

"I'm enjoying the view, and I've been putting my hand in the water sometimes to cool off," Ellen admitted.

"I've taken some scenic pictures for you along our route, and even one of the tour boat that went by us earlier." Rob kept a hold on the root holding them close to the bank.

"I can't wait to see the pictures you've taken." Ellen put her water bottle away.

"Shall we continue our boat ride?" he asked.

"I'm ready to head on when you are," Ellen replied.

They rowed until they reached a shallow bend in the river, making it difficult to go on. So they turned and headed back to the dock where they'd started almost two hours before.

Ellen sighed. She didn't want this outing to end.

*

Middlebury

Ezra glanced at the clock on the store wall. It was four o'clock—almost quitting time. *Let me think. . . What time would it be in Hawaii right now? As I recall, Nathan mentioned Hawaii is six hours behind us, so that would make it around ten in the morning. I wonder what Ellen's doing right now.*

Ezra stood with his back to the counter, continuing to stare at the clock. He hoped she had received his letter and would send him a response soon.

Ezra closed his eyes, visualizing Ellen's pretty face. He could almost hear her calling his name. "Ezra. . .where are you? Ezra, can you hear me?"

Ezra was jolted out of his musings when Nathan thumped his arm. "Hey, what's the matter with you? Didn't you hear Lenore calling for you from the back room?"

"Oh, sorry. I'll go see what she wants." With his face feeling as warm as bread fresh from the oven, Ezra hurried off.

When he entered the back room, Lenore stood with her arms folded, frowning at him. "How come you didn't answer when I called? Couldn't ya hear me shouting your name?"

"No, not at first. I mean. . . Well, I was deep in thought." He gave Lenore his full attention. "What'd ya need?"

She pointed to some shoe boxes on a shelf overhead. "I can't reach those and wondered if you'd get them down for me."

"Oh, sure thing." Ezra reached up and pulled down one box after another. "There you go, Lenore."

She looked up at him with a sweet, dimpled smile. "Danki, Ezra. It must be nice to be so tall."

"It does have some benefits. Is that all you needed?"

"Jah."

"Okay. I'll be heading for home soon. See you tomorrow, Lenore." When Ezra glanced at his reflection in the mirror on the back wall, he noticed his hair needed a trim. *Think I'd better see if my mamm will give me a haircut soon.*

As he headed back to the front of the store, Ezra found himself wishing yet again that Lenore was Ellen. It was probably no more than wishful thinking, but in truth, he hoped Ellen would end up working here again.

*

Wailua

"We should head back to the farm soon, but before we go, it might be fun to take the self-guided tour of the reconstructed old Hawaiian village," Rob said as he and Ellen left their kayaks.

Ellen smiled up at him. "From what I read on the brochure I picked up, it sounds quite interesting."

"Great! Let's go." Rob grabbed Ellen's hand and was pleased when she didn't pull it away. *I'm glad she likes being in my company because I sure enjoy having her close to me.*

As they walked through the thatched-roof structures, including a canoe house, birthing house, the chief's assembly house, and doctor's house, Rob enjoyed seeing Ellen's reaction. Based on the almost continuous smile on her face, he felt sure she was having a good time. Artifacts and storyboards explained each structure's purpose, and lush green gardens grew in and around the village, yielding traditional Hawaiian fruits and flowers.

Rob looked up as some heavy gray clouds moved in overhead, shadowing the sun.

He bent down to pick up a deep coral-colored Hibiscus that had dropped on the ground. Then, without so much as a thought, he tucked it behind Ellen's right ear, in front of her white head covering. "You look beautiful," he murmured. "Pretty as the flower behind your ear."

Ellen's cheeks colored, and she gave a slight dip of her head. "Thank you, Rob."

It began to rain, but they continued on. Rob wouldn't allow anything to interfere with their wonderful day.

As they finished their tour, he found himself thinking: *This day has been wonderful. I'll remember it long after Ellen is gone.*

CHAPTER 29

Kapaa

On the last Monday of August, Ken finally came home. As he sat on the couch, he remembered how nice it had been to roll out of the hospital into the sunshine after being cooped up for weeks. Even though he had emerged from the hospital in a wheelchair, he didn't care. Mandy and Mom were attentive, getting him into the car and making sure he was comfortable as could be.

Now as Ken reclined on the couch with his injured leg propped on a pillow, frustrations piled up. He'd been lying here, feeling useless for the past hour, watching his wife and mother scurry about trying to make everything just right for him. Well, nothing was right, and if he didn't gain full use of his left arm and leg, things might never be.

From what the doctor had said, Ken might always have a limp and be forced to use a cane. He couldn't believe how much his life had changed. Adjusting to it was grueling. Ken wondered how long it would take him to be somewhat normal again, and he couldn't stop thinking about all the problems he faced.

His jaw clenched as he looked at the twirling ceiling fan. *Mandy and I agreed to remain on Kauai to help Mom run the farm. If I'm not able to do the things I used to, then what good am I?*

Ken pulled himself to a sitting position and stared at his cast. *Sure can't sit back and watch Mom and Mandy do all the work. And watching Rob do everything will make me feel like even less of a man. It's my job to provide for my family, not some stranger I don't know well. Should have never gone surfing with Taavi and Rob that day. My place was here, taking care of things on the farm.*

Ken wasn't one to give in to self-pity, but he couldn't seem to help himself. The shark attack had changed everything—including Ken's outlook on life. He kept asking himself why God had allowed this to happen. Was it punishment for being selfish and running off to do something fun when he should have stayed home to help Mandy that day?

Grimacing, Ken ran his fingers through his hair. To make matters worse, he still dealt with pain and had to take medication to keep it under control. Ken didn't like taking pills, and except for an occasional ibuprofen for a rare headache, he had never been on any medications. But the shark attack had altered that. Now he had no choice but to do everything the doctor instructed—including taking pills for the pain. *I could use some good news about now.* Ken drummed his fingers on the sofa cushion.

Mandy came over and knelt on the floor in front of the couch. Smiling, she reached up and took hold of his hand. "There's something I need to tell you, Ken."

"Oh?" He hoped it wasn't anything negative. They'd already dealt with enough bad news.

She sat up and leaned close to his ear. "We're going to be parents."

Ken blinked several times, wondering if he'd heard her right. "Would you please repeat that?"

"I'm expecting a baby. It'll be born in late January or early February."

"Now doesn't that lift your spirits, Son?" Mom asked when she entered the room.

"How long have you known about this?" Ken directed his question to Mandy.

"Several weeks." She continued holding his hand.

"Why are you just now telling me this? Didn't you think I had the right to know I was going to be a father?"

"Of course you have the right, but I didn't want you to worry about me when you were going through so much yourself."

He let go of her hand and stroked her cheek with his thumb. "You're my wife. I'm always going to worry about you."

Mandy smiled. "Well, you needn't worry. I'm doing fine."

Ken's jaw clenched. "I'm also concerned because I don't know if I'll be capable of providing for my family now. It's obvious I'm not going to be able to do all the things I used to do around here."

"It's okay, Son." Mom moved across the room. "Rob is working here full-time, and Ellen has also been helping out."

"That's fine for now. But what's going to happen when Ellen goes back to Indiana? Rob can't manage things on his own, and Mandy sure won't be able to help."

"When Ellen leaves, I'll look for another person to assist Rob with his chores on the farm." Mom placed her hand on Ken's uninjured shoulder. "Let's not worry about all of that right now. You need to rest and concentrate on getting well. We have to trust God to work out the details for everyone involved."

✳

Ellen came into the house to get something cold to drink for her and Rob, when a knock sounded on the back door. Makaio and Luana stood at the door.

"Aloha!" Grinning, Makaio gave a nod. "We heard Ken came home today, so we wanted to come by and say hello."

"He's in the living room with Mandy and Vickie. I am sure he'll be glad to see you." Ellen led the way.

When they entered the room, Ellen held back, while Luana and Makaio greeted Ken.

"It's good to see you're back where you belong." Makaio gave Ken's good shoulder a squeeze. "And I'll bet you're tired of eating hospital food and lookin' forward to some of your mom's home cooking."

Ken nodded.

"How are you feeling?" Luana stood in front of the couch.

"About as good as can be expected, I guess." Ken looked over at Mandy. "Have you told them the news?"

She shook her head. "Not yet."

"What news?" Luana and Makaio asked at the same time.

"We're expecting our first baby." Mandy smiled, looking over at Ellen. "And my best friend has promised to stay until after the little one is born."

"Oh, my. . . Now, that is good news." Luana clapped her hands, before giving Mandy a hug.

Makaio also hugged Mandy. "Yes, it sure is good news. Congratulations, you two."

"Thank you." Mandy gestured for Luana and Makaio to take seats, and Ellen offered to get them something to drink.

"No, thanks. We just had lunch." Luana fingered her lei. "We have some news of our own to share."

"What is it?" Vickie asked.

"Our daughter and son-in-law are for sure moving to the Big Island, so. . ." Luana paused and looked over at Makaio. "Why don't you tell them?"

"Okay. After much prayer and consideration, Luana and I have made plans to sell our bed-and-breakfast and move to the Big Island too."

"We want to be near our ohana," Luana put in.

Ellen stood near Mandy, too stunned to say a word. She never expected Makaio and Luana would sell their B&B, much less leave Kauai. She couldn't imagine the possibility of visiting this island again and not seeing the Palus.

✳

Vickie sat in her room that evening, staring at the pile of bills that had accumulated this past month. While sipping on warm hibiscus tea, she wondered what her next move should be. In addition to debts of her own that had to do with the organic farm, Ken's hospital bills kept coming in. Even though he was out of the hospital, he'd still have to go to therapy sessions, and those wouldn't be cheap. Even with the help they'd gotten from their church, as well as the Amish community in Middlebury, Mandy and Ken were financially overextended. Truth be told, so was she. With a baby on the way, her son and daughter-in-law would need all the help they could get.

"So many memories," Vickie murmured. Looking around the bedroom, her gaze fell upon the picture hanging above her husband's dresser. *Oh, how I remember the day Charles gave me that painting.* It was an anniversary gift he had surprised her with many years ago—one he'd seen her admiring when they'd visited an art store. Charles told Vickie the beautiful colors of the Hawaiian sunset were a reminder of all the times they had walked hand-in-hand along the beach, watching the sun descend into the horizon as if the ocean had swallowed it whole. The painter had captured the sky's vivid colors, which reflected on calm ocean waves. Over the water, big beautiful clouds, darkened by impending dusk, hung in the sky. A palm tree stood in the foreground, and Vickie could almost see it swaying.

"One day he was here, and the next he was gone." Vickie reached up and touched the heart-shaped locket she wore around her neck, another gift from her husband. This one held a black-and-white picture of them on their wedding day. *I miss you, Charles.* Vickie's husband had been her strength, her rock. Charles would know what to do with this situation, but he wasn't here to ask.

She tapped her fingers on the desk, thinking things through. *Should I sell the farm and downsize?* The thought had crossed her mind several times since Ken's shark attack. The profit Vickie could make by selling the farm would help pay Mandy and Ken's expenses. From the looks of things, it would be a long time, if ever, before Ken could return to his duties on the farm. The sensible thing to do would be to sell it. *But will I be able to give up all these memories?* she wondered.

Vickie set the bills aside and sat on the edge of her bed. The responsibilities once shared with Charles fell on her shoulders now. *What would Charles want me to do if he were here? Is there a way out for all of us?* Vickie had to be the strong one and make some decisions on her own. She hoped she could make the right one and that if her husband was here, he'd be pleased.

CHAPTER 30

Middlebury

Ezra's heart beat a little faster as he sat on the front porch of his parents' home, holding an envelope. He'd picked up the mail for his mother and found a letter to him from Ellen. Of course, with mail coming from such a long distance, he figured it would take a longer time to get a response from her, but he'd almost given up.

Eager to know what Ellen said, he tore the envelope open and read:

> *Dear Ezra,*
>
> *I was surprised when I got your letter. It was nice of you to write. I miss my family and friends, but it's good I came to Kauai, because I'm needed here.*
>
> *Ken is out of the hospital now, but he has a long ways to go in his recovery.*
>
> *I've been working on the chicken farm with a young man named Rob. He seems to know a lot about chickens and many other things too. Several days ago we took a break from our work and rented some kayaks. It was hard to get the hang of it at first, but once I did, I had a lot of fun. Another time, Rob and I visited Spouting Horn, an amazing sight to see.*
>
> *Take care, and please tell my family I said hello.*
>
> > *Sincerely,*
> > *Ellen*

Ezra crumpled the letter in his hands. He'd hoped Ellen might say she missed him. But no, she'd mentioned some fellow named Rob.

His fingers tightened around the wad of paper. *Is Ellen interested in this man? All this hope of us being a couple may be for nothing. I wish she'd never gone to Kauai. If I could, I'd go there right now and bring her home.*

✳

Kapaa

Mandy sat in the rocking chair next to the couch where Ken reclined. It was hard to believe it was the first day of September. Ken had been home from the hospital five days, and with each passing day, his short-fused nature, along with depression, increased. He wouldn't take the pain medicine unless she forced the issue. Ken seemed to be holding in all his problems, along with the discomfort he had to deal with every day. Sometimes he acted worse than a cantankerous old grizzly bear.

She'd hoped the news of her pregnancy would help, but as Ken grumbled on about the future, he focused on his inability to do all the things he'd done before. It seemed that her being pregnant made things even worse, because Ken dwelled on what he wouldn't be able to do once their child grew older.

She glanced at him, lying there with his eyes closed. Was he sleeping or trying to tune her out as he sank deeper into his own little world of misery?

Mandy swallowed hard, struggling to keep from crying. Nothing seemed right in their lives anymore. What had happened to all their hopes and dreams for the future? She missed running the bed-and-breakfast and struggled with the desire to see her family back home. With the exception of their baby's arrival, there wasn't much to look forward to in the days ahead. There was no doubt about it—her faith was being put to the test. The question was, could she rise above her worries and remain firm in her beliefs?

"Are you two hungry?" Vickie asked when she entered the room. "It's almost time for lunch." She stopped and looked at Ken. "Is he sleeping?" she whispered to Mandy.

"I'm not sure. His eyes have been closed for half an hour or so."

"Maybe we should go into the kitchen so we can talk without disturbing him." Vickie took a step back.

Mandy was about to respond, when Ken's eyes snapped open. "I wasn't sleeping, and I wish you two would stop talking about me." He pulled himself to a sitting position.

Mandy flinched at her husband's sharp tone. The old Ken would never have responded like that. *I need to be more understanding*, she told herself. *I don't know how I would act if I were in Ken's position.*

"I need to talk to both of you about something." Vickie took a seat on the end of the couch by Ken's feet. "I've done some serious thinking and praying and have made a decision about the farm."

"What about it?" Ken's face was almost expressionless.

"I'm going to sell it and buy Makaio and Luana's bed-and-breakfast." Ken's eyebrows shot up, and Mandy's lips parted a bit.

"Why would you do that, Mom?" he asked.

"For one thing, by selling the farm it'll take care of the rest of your hospital bills." Vickie smoothed her hair back away from her face. "The B&B will also give us a nice place to live, while providing a decent income."

"Have you spoken to the Palus about this?" Mandy questioned.

Vickie nodded. "They are willing to sell it to me on the contingency that our place here sells within sixty days. And since you and Mandy have had experience running a bed-and-breakfast, I believe it will be a good thing for all of us."

"Humph! You really believe that's gonna happen?" Ken placed his scarred arm awkwardly across his chest. "Not many people can afford to buy a place as big as this, not to mention all the work involved in raising the chickens." He glanced down at the cast on his leg. "Besides, how much help do you think a cripple like me is going to be running any kind of business?"

Mandy wished her husband wouldn't be so negative. The idea of living in Luana and Makaio's B&B and helping run it appealed to her. Even though she wouldn't be living near her family, she would enjoy the prospect of having a place of business similar to what they had in Middlebury.

"I am sure there will be many things you can do, Son." Vickie touched his good leg. If nothing else, you can take care of the books and be in charge of all reservations."

Ken grimaced. "Yeah, right—that's just what I've always wanted to do. And what about all the indoor and outside maintenance? Someone will have to do that, you know."

"Yes, I'm well aware. If necessary, I'll hire someone for that." Vickie rose to her feet. "It's all settled, and I'm trusting God to work everything out. In the meantime, I'm going back to the kitchen to fix us all something to eat." She smiled at Mandy and hurried from the room.

"We need to give this a chance," Mandy said, looking at Ken. "If it's meant for us to move to the B&B, then the farm will sell in two months or less."

Ken's only response was a soft grunt, then he closed his eyes again.

Mandy left the rocking chair and leaned over to kiss his forehead. If the farm sold, and they bought the B&B, Ellen would be there to help out—at least until after the baby was born. That was a comfort in itself.

✳

Middlebury

Nora got down on her hands and knees to plant iris bulbs. She'd wanted to purchase some at the local market but hadn't gotten around to it yet. Then out of the blue, Birdie Mitchell had stopped by the other day, with a whole box of bulbs. Birdie said she needed to separate her bulbs and Nora was happy to accept the gift from her English friend.

Funny how things work out sometimes, Nora thought as she used the small hand rake to pull more dirt out of the depressions she'd made. *Now I'll have something to look forward to next year, when these flowers come up and bloom.* Nora sat back on her heels and looked at the area where she'd be planting the bulbs. The irises, Birdie told her, were a bluish, purple variety and would add even more color to this flowerbed. The irises would fit right in because Nora had planted perennials, bulbs and self-seeding annuals so that she didn't have to replant every year.

"I wonder how Ellen is doing." Nora sighed and continued talking to herself. "I miss her and can't wait until she comes home. I'll bet she's getting homesick and is anxious to get back to her family."

Nora's thoughts went to Ezra. *Once Ellen comes back, it sure would be nice if she became interested in Ezra. He's a hard-working, reliable man and would make a good husband for her.*

As she covered each bulb with dirt, Nora smiled. Although Ezra hadn't come right out and said it, she had an inkling his interest in Ellen was growing. Sometimes a person just knew these things.

✳

Kapaa

Shortly before noon, Ellen was surprised when Mandy came outside and said she wanted to speak with her. "Vickie has lunch on the table, and she wondered if you and Rob would like to join us."

Ellen smiled. "I'd be happy to, but Rob had an errand to run, so he's not here right now. He'll be ready to grab a bite to eat before he comes back this afternoon."

"Oh, I see." Mandy joined Ellen by the flowerbed she'd been weeding. While the chore had nothing to do with the chickens, it was something Vickie didn't have time for, so she'd asked Ellen to do it. Working in the flowerbeds was something Ellen enjoyed, especially back home when she'd helped her mother plant different flowers around their house. "Did Rob let Vickie know he'd be taking some time off?"

Ellen shrugged. "I'm not sure, but I assume he did. If not, then I'll let her know when I go inside for lunch."

"Okay, but before we go in, I wanted to make you aware of something Vickie shared with Ken and me a little while ago." Mandy slipped both hands into her skirt pockets. "My mother-in-law is putting the farm up for sale and hopes to buy Luana and Makaio's bed-and-breakfast."

Ellen's fingers touched her parted lips. "Well, now, that's a surprise."

"I know. She's doing it in order to pay Ken's hospital bills and also to provide us with a home and a job." Mandy placed her hands on her growing belly. "I never expected she would part with the farm, and I feel humbled by her generosity. Her husband's organic business is important to Vickie, and she is making a real sacrifice on our behalf."

"She wouldn't do it if she didn't want to." Ellen placed her hand on Mandy's shoulder. "How do you feel about this decision? Is helping run the B&B something you would like to do?"

Mandy rolled her neck from side to side, then reached up to rub a spot on the left. "I've given it some thought and believe it would be a good thing for us. But Ken is concerned he won't be able to do much to help out. And until the baby is born, and I'm back on my feet, my help will also be limited."

"Not to worry, my friend. As I've said before, I'll stay and help out for as long as you need me." Ellen was excited about the news Mandy had told her. She loved working at the B&B back home, and now she'd have the opportunity to work at the bed-and-breakfast she'd become familiar with here in Hawaii. *I should give my parents a call and give them an update on everything. I'm sure they'll understand my reasons for not coming home real soon.*

CHAPTER 31

*H*olding a glass of strawberry-guava juice, Ellen entered her room at the Palms Bed-and-Breakfast and sat on the bed. It was hard to believe this was the first Thursday of November. She couldn't understand how the last two months had gone by in such a blur. The farm sold the first week it was on the market; the sale of the B&B went through soon after; and Makaio and Luana moved to the Big Island to be with Aliana and her family.

The move from the farm to the bed-and-breakfast went well, with Vickie, Ken, and Mandy adjusting to their new positions. Vickie hired Rob to do the yard work and maintenance. Since Ken was still recuperating and Mandy wasn't up to doing much, most of the indoor work fell on Ellen's shoulders. She didn't mind, though. Helping at the B&B was more enjoyable than working around chickens all day and cleaning smelly poultry buildings. Besides, this home was familiar and reminded Ellen of the days she and Mandy stayed with Luana and Makaio. It seemed empty without the Hawaiian couple, though. It had been a tearful goodbye when they'd left for the Big Island, knowing she might never see them again.

Ellen's thoughts scattered when someone knocked on her bedroom door. "Come in," she called.

The door opened, and Vickie poked her head inside. "If you're not busy, I wondered if you'd like to help me decorate for Thanksgiving."

Ellen smiled. "I'd be happy to." Even though they had no guests scheduled to stay over the holiday, three couples were coming the week before Thanksgiving.

Vickie stepped into the room and shut the door. "I've said this before, but I want you to know how much I appreciate your willingness to stay and help out. I'm sure you'd rather be home with your family during Thanksgiving and Christmas."

"This is the second time I've been in Hawaii during the holidays," Ellen stated. "Mandy and I helped Luana decorate the B&B for Christmas while we were staying here."

"How do your parents feel about you being here now?"

"Mom and Dad miss me, of course, but they understand. And I enjoy being here to spend time with Mandy." Ellen almost added that she liked spending time with Rob, too, but kept those thoughts to herself.

Since Ellen and Rob both worked here, they saw each other every day. When things had been slow at the B&B, they'd gone on a few more excursions—one that included a trip to the lighthouse on the north end of the island. It had been fun, climbing to the top of the structure and looking out over the water. The Pacific Ocean looked enormous, making the Island of Kauai seem like a mere speck in the middle of it.

Pushing her musings aside, Ellen smiled at Vickie. "Would you like me to look through the boxes of decorations Luana left, to see what we can use, or do you have some of your own?"

"Mine are still in boxes we haven't gone through yet, so if you're able to find the ones Luana left, we'll use those. But before you begin, can you tell me how much you know about Rob?"

"Not a lot," Ellen replied. "Why do you ask?"

"Rob's a hard worker, but he doesn't say much, and whenever I try to engage him in conversation about something not work related, he clams up." Vickie took a seat on the end of Ellen's bed. "I don't know much about him, other than that he's Taavi's friend and shares expenses while living at Taavi's house. Rob seems honest and upright, but one can never be too careful."

Ellen tipped her head. "What are you saying? Has Rob done something to make you not trust him?"

"Nothing specific. However, his personal life is a mystery."

"Rob is a little private, even with me. But aside from that, he's been living with Taavi awhile, and Taavi seems to think highly of him."

"You're right, but it seems like he might be hiding something." Vickie smoothed the Hawaiian quilt on Ellen's bed. "I didn't have much chance to observe him when he worked at the farm. Now that Ken's out of the hospital, and since Rob's working here, I've had more opportunity to deal with him, and. . ." Vickie lifted her hand. "Oh, never mind. I'm probably being too cautious." She rose from the bed. "Let's get those decorations out now, shall we?"

"Of course." As Ellen followed Ken's mother from the room, she couldn't help wondering if Vickie's suspicions about Rob were legitimate. Could his unwillingness to talk about his past indicate that he was hiding something? If so, Ellen couldn't imagine what it might be.

✳

Ken sat on the lanai, watching Rob in the yard, hauling off a stack of limbs he'd cut from an overgrown tree. Ken could see their hired help had made good progress on the landscaping. Ken's mother had mentioned the other day that keeping things neat as a pin would help bring in new guests.

Ken wished it could be him out there doing the chores. He felt useless, and wondered if he'd ever be able to work again.

Ken heard his wife indoors, humming a church song. She seemed happier since he came home from the hospital and they'd moved to the B&B. Ken had certainly put her through enough heartache, yet she always bounced back and kept a cheerful attitude—at least in his presence and probably for his sake.

Ken stared down at his hands—one good—one badly scarred. The attack could have been far worse, but it didn't seem to help his situation right now.

What's my purpose in life these days? Ken's cast was off his leg, and the incision had healed, but he walked with a limp and relied on a cane. He could use his left arm for some things, but there was no strength in it. Even with therapy, he doubted he'd ever be whole again. How was he supposed to take care of his wife and baby? Would he spend the rest of his life watching Mandy work, while he gimped around, struggling to do the simplest things? And he'd never be able to surf again. Even if he could get up on a board, the thought of encountering another shark terrorized him.

"Oh, there you are, Ken. I've been looking for you." Mandy placed her hands on his shoulders.

He looked up at her from the cushioned wicker couch and forced a smile. "Did you want something? Because if you did, I probably can't do it."

Ken couldn't keep the sarcasm out of his tone, but felt bad the minute he said it. "Sorry, Mandy. I shouldn't have spoken to you like that."

"Apology accepted." She took a seat in the chair beside him, then reached over and took hold of his hand. "Feel this, Ken. Our baby is quite active this morning." She placed his hand on her stomach.

Ken drew in a sharp breath, and tears stung the back of his eyes as he felt movement beneath the surface of his wife's belly. His son or daughter was inside Mandy's womb and would make an appearance soon. Ken could either sit around feeling sorry for himself or figure out a way to take care of his wife and child and become the best dad he could be. He needed to count his blessings and be thankful God spared his life.

✳

The sun beat down on Rob's head. Even through his ball cap he felt the intensity of this warm afternoon. *Fall weather in Hawaii is sure different from what I dealt with on the mainland. I wouldn't go back there for anything, though.*

He glanced at the lanai, where Ken sat. He appeared to be watching him. Rob felt bad Mandy's husband was laid up and couldn't do certain things around the place. It had to be hard for Ken to sit and watch while others did most of the work. Rob gave Ken a brief wave, then bent to pick up another pile of branches he'd trimmed this morning. He was about to haul them across the yard, when Ellen came out of the house. His breath caught in his throat at the sight of her in a plain, but pretty lavender dress. *I wonder how she'd look in a Hawaiian mu-mu.*

"I brought some lemonade," she called, placing a tray on the picnic table.

"Sounds good. I could use a break." Rob put the branches on a pile and joined Ellen at the table.

"The yard looks nice," she commented as they took seats on the same bench.

"Thanks. What have you been up to today?"

She handed him a glass of lemonade. "I spent most of the morning helping Vickie decorate the B&B for Thanksgiving."

Rob reached under his cap and rubbed his forehead. "Oh, yeah. Guess that's coming up in a few weeks."

"Will you spend Thanksgiving or Christmas with your family?" Ellen drank from her glass.

He shook his head. "I told you before—they live on the mainland."

"I remember, but I thought some of your relatives might fly to Kauai to spend the holidays with you, or that you might go home for a few weeks."

"Nope." Rob drank the rest of his lemonade and set the glass back on the tray. "I have no desire to go home."

Rob figured from Ellen's slight grimace that she probably wondered why he didn't want to be with his family—especially during the holidays. Well, she wouldn't understand how things were, and he wasn't about to tell her.

"How long has it been since you've seen your family?" Ellen asked.

"A couple of years."

"How come?"

"It's complicated, and I'd rather not talk about it." Rob poured himself more lemonade and glanced over at her. "Why don't you tell me more about your family?"

"I've told you a little bit. What else would you like to know?" Ellen shifted on the bench.

"How many siblings do you have?

"Three younger sisters."

"No brothers, huh?"

She shook her head. "What about you? How many siblings do you have?"

"Two brothers and two sisters." Rob was quick to change the subject. "What does your family normally do for Thanksgiving?"

Ellen smiled. "We always have a big get-together with some of my aunts and uncles. This year, though, I'll be celebrating the holiday with Mandy, Ken, and Vickie." She scooted a little closer and offered him a cookie from the plate she'd also brought out. "I made chocolate-chip cookies last evening."

Rob reached for one. "They look good. Thanks, Ellen."

"You're welcome." She picked up a cookie and took a bite.

His heart beat a little faster as he gazed into her beautiful blue eyes. *Oh, boy, I'd better watch it. I'm falling for this girl.*

CHAPTER 32

When Rob entered the B&B to see if any inside work needed to be done, he discovered Ellen knelt beside a cardboard box in the living room, pulling off the tape that held the flaps together.

"Hey, is there anything I can do to help?" He went down on his knees beside her.

She looked up at him and smiled. "I found this box of fall decorations that I missed five days ago, and I discovered there are some Christmas things in here too. So, if you're not busy with something else, maybe you could help me separate things."

"Sure, I can do that." Rob pushed his bangs back off his forehead. "You have my undivided attention."

"All right then. Why don't we take everything out of the box and put them in two piles? The Christmas items over there, and the fall decorations over here."

"Sounds easy enough." Rob reached into the box at the same time as Ellen. When their hands touched, he clasped her fingers and gave them a squeeze. "This is a lot more fun than takin' care of squawking chickens, huh?"

Her cheeks colored slightly as she nodded. "Working here brings me such pleasure, like it did at the B&B Mandy and Ken used to own in Middlebury. I enjoy seeing to the needs of others."

"It shows, and you do it well. Mandy's lucky to have a good friend like you."

The pink that had erupted on Ellen's cheeks deepened. "I feel fortunate too. Mandy's a good friend. We've known each other since we were children."

Wish I'd known you when you were a girl. Things might be different for me now. Rob bit the inside of his cheek to keep from voicing his thoughts. He delighted in the sound of her voice.

They took turns pulling items from the box and placing them in piles on the throw rug. Ellen seemed to be fixated on the shiny globes she pulled out and held up to the light.

"Look at all these pretty tree ornaments." Ellen showed Rob one with a beautiful snow scene painted on the front. "I'd hate to see any get broken."

"Don't worry. I'll be careful with them." Digging deeper into the box, Rob felt something bristle against his fingers. "Well, look what I found." He lifted a bundle of synthetic mistletoe. "You know what this means?" Before Ellen could respond, he held it over her head, leaned close and gave her a kiss. He would have kissed Ellen longer, but when Mandy came in, he quickly pulled away.

Wide-eyed, she stopped in front of them and cleared her throat. "Am I interrupting something?" Mandy's tone was cautious.

"Umm. . .no. I was just helping Ellen sort through some decorations." Rob clambered to his feet. "Guess I'll go find Vickie and see what else she has for me to do before I head back to Taavi's place."

"Vickie's not here right now," Mandy said. "She went to the grocery store."

"Oh, okay. Guess I'll head out now then." Rob turned to go, but when Ellen called out to him, he turned back around.

"When you see Taavi, would you let him know that you're both invited here for Thanksgiving dinner? This morning, Vickie mentioned asking you to join us."

"Sounds good. I have no other plans, so I'll be here for the meal. I'm not sure about Taavi, but I'll extend the invitation." Rob gave a wave and headed for the door. The thought of a home-cooked Thanksgiving meal made his mouth water. Of course, spending the day with Ellen made it even more enticing.

✳

After Rob closed the door behind him, Ellen looked up at Mandy, who stood staring down at her with a disapproving expression. "What's wrong? You look *umgerennt*."

"I am upset. You seem to be acting careless around Rob, and why did you let him kiss you?"

Ellen's face tightened. "I am not being careless, and I didn't *let* Rob kiss me. It sort of happened when he held a piece of mistletoe over my head."

"I didn't see you pull away from him. It looked to me like you enjoyed the kiss."

Ellen couldn't deny her feelings, but she wasn't about to admit how she felt when Rob's lips touched hers. It was difficult to admit that her attraction to him grew. She might even be falling in love with Rob. But this didn't change the fact that she'd be going home in a few months, or that he was English and she was Amish. They were obviously not meant to be together, so she needed to set her feelings aside—however hard that would be as long as she remained on Kauai. But she'd already agreed to stay and help. Plus, she wanted to hold Mandy and Ken's precious baby. So while she was here, she would try not to let her feelings for Rob get in the way of good sense.

Mandy took a seat in the rocking chair and placed her hands across her stomach. "I'm sure the last thing you want from me is a lecture, but I'm concerned about you, Ellen."

"What are you concerned about?" Ellen took a seat on the couch.

"I've seen the way you and Rob look at each other whenever you're together, and it spells trouble." Mandy leaned back in the rocker. "It's obvious that you're falling for Rob, and you know the old saying: 'If you play with fire, you're bound to get burned.'"

Ellen's knuckles turned white when she clasped her hands together. "What is that supposed to mean?"

"You're Amish and have joined the church. If you and Rob were to pursue a relationship, and you left the church, your parents would be hurt."

"Yes, I know. I don't need the reminder." Ellen rolled her shoulders to release some of the tension she felt. "You fell in love with and married an English man. And now, you're living in Hawaii."

"My situation is different. I was not a church member when I married Ken."

"You're right, but Rob and I have made no commitment to each other, so you have nothing to worry about."

Mandy got the rocking chair moving. "I hope you can keep it that way. As much as I would love having you stay here permanently, if you gave up the Amish way of life to marry an outsider, you'd most likely have regrets."

"Do you have regrets?" Ellen blinked rapidly.

"I'm not sorry I married Ken, but I wish we could live near both of our families. It was hard on my folks when I chose not to join the Amish church." Mandy stopped rocking and came over to sit on the couch beside Ellen. "Please promise you'll give what I've said some serious thought before you make any decisions that could affect the rest of your life."

Ellen slowly nodded. "Danki for caring enough to express your thoughts."

"You're welcome." Mandy stood. "Now I'd better see if my husband needs anything." She offered Ellen a brief smile and left to find Ken.

Ellen leaned against the sofa cushions and rubbed a finger over her lips where Rob had kissed her moments ago. Could she give up the Amish life she'd always known to become English if her relationship with Rob became serious? She couldn't expect him to become Amish. While she'd heard of a few people who had given up their modern, English world to join the Plain faith, it had been a difficult transition. Some gave up and went back to their old way of life.

Ellen touched her hot cheeks and drew in a deep breath. *I am being silly for thinking about this. Rob has not said anything about loving me or suggested I leave the Amish church.* Mandy's lecture had confused Ellen. The only way she could put these thoughts out of her head was to get busy working again.

She knelt beside the box and began sorting things again. When her gaze came to rest on the mistletoe Rob had dropped back into the box, a shiver ran down her spine. She couldn't deny that she'd enjoyed his kiss. But since it was the first real kiss she'd received from a man, she had nothing to compare it with.

CHAPTER 33

Middlebury

*T*hanksgiving was always a busy time in the Lambrights' home, and this year was no exception. Visiting relatives were in the living room sitting by the toasty fire and talking to Nathan. Nora and her three daughters had been bustling around the kitchen all morning. Soon the turkey would be done, and it would be time to gather around the table. At least the house was filled with people, which would help take Nora's mind off Ellen's absence.

"Do you know what Ellen's doing today?" Lenore asked as she picked up a stack of plates to take them out to the dining-room table.

Nora grabbed some utensils from the counter, then turned to face her daughter. "I spoke with her yesterday, and she said they'd be having dinner at the B&B, and had invited Rob, the young man who works for them, as well as Ken's friend Taavi." She opened the oven to check on the turkey. The delicious aroma permeated the kitchen. "Ellen also mentioned that they don't have any guests at the bed-and-breakfast right now."

"Sounds like my granddaughter will have a nice Thanksgiving there in Hawaii." Nora's mother said as she entered the kitchen.

Nora smiled. "I hope so, Mama."

Darla took some glasses down from the cupboard, while Ruby got out the silverware. "Did Ellen say how Mandy and Ken are doing?" Ruby asked.

"Jah. Ken's injuries are healing, and Mandy's due to have her *boppli* on January tenth. Originally, they thought it would be February, but Mandy miscalculated."

"Will Ellen be staying on Kauai until after the baby arrives?" Darla questioned.

Nora nodded. "And did you hear that Mandy's folks are planning to go there?"

"Oh, really?" Grandma's silver-gray brows lifted. "To Kauai?"

"Jah. They've made arrangements to go to California on the train, and then they'll get on a cruise ship that will take them to Kauai. Once Mandy's folks arrive, Ellen plans to fly home." Nora could hardly wait for that.

✳

Kapaa

Mandy sat on the couch beside Ken, strumming her ukulele and enjoying the tantalizing aromas floating in from the kitchen. Even though she couldn't be with her family in Middlebury today, she felt content. It would be a few hours before their company arrived for the meal, so this was a good time to sit and relax. Beforehand, she'd helped Vickie prep the potatoes and make a tropical fruit salad. Ellen made the stuffing for the bird, along with her favorite dinner rolls.

Ken seemed at peace today, as he placed his hand on Mandy's stomach. "Our little fella—if it is a boy—is sure active today."

She smiled. "Yes, and I'll bet he will take after his father—strong and brave."

Ken's brows drew together. "I may have been those things once, but not anymore. Since the shark attack, I've felt like a weakling and a coward."

"You're not a coward. And you'll regain your strength. It's just gonna take time. Even if your physical abilities are limited, you can still do things to help around here." She placed her hand over his. "When Luana called last week to see how things were going here, she said how pleased she and Makaio are that we are the ones who took this place over for them. They worked hard establishing their business, and we don't want to let them down."

Ken moved his head slowly up and down. "You're right, Mandy, and despite my limitations, I'll do my best to help you and Mom in any way I can."

✳

"Everything tastes great." Taavi's gaze went from Vickie, to Mandy, and then Ellen. "Mahalo, ladies. You did a terrific job with this meal."

"Ellen did most of it," Vickie said. "She's an excellent cook and will make some lucky man a fine wife."

Ellen's face warmed. "I appreciate the compliment, but you and Mandy were a big help preparing this delicious Thanksgiving meal."

"I didn't do as much as you and Vickie." Mandy gave her stomach a few taps. "This little one has been sapping my energy, and I'm not up to doing much."

"It's not a problem." Vickie smiled at Mandy. "You need to rest whenever you can."

"Your mother-in-law is right," Ellen put in. "Even after the baby comes you'll need to take it easy."

"Since my folks are coming in January, and plan to stay several weeks, I'll have plenty of help."

Ellen wished she could stay longer, but her family missed her, and she needed to return home after Mandy's parents arrived. She glanced across the table at Rob and swallowed the piece of turkey she'd put in her mouth. He looked at her, too, and her heart skipped a beat. Did Rob realize their time was running out? *He must never know the way I've come to feel about him. Once I leave this island, whatever may have been between us, will be a thing of the past.*

Ellen blotted her lips with a napkin and focused on finishing her food. Wishing for the impossible only saddened her. Once she was back home and found a new job, she could put Rob and all the fun times they'd had together out of her mind.

✳

When the meal was over, everyone helped clear the table. Then the women went to the kitchen to do the dishes and put the leftovers away. Rob joined Taavi and Ken in the living room to watch TV and visit. Rob's mind wasn't on the conversation, however. All he could think about was Ellen and wishing he could spend some time alone with her today. Since she'd be going back to Indiana sometime in January, they didn't have much time left to be together. *I wonder what she would say if I asked her to stay. Could I put the past behind me and begin a relationship with Ellen? Would she turn me away if I told her about my past?*

Taavi bumped Rob's arm. "Hey, wake up. Did you hear the question Ken asked you?"

Rob jerked his head. "Uh. . .no, sorry, I did not." He looked at Ken. "What was it you asked?"

"I wondered if you play any musical instruments."

"Not really. I've fooled around with a harmonica a bit, but never got the hang of it. Someone told me once that playing a mouth harp isn't hard. All you need to do is blow and suck." He slapped his hand against his knee. "So I gave it a try, but it didn't help. Guess I'm not cut out to play an instrument."

Ken chuckled. "Makaio taught Mandy to play the ukulele. I bet she could teach you. Would ya like me to ask?"

"No, that's okay. I'll stick to outdoor sports like kayaking and leave the musical stuff to those who have talent."

Taavi looked at Ken and rolled his eyes. Rob figured his roommate thought he was ridiculous. But truthfully, he had a good reason for not wanting to learn to play an instrument—a reason that had left a scar on his heart. But he'd never talk about it—not to Ellen or even Taavi. The past was in the past, and it needed to stay buried. It was the only way he could deal with the unpleasant memories.

Rob stood up and moved across the room. What he needed right now was some fresh air, but he'd enjoy it more if Ellen went outside with him. He popped into the kitchen to see what she was doing, and found her putting a stack of clean dishes in the cupboard. "I need some air. Are you free to take a walk with me?" he asked.

"That sounds nice. I have a few more dishes to dry, and then I'll be ready."

Rob stood back and watched as she completed her task.

"When you two come back inside we'll have some pie and coffee," Mandy said as she put the clean silverware in a drawer.

Rob gave his stomach a thump. "Oh, boy. I'd better take a long walk if I'm gonna make room for any pie. I ate way too much turkey and dressing."

"I think we all did." Vickie put the last pot away. "Maybe in another hour or so we'll all have room for pie."

"I'm ready to go now." Ellen smiled up at Rob.

When they stepped outside, Rob reached for Ellen's hand and led her across the yard and down the street. It was a beautiful evening, with a light breeze to cool the warmth of the day. Several people sat on their lanais, and others were out walking.

Rob glanced at Ellen. He'd miss her when she left Kauai and wished he could ask her to stay. They paused to look at some colorful flowers growing in someone's yard. Except for the meal they'd eaten and the fall decorations placed throughout the B&B, it didn't seem much like Thanksgiving.

Ellen had a faraway look in her eyes. "It's funny to see flowers blooming this time of year. Back home the weather on Thanksgiving tends to be cold, and sometimes it snows. But inside, it's always warm and toasty, and the smell of turkey roasting goes all through the house. Dad usually has a fire going, and we all gravitate to the living room after the meal is eaten." Ellen snickered. "Dad and my uncles end up snoozing, while we women visit. In the background, the firewood would be popping and cracking. I can almost hear it."

Rob tried to visualize what she'd told him. He could only guess how much Ellen must miss her family today.

"About an hour or so after we eat, the desserts are brought out," she continued. "Along with what Mom bakes, my aunts bring a few desserts." Ellen sighed. "After indulging in the desserts, we're all stuffed—and then some. But oh, everything is always so good."

"What kind of desserts do you have?" Rob couldn't help it. Memories from past Thanksgivings flooded back to his mind.

"Mom usually makes a pumpkin pie and also mincemeat. My aunts will often bring home-made cookies or cake. A few days before the holiday, Dad freezes home-made vanilla ice cream." Ellen slowed her pace. "So on top of everything else, we end up having that too. You can only imagine how full we are by the end of the day."

Oh, I think I can. Rob's fingers itched to stroke Ellen's soft check. *You're beautiful, Ellen. I wish I'd met you a few years ago.*

✻

Middlebury

When Ezra pedaled his bicycle into the shoe store parking lot the day after Thanksgiving, he saw Nathan putting his buggy horse away in the corral. This was the busiest shopping day in the English world, and shoppers flocked to the shoe store as well.

The front door of the store was ajar, so Ezra figured Lenore must be inside. He parked the bike near the building and hurried into the store, where he found her sitting on a stool behind the counter. "How'd your Thanksgiving go?" Ezra asked.

"It was good. My aunts and uncles came, and all our family was together except for Ellen. It didn't seem the same without her." Lenore frowned. "Christmas won't be the same without her either. But she's doing a good thing by staying in Hawaii to help Mandy and Ken."

Ezra leaned on the counter. "Your sister's been there a long time. Any idea when she might be coming home?"

Lenore's face brightened. "She'll be back sometime in January, after Mandy has her boppli and Mandy's folks arrive to help out."

Ezra smiled. "That's good to hear." *I wonder if I should write her another letter, and express my feelings for her. Or I could just wait till she gets home.* Ezra's mind worked overtime as he thought about what he ought to do once Ellen returned home. One thing was for sure: he wouldn't waste any time. He'd already missed too many opportunities to let her know his feelings. *This time I'm going to be more direct.*

CHAPTER 34

Kapaa

*C*hristmas Day was overcast, with the promise of rain. Ellen stood on the lanai, looking out at the yard, and wondering if her parents had snow at home. More often than not they were blessed with a beautiful dusting of snow on Christmas Day. Sometimes it occurred as soon as Thanksgiving, and by Christmas there would be enough snow for a sleigh ride.

Today, more than ever, Ellen struggled to keep her feeling of homesickness under control. It might be Christmas, but the temperatures on Kauai seemed more like early summer.

Ellen longed to be back in Indiana. She would miss the evening hours, with a glowing fire in the living room and family members gathering around together to sing Christmas carols.

There were so many things she missed about home—starting with her family and friends.

Mom had called Ellen this morning to wish her a Merry Christmas, and she'd been able to talk to Dad, as well as her sisters. Hearing their voices brought tears to her eyes. *But I'm needed here right now*, she reminded herself.

Taavi planned to spend the day with his parents, so he had dropped by last night to wish them all a Merry Christmas. But Rob would be joining them for Christmas dinner. Ellen looked forward to spending the day with Rob. But each time they were together, her heart longed for more. She hoped someday Rob might come to Middlebury to visit. But seeing him there would only make it more difficult to say goodbye again. Sometimes she wished she'd never met Rob. Other times, Ellen found herself hoping he'd proclaim his love for her, and they could figure out some way to be together.

Ellen stepped into the kitchen to check the time. Rob should be here soon, and since there was nothing else to do at the moment, she decided to wait for him on the lanai.

She'd no more than taken a seat on the swing when Rob pulled his motor scooter into the yard. He looked handsome in his green shirt and dressy dark trousers. Ellen smiled when he got off and walked toward the house, carrying a small paper sack in his hands.

Grinning, Rob joined Ellen on the lanai and handed her the bag. "Merry Christmas! Here's a little something from me to you."

A tingling sensation swept up the back of Ellen's neck and across her face. "Oh, Rob, I appreciate the gift, but I'm sorry to say, I have nothing for you."

He took a seat beside her on the swing. "I didn't buy you a gift because I wanted something in return. Besides, being here with you is gift enough for me."

The homesickness Ellen had felt previously was replaced with goosebumps stretching from her head down to her toes.

Ellen struggled to find the right words. "Thank you, Rob. I'm glad you could join us today."

"Me too." Rob pointed to the paper sack. "Go ahead and open it."

Ellen reached inside and pulled out a bar of pineapple-fragranced soap, some coconut lip gloss, and a tube of Plumeria-fragranced hand lotion. "These are so nice. Thanks."

He clasped her hand. "Glad you like them."

"You look nice today. Is your shirt new?" The nearness of him caused Ellen to shiver.

"Yeah." Rob smoothed his shirt collar. "It's not what you're used to seeing me in, but I'm glad you like it."

"Shall we go inside now?" Even though she'd rather stay here with Rob the rest of the day, Ellen rose from the swing. "Dinner should be ready soon."

✳

As Rob sat at the table, enjoying a tasty meal and pleasant conversation, a sense of homesickness washed over him. *I wonder what Mom, Dad, and the rest of my family are doing today. Should I give them a call to say Merry Christmas? Would they be glad to hear from me, or would I be in for a lecture about being gone so long without contacting them?*

He shifted on his chair, while glancing at Ellen. Could she sense his unrest? Did she know he struggled with deep emotions today?

From her seat across the table, Ellen gave Rob a smile. *Sure wish she wasn't so sweet.*

He looked away, concentrating on finishing what was left on his plate. If Mandy had her baby within the next few weeks, this might be the last meal he'd share with Ellen.

When everyone finished eating, the women cleared the table. Ken said he was tired and wanted to lie down for a while, so Rob decided this would be a good time to call home. He excused himself and went out to sit on the lanai. If he was going to do this, he didn't want anyone to hear his conversation.

✻

"Rob left his cup of coffee sitting on the table," Mandy mentioned as she put some of the leftovers in the refrigerator. "I wonder if he wants it."

"I'll go see." Ellen went to the dining room and picked up Rob's cup. It was still warm, so she opened the door to the lanai, and was about to step out, when she saw Rob sitting in a chair with his cell phone up to his ear.

A rush of adrenaline shot through her body when she heard his spoken words.

"En hallicher Grischtdaag."

Ellen gasped. Rob had just wished someone a Merry Christmas in Pennsylvania Dutch. But how could it be? Rob wasn't Amish. He was English.

She stood quietly behind him and listened as he continued to speak in the Amish dialect. By now she could tell he was talking to his family since she heard him say *mamm* and *daed*. When Rob put his cell phone away, she cleared her throat.

He whirled around. "Ellen! How long have you been standing there?"

"Long enough to hear you speaking Pennsylvania Dutch." Ellen set Rob's coffee down on the table by his chair. "What's going on, Rob? Who were you talking to?"

"No one." His face flamed. "I mean, I left a message for my folks."

"Are—are you Amish?"

He nodded slowly. "I was raised Amish but never joined the church."

Ellen blinked rapidly, her body heat rising. "Why have you been lying to me about this?"

"I didn't lie—just didn't give you any details of my previous life. No one else on the island knows either."

Barely able to stand, she lowered herself into the chair beside him. "What are the details, Rob? Why did you keep the truth of your heritage from me? And what is the reason you are here on Kauai?"

He drew in some air and released it with a huff. "First of all, my name's not Rob Smith. I took that name on after I left my parents' home."

"What is your real name?"

"Rueben Zook. I was raised in an Amish home in Ronks, Pennsylvania." His face sagged. "Up until now, I've never told anyone about my Amish heritage, or that I changed my name after I ran away and came here with a new identity."

Ellen's fingers tightened around the band of her apron. "Why were you running from your past? Are you ashamed of the Amish way of life?"

Shoulders hunched, Rueben shook his head. "It's not that. I left because I killed my girlfriend, Arie Stoltzfus."

"What are you saying?" Ellen felt as if all the color had drained from her face.

"Arie and I were in the car I'd bought during my running-around years." He paused and rubbed his eyes. "As we approached the train crossing, I heard a whistle blow. She pleaded with me not to cross over, but I was sure I could make it." Rueben's hand shook. "The car stalled on the tracks. I got out and hollered at Arie to slide across the seat, but before she could make a move, the train slammed into my vehicle. I saw the whole thing happen, and I will never forget the sound of the crash. Somehow, I made myself walk toward the mangled car." Rueben's voice lowered to a whisper, and his breathing seemed erratic. "Arie would never laugh, sing, or play the guitar again. She was killed outright, and it was my fault."

Ellen sat in stunned silence as Rueben rocked back and forth, as though reliving the tragic event. "I've been angry at God ever since and vowed never to fall in love again." His eyes watered as he looked at Ellen and shook his head. "I'm sorry for letting you believe something might be happening between us. I can never return to my Amish heritage, and I can't commit to a relationship with you because you're committed to the Amish faith."

A sob rose in Ellen's throat and she leaped out of her chair. His confession only added to her confusion. She couldn't wait to go home and put this nightmare behind, but she had an impulse to take Reuben in her arms and comfort him for what he'd been through.

✳

Ronks, Pennsylvania

Elsie Zook sat in the phone shack, shaking her head tearfully as she replayed Rueben's message. After his sudden disappearance, nearly two years ago, this was the first time she'd heard from her son. He'd made no contact with anyone else in the family either. The joy of hearing his message was almost her undoing. Rueben had called to wish them a Merry Christmas, but said nothing about where he was or if he might be coming home.

She reached under her glasses and wiped away tears as they trickled down her cheeks. *I wish Rueben had left a phone number so I could return his call, but thank You, Lord, for nudging my boy to call home. I praise You, Jesus, for keeping my son safe and for letting me hear his greatly missed voice.*

She rested her forehead on the bench in front of her. *Oh, Rueben, why did you have to run off? Why couldn't you have stayed and let us help you deal with your grief over losing Arie? Don't you know how much we miss you? Doesn't it bother you that Arie's parents are grieving too?*

Elsie stood. *I must get in and share this with the rest of the family, who have gathered at home for the holiday.* She took a step toward the door of the phone shack, then paused to send up a silent prayer. *Dear Lord, please bring our son back where he belongs.*

CHAPTER 35

Lihue

*B*etween my job and yours, we haven't seen much of each other lately." Taavi reached for the loaf of bread Rueben set on the counter. "Christmas has come and gone, and I still haven't heard how your day went. Did you have a good one?"

Rueben's jaw clenched. This wasn't a conversation he wanted to have. Christmas was ten days ago, and he figured by now Taavi wouldn't bring the subject up.

He undid the top button on his Hawaiian-print shirt and rubbed the lower part of his neck. "It did not go well."

"How come? Didn't Ellen like the gift you got her?" Taavi popped a piece of bread into the toaster.

"She said she liked it. What she didn't like was finding out that I'm not who she thought I was."

"Huh?" Taavi tipped his head. "What are you talking about?"

Rueben recounted the whole thing—beginning with when Ellen overheard him speaking Pennsylvania Dutch while leaving a message on his folks' answering machine and ending with how upset she was because he hadn't told her the truth about his heritage right away.

Taavi's head jerked back, and he gave Rueben an incredulous stare. "All this time you've let all of us believe you were just some guy who'd come to the island to get a little sun and have some fun, when you were running from your past?"

Rueben nodded.

Taavi broke eye contact with Rueben. "I'm disappointed in you, man.

It hurts to know you've been feeding me a line and all the people close to you here. That's not cool."

"I'm sorry I deceived you. It was wrong, but I was ashamed to admit who I was and that I'm responsible for the death of the woman I loved."

"Carrying a burden like that is unhealthy. You've gotta forgive yourself and have faith that the Lord will help you through all this." Taavi looked at Rueben again and shook his head. "Without the Lord's help, you'll never put this behind."

"That's easy for you to say. You're not the one it happened to."

"Oh my dear *hoapili.*" Taavi placed his hand on Rueben's shoulder. "I wish there was something I could do for you."

"Well, there isn't, and I guess I'm not much of a friend." Rueben tossed a cluster of grapes in his lunch pail, along with the sandwich he'd made. The last thing he wanted was pity. "I've gotta go. I can't be late for work." Before Taavi could respond, Rueben grabbed his lunch and dashed out the door.

✳

Kapaa

Ellen fumbled with the fruit she'd finished cutting for their B&B guests. Ever since she'd learned the truth about the man she thought was English, she'd been a ball of nerves. Her emotions were so mixed, she could hardly think straight. And today, with Mandy going into labor, she was even more apprehensive. Mandy, Ken, and Vickie went to the hospital around three in the morning, but so far Ellen hadn't heard a word. Ellen wanted to be at the hospital when the baby was born, but someone had to be here to take care of their B&B guests.

She placed the kiwi, papaya, and pineapple slices on a platter and went to the refrigerator to get a carton of eggs supplied by the new owners of the organic farm. Ellen was about to crack the first egg into a bowl, when Rueben entered the kitchen. He moved past her to get a bottle of water, but didn't say a word. He didn't even look at her.

Ellen flinched. *If only he'd been honest with me from the beginning. "Mer sedde immer ehrlich sei,"* she mumbled.

Rueben stepped in front of her and tilted his head. "We should always be honest, huh? Have you forgotten that I speak Pennsylvania Dutch and knew exactly what you were saying?"

"Rob. . . I mean Rueben. It's not easy getting used to you being Amish when all along you led me to believe you were English."

He lowered his gaze. "I couldn't get up the nerve to tell you because I was afraid of your reaction."

"I would have reacted better if you'd been truthful from the beginning. Aren't you aware of what the book of Proverbs says about dishonesty? 'Lying lips are abomination to the Lord: but they that deal truly are his delight,'" Ellen quoted.

Rueben glared at her. "I don't need a reminder. I've been lying to myself for years."

"It's not your fault Arie didn't get out of the car when you warned her."

"No, but I am to blame for trying to beat the train. I am a *glotzkopp*, and because of my stubbornness, Arie is dead. She was too young to have her life end that way."

"So what are you going to do—stay here on Kauai the rest of your life and try to bury your past?"

He nodded. "The farther I am from home, the less likely I'll think about what happened."

"Do you truly believe miles or even an ocean will change all that?" Ellen tried to be sympathetic, but her nerves were on edge. "I've never mentioned this to you before, but ever since I met you, I felt there was something sad behind your eyes. This weight you carry will eventually beat you down, if it hasn't already." Ellen paused, then added, "Rueben, you deserve to be happy."

"I can't go back and look my family in the eyes, or Arie's folks either." He scuffed the toe of his sneaker against the tile. "And happiness—well, that's the last thing I deserve."

"Don't you care how much they must miss you?"

He shrugged. "They're better off without me."

"Rueben, you can't mean that."

"I do."

Ellen looked away. She wanted to say more, but heard their guests coming into the dining room, awaiting their breakfast. "We can discuss this some other time if you like. Right now I have guests to feed." She moved over to the stove.

Rueben grabbed a second bottle of water and went out the back door.

✳

Lihue

Ken sat beside Mandy's hospital bed, fretting. It seemed like she'd been in labor a long time. He wondered if something was wrong. The nurse who'd checked on her recently assured them everything was fine, and that many women experienced a long labor with their first child. Still, it was hard not to be concerned. He and Mandy had been through a lot since coming to Kauai, and he hated to see her suffer during labor. Ken was glad that for the moment at least, she'd dozed off.

He looked over at his mother reading a magazine in the chair across the room. *I wonder if Mom suffered much when she gave birth to me or my brother.* His fingers clenched. *I can't believe Dan didn't bother to come see me after the shark attack. What kind of brother is he? For that matter, he's been no support to Mom since Dad died.*

Ken felt thankful Ellen had come to help out and that his mom had hired Rob. Although, from what Ellen had told him and Mandy the day after Christmas, Rob wasn't even the young man's name. It was hard to understand how Rob, a.k.a. Rueben Zook, could lie about his Amish heritage and run away from home. His situation seemed similar to Ken's brother, only they'd left home for different reasons. And at least Dan wasn't trying to hide his identity.

People can make all kinds of excuses for the things they do, Ken thought, *but it all boils down to one thing: everyone is responsible for the way they deal with what life throws at them, and I'm certainly no exception.*

It had taken a while, but Ken had finally accepted the fact that he had to learn to live with his disability and stop feeling sorry for himself. It wasn't like he was completely incapable of doing things. He just couldn't do all the physical chores he used to do. But he would do what he could and leave the rest to Rueben, or whomever Mom chose to hire in the future at the bed-and-breakfast.

Ken's cell phone rang, and Mandy's eyes opened. "Sorry for waking you, honey. I forgot to silence my phone. Is there anything I can get you?"

"No. Go ahead and see who's calling."

Ken answered the call and was surprised to hear Mandy's mother on the other end.

"Hello, Ken. Nathan and I are at the port where the ship came in, and we need a ride to the B&B," Miriam said.

Ken slapped the side of his head. He knew Mandy's folks were supposed to arrive today. He just hadn't expected it to happen this early. He looked at his mother. "Mandy's folks are here already, and they a need a ride. Would you mind going to pick them up? I know they'll want to come here."

"Not a problem." She rose from the chair and picked up her purse. "I'll be back soon."

Ken got back on the phone with Miriam and told her his mother would come to get them.

Mandy looked over at Ken with a wide-eyed expression. "The pains are coming harder now. Oh, I hope my folks get here before the baby is born."

CHAPTER 36

Kapaa

J can't believe you're leaving in the morning. The time you've been here has gone too fast." Mandy slipped her arm around Ellen's waist as the two of them stood looking down at the baby, asleep in his crib. "I appreciate all the help you've given, as well as the emotional support I needed. I'm going to miss you so much."

Ellen swallowed hard, hoping she wouldn't break down. "I'll miss you too. Maybe when little Isaac Charles is older you can come to Middlebury to visit. I'm sure everyone in your family would like to meet him."

"I know they would, and we will do that whenever Ken is up to traveling." Mandy smiled. "Maybe you can come back to Kauai to visit us sometime."

"That would be nice." Truth was, Ellen didn't think she would ever return to Kauai or any of the other Hawaiian Islands. Unless it was another emergency, she wouldn't be able to fly, and coming by cruise ship didn't seem possible anytime in the near future either.

Ellen thought about Mandy's parents and how difficult it would be when the time came for them to return to Indiana. Miriam and Isaac had been a big help since they arrived. But they'd stayed with their new grandson and his parents only ten days, and would be going home in a few weeks.

Ellen wondered if Isaac or Miriam resented Mandy marrying Ken. If they did, they'd never shown it. They had always been kind and loving toward him. When a son or daughter married outside the Amish faith, it was difficult enough. But being separated by so many miles made it worse.

I could never marry outside the faith or move thousands of miles away, Ellen told herself. *I would miss my family, and they would miss me.*

Her thoughts went to Rueben. It was hard to believe he hadn't seen his family since he'd left home almost two years ago. Ellen understood the guilt he must feel over his girlfriend's death, but staying away from family and friends was selfish and hurtful. If Rueben had remained in Pennsylvania, his parents or church ministers could have helped him deal with the grief and guilt.

Ellen dreaded going to the airport tomorrow—not just saying goodbye to her friends, but having Rueben drive her there in Ken's SUV. When Rueben heard Vickie would be taking Ken to a doctor's appointment in the morning and had guests checking in during the afternoon hours, he'd volunteered to see that Ellen got to the airport.

Since Christmas, Rueben seemed to be avoiding Ellen, so it seemed strange he wanted to see her off. The thought of being alone with him, even for the short drive to the airport, sent shivers of apprehension through her body. Ellen hoped she wouldn't break down when she said goodbye to Rueben. She cared for him and was angry with herself for allowing it to happen.

Ellen turned her focus on the baby again. His little eyes were open, and he seemed to be smiling at her. She looked at Mandy. "Would you mind if I hold him for a while?"

"Of course not." Mandy gestured to the rocking chair in her bedroom. "Why don't you sit there and rock him? I have one little request from you first, though."

"What do you want me to do?"

"I would like to take a photo of you holding him, so I'll have this memory to look back on." Mandy's eyes misted.

"Okay. I'm all right with that." Ellen picked up the baby and took a seat in the rocking chair.

Mandy got her camera and took a couple of pictures. "Okay, Ellen, you can keep rocking the baby while I go visit with Mom and Vickie. Ken and Dad are both dozing in the living room, so they're not good company right now." Without a sound, Mandy slipped out of the room.

As Ellen rocked baby Isaac and stroked his silky dark hair, she closed her eyes and imagined what it would be like to have her own precious child.

❋

Lihue

When Rueben drove Ellen to the airport the following morning, he tried to think of something to say. What was there to talk about? He'd messed things up with his deception. He'd ruined any chance of a relationship with her, and now she was going home.

I can only imagine what Ellen is thinking. She's committed to her church and Amish family, so I can't ask her to stay. Rueben blew out a breath. *Besides, even if she were willing to give up her Amish life, I'm not ready for a commitment to another woman.*

Rueben had left a trail of bad decisions—at home and here on Kauai. He didn't trust himself not to make more.

Rueben's thought went to his friend Taavi. *He said I need to have faith that the Lord will help me deal with all this, but I'm not sure I can. My faith in God faltered after Arie died, and I began blaming myself.*

He glanced over at Ellen. Her posture was rigid as she stared out the passenger window. *She's probably as uncomfortable as I am right now. Is there anything I can say to make things better before we part ways?*

As they drew closer to the airport, Ellen looked over at him and said, "I appreciate the ride, but you can just drop me off at the terminal. That way you won't have to pay for parking or trouble yourself any further."

"It's no trouble." Rueben shook his head. "I want to take your luggage in for you."

"I can manage."

"Your suitcase is heavy, and you'd have to lift it onto the conveyor belt where they check for items that can't be taken off the island." Rueben drove Ken's car into the parking lot and turned off the ignition. Then he got out and took Ellen's suitcase and carry-on tote from the back of the vehicle.

When Ellen exited the car, she carried her tote, while Rueben pulled the suitcase. He kept his steps slow, trying to delay the inevitable. If only he could make time stand still. *Why can't I remember what I wanted to say to Ellen?* Last night in bed, he'd rehearsed what he wanted to tell her, but now all he could do was grope for the right words to say.

Rueben had made sure Ellen was here in plenty of time, so she wouldn't miss her flight. They walked side by side, but no words were uttered between them. When they approached the conveyor belt, Rueben lifted the suitcase for her and picked it up on the other side. Then he waited as Ellen went to the counter and got her boarding pass. Once that was done and the luggage had been sent through, he began walking with her again.

As they came closer to the security line, Rueben began to panic. He still hadn't said what was on his mind, and he was almost out of time. "Wait, Ellen." He touched her arm. "There's something I need to say."

She stopped walking and turned to face him.

"Listen, I want to apologize again. I was wrong to deceive you."

She nodded.

A quick look around, and his eyes honed in on a couple who were saying goodbye with a hug and lingering kiss. He looked back at Ellen, wanting nothing more than to kiss and hold her the same way. His throat felt so dry he struggled to swallow. For this one moment, it felt as if they were the only two people in the terminal. No sounds could be heard, except for the beating of his own heart drumming in his ears. It was only he and Ellen, and as she looked up at him, Rueben felt as if he were drowning in her beautiful blue eyes.

He reached for her hand, and was pleased when she didn't resist. "I care for you, Ellen, and if things had been different, I think we could have begun a serious relationship." He paused and moistened his lips. "But I'm sure you realize under the circumstances a future for us is not possible."

"I know." Ellen's eyes glistened with tears. Her thumbs rubbed against his fingers, and her touch nearly drove him insane. "I hope someday you'll go back home and make things right with your family."

Rueben shook his head forcefully. "That's not possible. I can never return to Pennsylvania." He pulled Ellen closer and gave her a hug. *I can't believe I'm letting her go.* His mind thought one thing, but his heart said the opposite. "Goodbye, Ellen. I wish you all the best."

"I wish the same for you." Ellen turned and hurried toward the ever-growing security line.

As Rueben watched her go, the lump that had formed in his throat thickened. Then, as the line started moving, she was out of sight, swallowed up by those passengers who had followed. *If things were different, I'd go with her.*

✳

Over the Pacific Ocean

Tears streamed down Ellen's face as she looked at the pictures Rueben had printed for her from several of their outings, including the one he'd taken of them at Spouting Horn. Saying goodbye to Mandy and her family had been difficult, but leaving Rueben had been heart wrenching. Her head told her there was no chance of a relationship with him, no matter how much she longed for it. Her heart ached, thinking about Rueben's estrangement from his family. Surely they had to miss him, and no doubt he wanted to be with them. If he could get past the guilt, Rueben might be able to go back to Pennsylvania and reestablish a relationship with his family, even if he chose not to stay there permanently.

Unable to drink the water a flight attendant had given her, Ellen watched the huge thick clouds hanging weightless in the sky like giants. *Rueben is wrong.* She squeezed her fists until her fingers ached. *Things could be different if he wanted them to be. Why won't Rueben release his guilt and give his burdens to God?*

Ellen never expected her trip to Hawaii would turn out the way it had. She'd gone there to help Mandy but had fallen in love with a man she could not have a future with. Even as the distance between them grew longer, how could her feelings be reversed?

Maybe once I get home and into a routine again, it will be easier to forget I had feelings for Rueben. Ellen closed her eyes. *I will pray for him. And also for his deceased girlfriend's family. They all have to be in pain.*

When her plane landed in Seattle, Ellen would spend the night at a hotel near the airport. Tomorrow morning, she would board another plane and should arrive in South Bend, Indiana, that evening. She looked forward to being reunited with her parents and sisters, although this homecoming would be bittersweet. *I hope the old saying "absence makes the heart grow fonder" won't hold true for me.*

CHAPTER 37

South Bend, Indiana

On January sixteenth, Ellen stepped off the plane that had brought her back to her home state. The problem was, it didn't feel like home. After being in the Aloha State almost seven months, sometimes she had begun to feel it was where she belonged. Already, she missed Mandy and everyone else who'd become like family to her.

Pulling her cape tighter around her neck, Ellen had almost forgotten how cold January could be here in the Midwest. A shiver went through her body, making those warm temperatures she'd become so accustomed to that much harder to leave behind. Her cape felt heavy and bogged her down. The gray and dismal sky had no life to it.

As her feet walked on Indiana soil, Ellen's heart remained in Hawaii with Rueben. She'd thought of little else the whole trip home. Would she be able to shed the feelings that had grown within her for him?

Ellen made her way to baggage claim. The best antidote for thinking too much was work, and she hoped to remedy that by finding a job right away.

As Ellen approached the carousel to wait for her luggage, she spotted her mother and sister Ruby. Tears sprang to her eyes. It was so good to see them.

Mom enveloped Ellen in her arms with a hug so tight it nearly left her breathless. "Oh, Daughter, we've missed you something awful. It's *wunderbaar* to have you home."

Ellen could barely get the words out. "I've missed you too."

When she pulled away from her mother's embrace, Ruby gave her a hug. "*Ach*, you're so tan. And here it is the middle of winter."

Chuckling, Ellen shook her head. "Not in Hawaii. Well," she corrected herself, "technically it is winter there, but you'd never know it by the beautiful warm weather they have."

"Bet you're going to miss it." Ruby pointed to the luggage, circling on the carousel. "Look, there's your suitcase coming off now. I'll go fetch it for you."

While her sister raced off to get the luggage, Ellen grinned at Mom. "You'd think she was *eiferich* to get me home."

Mom's face broke into a wide smile. "We've all been eager for that, Ellen. You've been gone much too long. And since Ruby and Darla decided not to go to Florida this winter, it'll be nice to have all of my daughters at home."

"Jah, it will be nice, but I wouldn't have felt right coming home sooner, when Mandy needed me so badly." Gripping her tote with one hand, Ellen placed the other hand on her chest. "She and Ken have been through so much these past several months. They were ever so thankful for all the support they received—not just from me, but from everyone who helped with Ken's hospital, doctor, and therapy expenses."

Mom squeezed Ellen's arm. "You did a good thing by going there."

Ruby returned with the suitcase. "Are we ready to go?"

"Jah." Mom slipped her arm around Ellen's waist. "Our driver's waiting outside the terminal, so we'd best not keep her waiting."

"I assume Dad and Lenore must be working in the store this afternoon," Ellen said as they all began walking.

Mom nodded. "You'll see them at supper in a few hours."

"What about Darla? Will she be there, too, or is she scheduled to work at the restaurant this evening?"

"She's there right now," Ruby spoke up. "Darla was able to work the breakfast and lunch shift, so all our family will be together for supper."

"I'm glad." Ellen swung her tote bag as she stepped lightly. Despite missing her friends in Hawaii, it felt good to be home.

*

Middlebury

"How come you're panting for breath?" Ezra asked when he saw Lenore coming in the back door of the shoe store.

"I was out in the storage shed putting some boxes of shoes away that a customer didn't buy." Lenore blew on her hands and hung up her shawl. "It's cold out there, and I ran all the way back to the store."

He gave a nod. "Guess that's why your *gsicht* is red too."

Lenore touched her nose and snickered. "Bet my *naas* is as red as my face." She glanced at the clock on the far wall. "Oh, good. It's almost quitting time. I can't wait to go home."

"Are ya doing anything special tonight?" he asked, grabbing a pen.

"Jah. Mom hired a driver so she and Ruby could go to South Bend to pick Ellen up at the airport. We're gonna have a celebration supper tonight, and Mom's cookin' Ellen's favorite meal."

"That's great news." Ezra's cheekbones almost hurt from smiling so hard. "Say, what is Ellen's favorite *iems*?"

"Noodles over mashed potatoes." Lenore took a seat on a nearby stool. "Why do you care about my sister's favorite meal?"

Ezra couldn't help noticing how Lenore eyed him with suspicion, but it didn't stop him from blurting out what he wanted to do. "Think I may drop by later on to say hello."

Lenore's eyebrows squished together. "Are you sweet on my sister? Is that why you asked me about her so many times when she was gone?"

A warm flush crept across Ezra's cheeks. After working with Lenore all these months, he'd learned that she wasn't a bit shy about coming to the point. To his relief, some customers came into the store just then. Nathan began talking to one of the men, and Ezra quickly headed for the other Amish man.

He wasn't about to answer Lenore's question. The last thing he needed was Ellen's little sister blabbing to Ellen about his intentions or spreading gossip around the community. If anyone did the telling, it had to be him. Now he needed to find the right time to do it.

✳

"It's sure nice to have you back home with us." Ellen's dad smiled at her from his seat at the head of the table. "Didn't seem right with one of my *dochder* missing."

Ellen returned his smile. It was nice to be missed, and it felt good to be home, sitting around the table with her dear family. From what she could tell, nothing had changed since she left.

Ellen took a bite of mashed potatoes. *Rueben should be with his family as well, but he chooses an unyielding life.*

"Tell us all about your time on Kauai." Darla leaned forward as she gazed at Ellen from across the table. "Did you get to do anything fun while you were there?"

Ellen nodded, thinking about all the things she and Rueben had done. "But of course, most of my time was spent helping at the organic farm, and later, the B&B Ken's mother bought from Luana and Makaio."

"I imagine you enjoyed working at the bed-and-breakfast more than taking care of smelly *hinkel*." Lenore wrinkled her nose.

Ellen laughed. "I didn't mind helping care for the chickens, but you're right—working at the bed-and-breakfast was more enjoyable."

"What kind of fun things did you do when you weren't working?" Darla asked.

Ellen blotted her mouth with a napkin. Could she tell them without letting on that she cared for Rueben? "Well, I got to see Spouting Horn again." She paused for a sip of water. "Another time, I was able to tour a replica of an ancient Hawaiian village."

"Did you go alone?" Lenore questioned.

Ellen swallowed hard. "No, I went with—"

A knock sounded on the front door, bringing their discussion to an end.

Mom went to see who it was, and returned to the dining room with Ezra. Holding a cardboard box in his hands, he moved toward the table. "My mamm made two apple pies today, and I brought one over to share with all of you." His gaze moved to Ellen, and he offered her a wide smile. "Welcome back. I bet you're glad to be home."

She nodded.

Mom took the box from Ezra. "Tell your mamm we said danki. It was a nice gesture."

With hands in his jacket pockets, Ezra rocked back and forth on his heels. "Well, um. . .guess I'd better head for home."

"Oh, don't rush off," Mom was quick to say. "Have a seat at the table and join us."

He glanced at Ellen again, then back at Mom. "It's nice of you to offer, but I already ate supper."

"That's okay," Mom said. "You can visit with us while we eat, and then we'll have some of that pie your mamm made, along with hot coffee." Grinning, she hurried from the room.

Ellen pursed her lips. *It seems odd that Mom would be excited about a pie, when she made my favorite banana whoopie pies for dessert.*

Ezra went over to one of the empty chairs at the table and sat down.

"How's the weather out there?" Dad asked. "When Lenore and I came home from the store earlier it looked like it might snow."

"No snow yet." Ezra looked at Ellen again. "Think ya might come back to work at the store?"

She shook her head. "Dad has plenty of help with you and Lenore working there. I'll start looking for a job elsewhere soon."

Ezra cleared his throat louder than Ellen thought necessary. "There's to be a young people's gathering, with a bonfire, at your friend, Sadie's soon. Think ya might go?"

Before Ellen could respond, Ruby blurted, "Darla and I will be there, and I'm sure our sister will go too. Right, Ellen?"

Ellen nodded. What else could she do? There was nothing like being put on the spot. She would most likely go because it would be nice to see all her friends again.

She rose from her seat. "Think I'll see if Mom needs any help in the kitchen."

Ellen had no more than entered the adjoining room, when Lenore showed up. "Know what I think?" she whispered to Ellen.

"What?"

"I think Ezra likes you. I'll bet he's gonna ask if he can take you home after the get-together."

Mom gave a curious look their way, but didn't say anything. Ellen noticed a faint smile on her mother's face as she continued to cut the pie.

Hoping Ezra hadn't heard their conversation, Ellen leaned closer to

Lenore and whispered, "Why would you say something like that?"

"'Cause the whole time you were in Hawaii he kept asking questions about you." Lenore rolled her eyes. "And didn't you see the way he looked at you when he sat at the table? I'm certain that poor fellow's in love with you."

Ellen's face warmed. *Could it be true? Is Ezra interested in me? If so, what should I do?*

CHAPTER 38

The day after Ellen returned home, she decided to pay Sadie a visit. Since it was Wednesday, Sadie would be working at the hardware store. She looked forward to visiting her friend and hoped she and Sadie could go out to lunch during her noon break.

As Ellen headed down the road toward Shipshewana, it felt a bit strange to be traveling by horse and buggy again. During her time in Hawaii, she'd gotten used to either riding in a car or on the back of Rueben's motor scooter. She'd enjoyed all those times spent with Rueben and hadn't even minded getting windblown on the back of his scooter. Truthfully, Ellen had found pleasure in everything she'd done with Rueben.

"There I go, thinking about him again." Ellen clamped her mouth shut. How long would it take her to get past the feelings she had for him? Perhaps the longer she was home, the more distant her memory of Rueben would become. She hoped so, because it did no good to pine for something she couldn't have.

Soon another buggy came from the opposite direction. As it drew closer, Ellen realized it was Ezra's mother. They greeted each other with a hearty wave, and their horses trotted on.

Ellen reflected on Lenore saying the other night that she believed Ezra might be in love with her. "What nonsense." She snapped her horse's reins. "Let's go, Flame. It'll be lunchtime soon, and we need to get to Shipshewana."

✳

Shipshewana

When Ellen entered the hardware store, she found Sadie behind the counter, but there were no customers at the moment.

As soon as Ellen stepped up to the counter, Sadie put down her note-pad and leaped off the stool. "Ellen! What a joy it is to see you. When did you get home?"

"Yesterday, late afternoon." Ellen hugged her friend. "If you haven't taken your lunch break yet, I thought we could go to the little café in this building and visit while we eat."

Sadie nodded. "I haven't eaten yet. It'll be great getting caught up and hearing all about your trip."

Ellen smiled and slipped off her outer bonnet. Even though she'd written Sadie several letters, she hadn't told her everything—especially about Rueben.

Sadie informed her boss she was going to lunch, and the two of them headed down the hall to the restaurant. After placing their orders at the counter and finding a place near the back, they took a seat.

Sadie leaned forward, with her elbows on the table. "I'm eager to hear how Mandy and Ken are doing, and also their boppli."

"That baby is adorable. Little Isaac has Mandy's brown hair and Ken's blue eyes, but that could change as he grows older." Ellen took napkins from the holder for her and Sadie. "Mandy's doing well and getting her strength back."

"How about Ken? Is he getting along better now?" Sadie asked.

Ellen nodded. "He uses a cane and has some limitations, but Rueben's there to help out, so they're getting along as well as can be expected."

Sadie tipped her head. "Who's Rueben? I thought you said Ken's mother hired a young man named Rob to do the yard work and mainte-nance at the bed-and-breakfast."

Ellen's shoulders hunched. "Rueben Zook is Rob Smith's real name. He was raised in Pennsylvania, and his parents and siblings are Amish."

"What?" Sadie's brows lifted high on her forehead. "Tell me more."

"It's complicated. That's why I wanted to share this with you in person and not in a letter or phone call."

Sadie leaned closer. "You have my undivided attention."

Ellen explained everything about Rueben's situation: his girlfriend, the accident, and why he'd hidden out in Hawaii.

"It hurt me deep inside when he admitted this to me." She lowered her head. "If Rueben cared for me, like he said, then he should have been honest from the beginning."

"Is he ashamed of his Amish heritage?"

"I don't believe so. It has more to do with Rueben blaming himself for his girlfriend's death and being unable to face her family or his."

Sadie rubbed the bridge of her nose. "It's a good thing you didn't show your romantic side and get involved with him. He's not an honest person."

"To be frank, I do have strong feelings for Rueben." Ellen fingered her napkin. "But I'll get over it. It's just going to take some time."

"You should get a job so you'll be too busy to think about Rob—I mean, Rueben." Sadie shifted against the back of her seat. "And if someone asks you out on a date, you should go."

Ellen shrugged. "I'll consider it."

✳

Kapaa

Mandy smiled, watching her father sitting in the recliner, holding his precious namesake. Mom sat near him, watching little Isaac. "He's such a good boppli."

"Jah," Dad agreed.

What a precious sight to see her parents' joy as they interacted with their newest grandchild. Mandy wished Mom and Dad could stay here permanently, but they needed to return to their family and Dad's job back home. They would board a ship next week that would take them to California. Then it would be a train ride to Indiana.

Mandy moved closer to Ken on the couch and reached for his hand. It comforted her to see his strength returning and know that he had accepted his limitations with a more positive attitude. For a while, she'd been worried about his emotional state, but since the baby came, Ken seemed much calmer and upbeat. Their lives seemed to be back on track, although it did seem strange to be living in the home that used to belong to Luana and Makaio. She missed their smiling faces and gentle spirits. Maybe someday she, Ken, and little Isaac could fly to the Big Island for a visit. It would be fun to meet Makaio and Luana's newest granddaughter too.

Mandy thought about Ellen, and how much she missed her. It was selfish, but she wished things could have worked out between Ellen and Rueben and that they could live in Indiana. It was strange how her thinking had changed, because Mandy hadn't wanted Ellen and Rueben to develop a relationship at first—not until she learned that Rueben had been raised Amish. If only he'd get right with God and go back to his family, there could be a possibility of him and Ellen getting together. But Rueben seemed determined to wallow in self-pity, letting the guilt of his girlfriend's death swallow him up like a bottomless pit. All Mandy and Ken could do was continue to pray for Rueben.

Mandy sighed, shifting positions. *Guess some things just aren't meant to be. I'm sure someday Ellen will find the right man and get married.*

✳

Needing a break from his work in the yard, Rueben entered the kitchen and got a piece of fruit from the refrigerator. As he ate the papaya, he watched the middle-aged Hawaiian woman who'd been hired to take Ellen's place. She moved about the kitchen, helping Vickie get a midday snack ready for the two couples currently staying at the B&B. Every time he saw the native woman, he thought about Ellen and how much he missed her.

Well, I can't stand around here all day, feeling sorry for myself. Rueben wiped his hands on a paper towel and headed back outside.

He'd begun watering some of the plants, when Ken came out of the house. Using his cane, Ken limped over to Rueben and stopped in front of him. "How long are you gonna let this go on?"

"What?"

Ken gestured to the picnic table. "Let's take a seat. I'm more comfortable sitting down."

"Okay." Rueben turned off the spray nozzle and put the hose on the ground. As he followed Ken across the yard, he could almost predict what this conversation would be about.

Rueben took a seat on one side of the table, and Ken seated himself on the other.

"I've been watching you mope around here ever since Ellen left, and I think you were foolish for letting her go." Ken stared right at Rueben, as though daring him to say otherwise.

Rueben lifted his shoulders. "She needed to go home. Her place is with her family, not here on Kauai."

"I'm well aware, but you should have gone with her."

Rueben shook his head with force. "No way! I can't go back to the mainland and face my demons."

Ken groaned. "Thanks to the shark attack that nearly took my arm and crippled my left leg, I've had to face my own share of uncertainties."

"Yeah, I know."

"I also lived near the Amish the first two years of my marriage, and I've come to know Amish values, as well as their ways."

Rueben massaged his forehead. "What are you getting at?"

"If you return to Pennsylvania and talk to your deceased girlfriend's family, I'm bettin' they'll offer their forgiveness right away." Ken leaned forward. "As I'm sure you must be aware, the Amish realize that without forgiveness there can be no healing."

With both hands clutching his stomach, Rueben rocked back and forth. It was difficult to speak, or even think. Before he could ask anyone else's forgiveness, he needed to forgive himself. The agony he felt over Arie's death screamed for release.

Rueben's shoulders shook as he rested his head in the palms of his hands. *Dear Lord, forgive me for what I did. Give me the courage to go home and face my deepest fears.*

CHAPTER 39

*N*ow buck up and stop feeling sorry for yourself, Mandy thought as she changed her little one's diapers. *Living here isn't so bad, and you have much to be grateful for.*

Baby Isaac gurgled and kicked his tiny feet. "Look at you, my little sweetie. You just wanna go, don't you?" Mandy chuckled, in spite of her melancholy mood. Her bundle of joy overwhelmed her heart with happiness. She loved watching everything about her tiny son: his smiles, when he slept, and even his healthy cries, letting her know he was hungry. Isaac was two weeks old, and other then when he was hungry, he hardly ever cried.

Mandy, Ken, and Vickie were good about taking pictures of the newest family member. Mandy planned to mail pictures to her parents, so they could share in the things they'd be missing as this little one grew.

Vickie had sold her car a week ago and bought a minivan so she could carry more passengers. This morning, Vickie had driven Mom and Dad to the port in Lihue so they could begin their return trip to the mainland. Of course, Mandy, Ken, and the baby went along. It had been difficult saying goodbye to her parents, especially because Mandy didn't know when she might see them again. Their future was uncertain, but at least she and Ken had been blessed with a healthy child.

Mandy was grateful for Vickie. In addition to paying off the remainder of Ken's hospital bills with the money she'd earned from the sale of the farm, Ken's mother had provided an income for them by buying the B&B. She was a good grandma, loving mother, and the best mother-in-law a girl could ask for. It was a shame Vickie's other son didn't care enough to come see her or his brother, not to mention his first nephew.

Mandy lifted Isaac into her arms and kissed his soft cheek. *If my folks could come here all the way from Indiana, surely Dan could fly to Kauai from California.* She'd been praying since the time Dan and his wife left Kauai that things would work out for the best for all of them. She just never expected Dan would stay away so long.

As Mandy headed down the hall toward the living room, she spotted Rueben's baseball hat on the entry table. In addition to taking Mandy's folks to the ship, Vickie had dropped Rueben off at the airport.

Ken had told Mandy about his conversation with Rueben last week, and how Rueben had asked God to forgive him. She wondered if Rueben might end up staying in Pennsylvania. Either way, she hoped things worked out well when he met with Arie's family.

✳

"Where would you like me to put this vase after I throw out the wilted flowers?" Kamilla, the woman who'd taken Ellen's place, asked Vickie as they worked together to clean one of the guest rooms.

"I keep all my vases in the lower cupboard on the right side of the kitchen sink," Vickie responded. Since Kamilla had only been working here a few weeks, she hadn't learned where everything should go.

"Okay, I'll take care of that now." Kamilla sent a smile in Vickie's direction and hurried from the bedroom.

Vickie hummed to herself as she opened a window to air out the room. She inhaled deeply, watching the sheer curtains blow inward as the breezes filtered through. It had rained yesterday, and the fresh air felt cleansing.

Things were running smoothly at the B&B, with the new people she'd hired to replace Ellen and fill in for Rueben while he was gone. Even, so, it didn't feel right without them. Ellen was always so cheerful and didn't have to be asked to do the chores. Kamilla, on the other hand, sometimes seemed unable to make a decision on her own. Perhaps, being new, she was overly cautious, not wanting to overstep her bounds.

In some ways, Vickie wished Ellen could have stayed on, but it was unrealistic to expect her to remain when her family was on the mainland. Besides, to stay would have meant Ellen would have to give up her Amish way of life, as Mandy had done. Only Mandy had never joined the church, so that made it easier.

Pilipo, the man taking Rueben's place, was a hard worker, but he rarely said anything unless spoken to. The only time she heard him talking was when he had his cell phone up to his ear.

Rueben, who'd once seemed like an introvert, had become outgoing and made conversation with the B&B guests when they were in the yard.

Pulling her thoughts in another direction, Vickie picked up the feather duster. She was about to tidy up the top of the dresser, when Kamilla called her from the kitchen. "You're wanted on the phone, Mrs. Williams."

Vickie stuck her head out the open doorway. "Can you take a message?"

"It's your son."

Vickie pushed an errant piece of hair away from her face. "Did you say someone needs to speak to my son? If so, Ken's on the lanai with Mandy and the baby."

Kamilla stepped into the hall. "The call's not for Ken. The man on the phone said he's your son, Dan, and he wants to speak to you."

Vickie's heart raced as she dropped the duster and rushed down the hall. Her hand trembled when she picked up the phone. "Aloha, Dan."

"Hi, Mom. How's it going? Are you, Ken, Mandy, and the new baby doing okay?"

"We're fine." Vickie took a seat at the table. It was good to hear Dan's voice. "Ken's getting by with the use of his cane. Mandy and little Isaac are doing well too. How about you and Rita?"

"We're both good." Dan cleared his throat. "Uh, the reason I'm calling is because I owe you a long-overdue apology."

"Oh?"

"I let you down by leaving Kauai soon after Dad died, and I'm sorry. I've been afraid to come back and face the loss I felt when he died." Dan paused, and Vickie heard him blow his nose. "Rita's settled in here with her family, so it wouldn't be fair to uproot her. But we'd like to come to Kauai for a visit soon, if that's okay with you."

Joy bubbled in Vickie's soul. She'd almost given up on her son returning home, even for a visit. His apology moved her to tears. "I forgive you, Son. You and Rita will always be welcome to come and stay for as long as you like. We have a room we don't rent to our guests. It's for family and close friends when they visit. Please let us know whenever you're free to come, and we'll roll out our Hawaiian welcome mat."

Dan chuckled. "Since we have that settled, I'd like to talk to Ken now, if he's available."

"He's on the lanai with Mandy and the baby. I'll take the phone out to him."

"Okay. Mahalo, Mom."

Vickie stepped onto the lanai and smiled when she saw Ken stretched out on the hammock with the baby across his chest. Mandy sat on the porch swing, reading a book.

"Your brother's on the phone. He wants to talk to you, Ken." Vickie went to the hammock.

Ken's eyes widened. "Okay, Mom. Would you mind taking Isaac so I can sit up?"

She leaned over and swept her precious grandson into her arms. The warmth and sweet scent of the little guy's baby lotion brought back pleasant memories of when her boys were babies. Oh, how she missed those days when she and Charles raised their children together. But now she had something else to look forward to.

Ken sat up and swung his legs over the side of the hammock, while Vickie took a seat on the swing next to Mandy. She patted the baby's back and was rewarded with a burp.

✳

"Hi, Dan." Ken held the phone close to his ear. "How are things in California?"

"Everything's fine here, but I didn't call to talk about me. I called to tell you how sorry I am for running out on you and Mom after Dad died. I was selfish and should have had the courage to stay and help out—not leave you stuck with all the responsibility." Dan paused a few seconds. "I should have been there for you after the shark attack too. Will you forgive me, Brother?"

Ken swallowed, in an attempt to push down the lump in his throat.

" 'Course I forgive you. I just wish you didn't live so far from us now."

"I know, but Rita's family is here, and. . ."

"No need to explain. I understand where you're comin' from." Ken smiled when Mandy came over to stand by his side. He appreciated it even more when she put her hand on his shoulder and gave it a squeeze.

"We hope to visit Kauai soon," Dan said. "I'm looking forward to holding that new nephew of mine. Is it him I hear gurgling in the background?"

"Yeah, that's my son. I can't wait for you to meet him."

"I'm anxious too. As soon as we get reservations made I'll let you know."

"We'll look forward to that."

"I'll call again soon. It was great talking to you and Mom."

"Same here. Oh, and be sure to say hello to Rita for us."

"Will do. Please tell Mandy I said the same."

When Ken hung up he took Mandy's hand. "I think things are gonna be okay with me and Dan. That's one burden lifted from my shoulders."

She bent down and gave him a kiss. "I'm so glad."

✳

Over the Pacific Ocean

Rueben fidgeted in his seat, trying to find a comfortable position. He'd booked his airline ticket in coach, and there wasn't much leg room for a man of his stature. Looking beyond the extended seats and into first class ahead of that, he wished he'd spent the extra money for a better seat. He'd only have to put up with the cramped quarters a few more hours. Then he could get off the plane in Seattle and stretch his legs.

Rueben glanced at his Hawaiian-print shirt. Then he got to thinking about the hat he'd left behind. *No problem. I'll get it when I go back to Kauai.* Unless things went better than he hoped, Rueben probably wouldn't stay in Pennsylvania.

He had mixed feelings about seeing his family again. While it would be great to visit and catch up on their lives, they might criticize him for running off to Hawaii instead of staying home and dealing with Arie's death.

Rueben dreaded more than anything seeing Arie's folks and not knowing what their reaction would be. He hoped they'd forgive, but his nerves were on edge. *Oh man.* Rueben glanced at his cell phone to check the time. *After punishing myself since the accident, getting criticized by Arie's folks can't make me feel any worse. But thanks to Ken, I decided to go home, and I plan to see it through.*

The man sitting next to Rueben began to snore, so Rueben slipped on his earphones to drown out the aggravating noise. He could have paid to watch a movie, but right now all he wanted to do was close his eyes and try to relax. Rueben had made a mess of things in his young life, and if nothing else, he needed to make things right with Arie's parents. Unfortunately, it may be too late for him and Ellen.

CHAPTER 40

Ronks

Rueben sat on the edge of the bed in his old room, staring out the window at the dismal winter weather. The backyard, covered with snow, sat in sharp contrast to the murky gray sky. He heard someone downstairs stoking the wood stove, but the heat hadn't made it to his chilly room.

As soon as Rueben woke up, he felt an ache above his eyes. Using his fingers to massage the area, Rueben moaned. "I don't need a *koppweh* today."

Rueben had arrived at his parents' home late Thursday evening. He'd rented a car after his plane landed in Philadelphia and gone straight to Ronks. He wasn't surprised that Mom, Dad, and his siblings had greeted him with warm embraces. What had surprised Rueben was they thought he'd come to stay. When he explained his reason for returning home was to make things right with Arie's folks, Dad had given him a stern look and said, "So you're not going to take classes and join the Amish church?"

Rueben said he hadn't made up his mind, and Mom started to cry.

"Don't know why they're trying to push me to join the Amish church," Rueben mumbled as he slipped on a pair of jeans. "I just got back and don't know yet if I'm staying." He bent to tie his shoes.

He realized how hurt his family must feel; especially when he'd told them this trip was mainly to see Arie's parents. He'd need to apologize for that.

Rueben put on a shirt and made his way downstairs, where he found Mom in the kitchen, fixing breakfast.

"Guder mariye." She offered him a pleasant smile. "Did you sleep well, Son?"

He nodded, choosing not to mention his headache. "Good morning. It felt strange to wake up to a cold room, though. I'm used to the warm, balmy weather in Hawaii and being able to open windows most of the time."

Mom pursed her lips, looking at Rueben over the top of her metal-framed glasses. "Why Hawaii, Rueben? If you had to leave home, what made you go so far away?"

"I've always wondered what the Hawaiian Islands were like." He took a glass down from the cupboard and poured orange juice from the container on the kitchen table. "I was sure nobody would know me there and figured it was a chance to start my life over and leave the past behind. Thought it would be easier to be around strangers." He laid a hand against his chest. "'Course, the past has a way of catching up to a person, and when it does, there's no place one can hide. Miles—and certainly not an ocean—didn't help me forget."

Mom clucked her tongue while shaking her head. "You should have stayed here, Rueben, and let us help you deal with Arie's death."

"I didn't want anyone's help. I needed to deal with it my own way." He sank into a chair at the table. "Thought I was doing a good job of it too. That is, until Ellen came along."

Mom quit stirring the pancake ingredients and came to join him at the table. "Who's Ellen?"

Rueben drank his juice, and then told his mother all about Ellen.

Mom pushed her glasses higher on her nose. "Are you in love with her, Son?"

"Yeah, but I can't even think about pursuing a relationship with Ellen till I talk with Arie's parents and seek their forgiveness."

Mom gave Rueben's arm a loving pat. "You need to go talk to Marcus and Susan soon."

"You're right, Mom." Rueben rose from his seat. "And I'm goin' over to see them now before I lose my nerve."

"What about breakfast?" she called as he grabbed his jacket and headed for the back door.

"The juice was enough. I'll see you when I get back. Maybe I'll be hungry by then."

✳

After leaving Arie's parents' home, Rueben sat in his car, staring at the dreary landscape before him. He couldn't believe Susan and Marcus had forgiven him for being the cause of their daughter's death. Rueben would always remember the way Susan touched his arm and said, "Of course we forgive you. After all, it was not your fault Arie didn't get out of the car when you warned her that the train was coming."

"Maybe she didn't realize how close it was and thought she had plenty of time," Marcus had added. "I'm sure Arie wouldn't have stayed in the car if she'd known what would happen."

Rueben rubbed his forehead, where the headache had been earlier. *But it was my fault for trying to beat the train.* He had told Arie's parents that, but they'd said they didn't hold him responsible for their daughter's death.

He closed his eyes. *They've forgiven me, Lord. Now I need to forgive myself and try to get my life back on track. But where do I begin? How do I start over?*

Pulling his cell phone from his pocket, Rueben opened his eyes. It was ten o'clock, which meant in Kauai, it was the wee hours of the morning, so he couldn't call Mandy. He would go back to his parents' house and wait till everyone at the B&B would likely be up before calling to ask for Ellen's address. Tomorrow after breakfast, Rueben would tell his folks goodbye and head for Indiana. According to his GPS, Middlebury was an eight- or nine-hour drive from here. But if the weather didn't cause a delay, he should make it by Saturday evening.

✳

Middlebury

"I don't know about you, but I'm sure looking forward to the young people's gathering at Sadie's." Holding the horse's reins with one hand, Darla reached across the buggy seat and tapped Ellen's arm. "Did you hear what I said?"

"Jah, I'm sure it will be fun." Truthfully, Ellen would prefer to stay home this chilly Saturday evening, but Sadie had mentioned her dad planned to build a bonfire in their yard. As long as she stayed close to its warmth, she probably wouldn't be cold.

This was Ellen's first young people's outing since she'd gotten home, and she looked forward to a time of singing, eating, and socializing. Hopefully, it would help take her mind off Rueben and wondering what he was doing in Hawaii. She'd also been thinking about Mandy, hoping things were going okay at the bed-and-breakfast now that she and Mandy's parents weren't there to help out. Vickie had hired a native woman to take over her position. No doubt, things were working out.

"Too bad Ruby has to work at the restaurant until eight." Darla broke into Ellen's musings. "Yesterday she thought she'd be able to join us tonight, but then the manager asked if Ruby could work someone else's shift who'd called in sick."

"There will be other gatherings." Ellen pulled her cape a little tighter around her neck. During the holidays on Kauai, she'd missed seeing snow. Now, as a chilly breeze blew in through the cracks around the buggy door, she longed for warmer weather.

Ellen saw the glow from the bonfire and smelled the scent of wood smoke as they approached the large white farmhouse where Sadie lived.

"Here we are." Darla led their horse and buggy down the lane and up to the barn, where several other buggies were parked. They both got out, and Ellen helped her sister unhitch the horse.

While Darla led him to the barn, Ellen took the container of brownies she'd brought along into the house. She found Sadie in the kitchen, getting paper cups, plates, and plastic utensils from the cupboard.

Sadie smiled when Ellen set the brownies on the table. "*Willkumm!* I'm so glad you came." She placed the items she held on the counter and gave Ellen a hug.

"I'm glad I did too. The big bonfire looks inviting."

"Dad was having fun getting it built." Sadie glanced past Ellen. "Did Darla and Ruby come with you?"

"Just Darla. Ruby had to work." Ellen looked out the window, where the yard was aglow from the fire. "Who all is here?"

"Let's see. . .Mary Ruth Zimmerman and her boyfriend, Andrew; the Lehman sisters, Sharon and Debra. Ezra Bontrager is here too, and so is. . ."

Ellen's thoughts drew inward. It was a silly notion, but she wished Rueben could be with her tonight. How nice it would be to sit around the bonfire with him and roast marshmallows.

✳

As Ezra sat close to the fire, roasting a hot dog, he watched Ellen sitting between Darla and Sadie.

Ellen's sure pretty. I'm glad she's back from Hawaii and came here tonight. I wonder what she'd say if I asked if I could take her home? Think I might muster the courage to ask.

Ezra let go of his roasting stick with one hand to scratch an itch on his nose. In the process, he almost lost his hot dog. He grabbed the meat in time, and finished roasting it just the way he liked—not too blackened, but heated all the way through.

After placing the meat in a bun, Ezra got up from his folding chair and walked over to the picnic table where the condiments, chips, and baked beans had been set. His stomach growled, thinking how good this meal would taste. He was glad everyone had prayed silently before the food was set out. That meant he could dive right in.

While Ezra squirted ketchup on his hot dog, he overheard Ellen talking to Sadie.

"Have you heard anything from Rueben since you left Kauai?" Sadie leaned close to her friend.

Ellen shook her head. "I've thought about sending him a letter, or even calling the B&B. But I'm not sure if. . ."

Ezra's jaw clenched as Ellen moved to the back of the line, where others waited to get their food. His frustration mounted, unable to hear the rest of her sentence. He wanted to know what else she'd said to Sadie about this fellow Rueben. Who was he anyway, and why would Ellen want to call or write to him?

Ezra remembered Ellen mentioning in the one letter she'd written him that she'd done some fun things while on Kauai with someone named

Rob. But she hadn't said anything about anyone named Rueben.

He finished dishing up, and walked toward the end of the line on the way back to his chair by the fire. As he strode past the young women, he heard Sadie say, "You shouldn't have let yourself fall for him, Ellen. You should keep your focus here, not on someone you met on Kauai."

Ezra hurried past, barely able to hang on to his plate. It wasn't the cold causing his hands to tremble. Unless he was mistaken, Ellen was in love with this Rueben.

He took his seat and stared at the food on his paper plate, no longer hungry. Ezra picked up his soda can to take a drink and ended up sloshing it on his sleeve. *How can Ellen be in love with Rueben? Why, the guy isn't Amish, so how could it work?*

Ezra wiped his sleeve with a napkin. *Maybe I've been fooling myself, thinking I had a chance with Ellen. Truth is, she's never given any indication that she has feelings for me. Could be it's time to move on.*

Ezra glanced in Ellen's direction. *Or maybe I ought to let Ellen know how I feel about her and see how she responds. After all, I'm here, and this fellow from Kauai is not.*

CHAPTER 41

When Rueben's vehicle drew closer to the address Mandy had given him for Ellen, his palms grew sweaty. He remembered during his phone conversation with Mandy, she had said she and Ken would pray for a good outcome. The Lord had been working in his life each day since he'd had the talk with Ken, and Rueben's faith was growing.

Holding the steering wheel with one hand and wiping the other on his pant legs, Rueben began to fret. *What if Ellen doesn't want to see me? I hope I didn't make a mistake coming here.*

He drew a quick breath. *But I'm here now, so I may as well see it through.*

Rueben drove up the snow-covered driveway and parked his car near the barn. He got out quickly, before he lost his nerve, and sprinted for the house, unmindful of the slushy snow.

He stepped onto the porch and hesitated at the door before he knocked. A striped feline sauntered up to Rueben, meowing and pawing at his leg. Rueben looked down and chuckled. "Are you as cold as I am, kitty?"

When the door opened, a young Amish girl, who looked a lot like Ellen, greeted him. "Can I help you?"

"Umm. . .is this where Ellen Lambright lives?" Rueben's mouth felt numb. He struggled to get his words out.

"Jah, but my sister's not here right now."

Rueben blew on his cold hands. "Would you mind telling me where she is? I need to speak with her."

She tipped her head. "About what? Who are you anyway?"

"Oh, sorry. My name is Rueben Zook. I met Ellen in Hawaii." He leaned against the door frame. "And who are you?"

"I'm Lenore."

Rueben smiled. "Ah yes, she told me about you."

Lenore stared up at him with a placid expression. "You must be from Hawaii all right, 'cause your face is so tan."

"Yes I am." He glanced at the snowflakes drifting down, as though in slow motion. "Would you please tell me where your sister is?"

"She went to her friend Sadie's place. There's a young people's gathering there tonight." Lenore crossed her arms over her chest. "I wasn't invited, 'cause I'm only fifteen. The others who'll be there are all courting age."

"Can I have the address? I need to talk to Ellen right away."

The girl's jaw jutted out. "Guess it's okay. I'll be right back." She stepped inside, leaving Rueben on the porch to shiver and wait. Through the slightly open door, he watched the contented tiger cat take a bath near the entrance table. *At least the feline is allowed inside. But I'm a stranger to Ellen's sister, so what can I expect?*

Rueben blew on his hands again. He wished he'd thought to buy a heavier coat before he left Pennsylvania. And he didn't have warm gloves either. The lightweight jacket Rueben wore did little to keep out the chill.

A few minutes later, Lenore returned and handed Rueben a slip of paper. "Here's Sadie Kuhn's address."

"Thanks." Rueben stepped off the porch and hurried back to his car. His stomach fluttered at the thought of seeing Ellen. He hoped this wasn't a mistake.

✳

By the time Rueben reached the address Lenore gave him, the snow was coming down harder. He pulled onto the driveway and parked his car near several black-topped buggies. Thanks to the glow of the bonfire on one side of the yard, he had no trouble seeing where the carriages were parked. The Indiana buggies were different from those in Lancaster County, where the tops and sides were gray.

Rueben got out of the car, and was about to head toward the group of people sitting around the fire, when he spotted Ellen. She stood next to one of the buggies, talking to a young Amish fellow. The man stood close to Ellen. His head was mere inches from hers.

Heart pounding, Rueben stepped into the shadows and watched. He wasn't close enough to understand what they said, but his throat tightened when the man put his hand on Ellen's shoulder.

I'm too late. Ellen already has a suitor. Who knows—maybe they'd been courting before Ellen went to Kauai. She had never mentioned having a steady boyfriend, but that didn't mean she wasn't being courted.

Rueben rubbed his arms as he made his way back to the car. The icy chill he felt had nothing to do with the wintry snow drifting down from the sky. He should have made things right with Ellen before she left Kauai, and now it was too late. Rueben would find a place to stay the night and then leave for Pennsylvania in the morning. He'd spend a week or so with his family before returning to Kauai. Without Ellen in his life, there was nothing here for him.

✳

As a car backed down the Kuhns' driveway, with its headlights shining in her face, Ellen shielded her eyes and stepped away from Ezra's buggy. She couldn't make out the driver but wondered if he or she was an English neighbor or perhaps someone who was lost and had used this driveway to turn around. Of course, the vehicle hadn't actually turned around—it had backed down the driveway, going faster than it should, especially in the snow.

"I wonder who that was," Ezra commented.

Ellen shook her head. "I don't know."

"Well, whoever it was, they nearly blinded us with their bright lights." Ezra spoke in a high-pitched tone.

Ellen glanced at her friends by the bonfire. "We should get back. Sadie's probably wondering where I went."

"Okay, but there's one more thing I want to say." Ezra shuffled his feet, making a horseshoe design in the snow. "I'm glad you came out to your sister's buggy to get your gloves. It gave me a chance to speak with you alone, but I didn't get everything said."

Ellen stirred restlessly, shivering as she shifted her weight from one foot to the other. She could hardly feel her toes, as the cold seeped into her shoes. Ezra had already asked if he could court her, and Ellen had told him that she was sorry, but she didn't see him as anything more than a friend. She hoped he didn't think he could change her mind. "What else did you want to say, Ezra?"

He reached out his hand, like he might touch her arm, but then let it drop to his side. "Earlier, I heard you tell Sadie about some other fellow."

All Ellen could do was nod.

"Well, after thinking it over, I realized you and I are not meant to be together. So I wanted you to know that there are no hard feelings. I want you to be happy, and if it's not with me, then I hope you find someone else."

Ellen smiled. "Danki, Ezra. I wish the same for you as well."

"Okay, then. Now that we have that settled, let's go roast some marshmallows."

Hobbling on near-frozen feet, Ellen followed Ezra back to the bonfire. She was glad they'd had this opportunity to chat. The one thing that puzzled her, though, was why, if he was interested in her, he'd been so bossy when they'd worked at Dad's store together.

It was nice of Ezra to say he hoped I would find someone else, but the man I love lives in Hawaii. I wish now I'd never met Rueben or discovered his past.

❋

When Ellen and Darla arrived home from Sadie's that evening, Ellen said she was tired and headed for her room. She was almost to the door, when Lenore stepped into the hall from her bedroom. "How'd the gathering go this evening?"

"It was nice." Ellen smoothed her sister's long hair away from her face. "I'm surprised you're still up. The house was dark when Darla and I came in, so I figured everyone had gone to bed."

"I waited up for you."

"How come?"

"Wanted to find out what the tan fellow from Hawaii said when he saw you."

Ellen's brows drew inward. "What are you talking about?"

Lenore motioned for Ellen to come to her room and shut the door. "He said his name was Rueben, and that he'd met you in Hawaii. When I said you weren't here, he asked where you'd gone." Lenore took a seat on the edge of her bed. "Wasn't sure if I should tell him, but I ended up giving him Sadie's address, 'cause he said he needed to talk to you."

Ellen collapsed on the bed beside her sister. She never expected Rueben would show up here. But there was no reason Lenore would make up such a story.

"So did he get to Sadie's? And did he tell you what he wanted?" Lenore tugged on Ellen's dress sleeve.

"No, I never saw Rueben." Ellen brought her hands up to her face. *Could Rueben have been driving the car that came into the Kuhns' yard? But if it was him, why'd he leave without looking for me?* Ellen jumped up and raced for the door.

"Where ya goin'?"

Ellen looked back at her sister. "Out to the phone shack to make a call."

"At this hour?" Lenore yawned and stretched her arms out to the sides. "Nobody we know will be in their phone shack to check for messages this late at night. Don't you think you ought to wait till morning?"

"The phone call I'll make is to Mandy. It'll be early evening on Kauai— not close to midnight, like it is here."

"How come you're callin' her?"

"To ask for Rueben's cell number. I'm sure either she, Ken, or Vickie must have it." Ellen didn't wait for her sister's response. She grabbed the flashlight from Lenore's dresser and hurried from the room. If Rueben had shown up at Sadie's house, she needed to find out what he wanted.

Chapter 42

When Rueben woke up the following morning, he felt as though his head had been stuffed with cotton. He didn't know if it was from jetlag or not getting enough sleep the night before. After returning to the Pleasant View Bed-and-Breakfast, where he'd booked a room in Middlebury, he'd lain awake for several hours.

As he lay there, looking around his room, Rueben compared the B&B to the one on Kauai. This place had a country vibe, with its rustic furniture and dried flowers, unlike the Palms Bed-and-Breakfast, which featured tropical décor and wicker furniture. There was a brightness to the Hawaiian B&B and a scent of flowers when the windows were open, allowing the warm breezes to come in.

Rueben sat up in bed, stretching his arms over his head, then plopped back down in the warm sheets. He had asked God's forgiveness, as well as Arie's parents', and was certain he'd been forgiven. One would think that should be enough, but it wasn't. Rueben had prayed about things last night and come to the conclusion that he needed to speak to Ellen before returning to Kauai. If there was even a chance she might choose him over the man he'd seen her with, he had to take it. He was determined to let her know how he felt, and it was worth the risk of rejection just to see her one more time. If Ellen sent him away, he'd have to come to grips with it, because more than anything, Rueben wanted her to be happy.

Since it was nine o'clock, Rueben figured Ellen would be in church with her family. So he'd hang around the B&B all morning and go back to Ellen's house this afternoon when she would likely be home. He had paid for one more night here and didn't have to check out until Monday morning, at which time he would head for Pennsylvania.

✳

Rueben arrived at the Lambrights' home shortly before four that afternoon.

Sure hope Ellen's here this time and I can speak with her face to face.

His steps were solid as he made his way through the snow and up to the porch. After two knocks, the front door opened.

"Oh, it's you again." Ellen's youngest sister, Lenore, looked up at him with a curious expression. "If you came to see Ellen, she's not here."

"Again?" He frowned. "Where is she this time?"

"Ellen went to visit some of her friends, and I'm not sure where she is right now or when she'll get home."

"Can I speak to one of your parents? I'd like to leave a message for Ellen." Rueben didn't trust the girl to give her sister a message.

Lenore shook her head. "My folks aren't here either. They're also out visiting."

Rueben groaned inwardly. This conversation wasn't taking him anywhere.

"If you have a piece of paper I can write on, I'll leave my number for Ellen."

"Okay, I'll go to the kitchen and get a notepad."

Lenore disappeared, and Rueben stepped into the entryway. He wasn't going to remain in the cold this time.

As he waited for Lenore to return, Rueben peeked into the living room. He saw a fireplace with two chairs on either side. At the other end of the room sat a large couch, recliner, and a rocking chair. The room had a warm, inviting feel. He fought the temptation to take a seat by the fire to warm his gloveless hands. *This must be where Ellen's family gathers after their holiday meals*, he thought, remembering what Ellen had described.

A few minutes later, Lenore came back with a pen and tablet. "Here ya go." She handed them to Rueben.

Holding the tablet steady in one hand, he wrote the number where Ellen could reach him and handed the tablet back to Lenore. "Would you please give this to her when she comes home?"

"I'll let her know." Lenore nodded and closed the door.

Rueben hoped the young girl would follow through. At the rate things were going, he wondered if he'd ever connect with Ellen.

✳

By the time Ellen returned home, it was late and the house was dark. She figured her parents and sisters were all in bed. It has been a long day, but she'd enjoyed her time with Sadie and their friend Barbara.

Ellen smiled, thinking about Gideon and what a good husband he was for Barbara. He had volunteered to watch their daughter, Mary Jane, so his wife could spend time with Ellen and Sadie.

The time Ellen spent today with two good friends was enjoyable, but she wished Mandy could have joined them, like she used to before moving to Kauai.

As Ellen stood in the hallway with her flashlight, she noticed a familiar aroma. It smelled like the musky aftershave Rueben wore. *Could he have been here again? If he did stop by, surely someone would have left me a note.*

She hurried to the kitchen, and looked on the table. No note there. Nothing on the counter or roll-top desk either.

Ellen tucked in her upper lip. *This is silly. If Rueben came by, someone would have told me. What I need now is a good night's sleep. Tomorrow morning I'll do some shopping and continue my search for a job.*

Ellen's mind shifted gears, remembering how she'd called Mandy to get Rueben's cell phone number. After their short but meaningful talk, Ellen had tried calling Rueben. All she got was his voice mail. Before coming into the house, she'd stopped by the phone shack to check for messages. There were none. If Rueben had come by to talk to her, why hadn't he answered her call? Should she try calling him again in the morning?

CHAPTER 43

Rueben took a seat at the dining-room table, where several plates had been set out. Apparently, he wasn't the only one staying at this bed-and-breakfast.

Glancing at the clock on the far wall, he thought about the cell phone he'd accidentally left at his folks' in Pennsylvania. In addition to using it for calls, he relied on the phone to check the time.

"Hi, I'm Tom. Where you from?" A tall, bald man entered the room and reached out to shake Rueben's hand.

"My name's Rueben. I'm originally from Pennsylvania, but my current home is the Island of Kauai."

The man's brows lifted as he took a seat across the table. "What brings you to Indiana?"

"Umm. . . Guess you might call it business."

"What kind of business?" Tom leaned against the chair, cupping his chin with one hand.

"It's of a personal nature." Rueben felt as if he were being interrogated. He wished their B&B hostess would bring on the food so he could eat and be on his way. He'd learned earlier that he hadn't received any phone calls, so he assumed Ellen either didn't want to talk to him or hadn't received his message.

I'll give it one more try before I head out of town, Rueben told himself.

✳

When Rueben arrived at the Lambrights' place, he spotted a young Amish woman coming out of the barn. It wasn't Lenore this time, but she had the same hair color. He figured she was one of Ellen's other sisters.

"Hello. My name is Rueben Zook." He approached the girl. "Ellen and I worked together in Hawaii. Is she at home?"

She looked at him strangely and tilted her head. "Ellen went to the shoe store to give Ezra Bontrager something he left when he was at our house last week.

Rueben reached under the baseball cap he'd bought the other day, and scratched his head. "Who's Ezra?"

"He works for our dad. He and Ellen went to school together, and a few days ago he asked if he could court her, but. . . Achoo!" She pulled a tissue from her jacket pocket and wiped her nose. "I don't mean to be rude, but I need to get back in the house. Do you have a message for Ellen? I'll give it to her when she gets home."

"No that's okay. She doesn't need to know I was here." Feeling as though he'd been kicked by a horse, Rueben headed back to his car. Ellen had a suitor, and he would do nothing to come between them.

✳

Shipshewana

After filling his tank at a gas station, Rueben stopped in Shipshewana. He'd heard it was an interesting town with lots of gift shops and restaurants. Since his mother's birthday was coming up, he would look for a gift in one of the stores.

Coming to Indiana had been a waste of time as far as connecting with Ellen. Now that he knew she was being courted by someone, there was nothing to do but go home and try to forget he'd fallen in love with her.

Rueben pulled into a parking spot and went into one of the buildings. He browsed around in the hardware store and then the store across the hall, hoping to find the right gift for Mom.

When he headed down the nearest aisle, a gray-haired English woman stepped in front of him with her cart. As Rueben tried to skirt around her, he spotted a young Amish woman at the end of the aisle and realized it was Ellen. His heart skipped. *What should I do? Should I make myself known or get out of the store before she sees me?*

Rueben didn't want to draw attention to himself by shouting Ellen's name, so he backed away from the English woman's cart and went down the next aisle, thinking he'd start up the previous aisle. But by the time he'd gone the rest of the way down the first aisle and headed up the next one, there was no sign of Ellen.

Rueben was on the verge of calling her name when someone from behind tapped his shoulder. He whirled around. It was the same woman who'd blocked his way in the previous aisle.

"Excuse me, sir, but do you know where I might find women's shoes?"

"Sorry, Ma'am, but I don't work here. It's my first time in this store. Maybe there's a clerk around who can point you in the right direction."

"Okay, thank you." The elderly lady pushed her cart toward the front of the store.

I hope Ellen is still in here. A sense of urgency welled in Rueben's soul. He didn't want to miss an opportunity to talk with her before she left the store, if for no other reason than to tell her that he'd returned to Pennsylvania to talk with Arie's folks.

Rueben was about to head down another aisle, when a young woman came up to him.

"I can't reach that hat. Would you mind getting it for me?" she asked.

Rueben couldn't ignore her request. "Sure. Which hat did you want?"

"That one." She pointed to a wide-brimmed straw hat. "It's my dad's birthday, and he needs a new hat."

Rueben got it down for her. "Here you go."

"Thanks." With a sweet smile, the woman moved on.

"At this rate, I'll never get to see Ellen," Rueben muttered. In an act bolder than anything he'd ever done, he cupped his hands around his mouth and shouted, "Ellen Lambright, if you're still in this store, I need to talk to you. I'm in the aisle where the men's hats are sold."

Rueben remained where he was and waited. The people around him stared, but he didn't care. Several seconds went by, and Ellen appeared at the end of the aisle. "Rueben?"

Nodding, he moved toward her.

With eyes as blue as the ocean, Ellen stared at him, motionless. She was the prettiest thing he'd ever seen. More beautiful than the islands he'd left behind.

As Rueben approached, two redheaded girls showed up out of nowhere. Laughing and poking each other, they ran in front of him.

Rueben looked at Ellen and lifted both hands, while she stood with one hand over her mouth. He saw her dimples, and knew she was stifling a chuckle.

"There you two are." A frazzled, pregnant woman entered their aisle, pushing an overflowing cart of items. She shook her finger at the girls. "You kids come with me right now. If you don't behave, there'll be no ice cream after lunch."

That seemed to quiet the rambunctious children. Rueben watched as the pouting girls went to stand beside their mother's cart. She looked up at him. "I hope these rascals didn't bother you too much."

"It's okay. No harm done. I was a kid once too."

As the woman and her children walked away, one of the little girls turned to look at Rueben. He winked before she disappeared around the corner.

Rueben started walking toward Ellen again. She did the same. He would not let her out of his sight now. As they approached each other, Ellen spoke first. "Rueben, I'm surprised to see you here. I've tried to call you several times, but you haven't responded to any of my messages."

"That's odd. The owner of the bed-and-breakfast where I stayed said I had no messages." Rueben scratched his head. "Didn't your sister give you the piece of paper I wrote the phone number on?"

"No. When Lenore said you had stopped by, I called Mandy to ask for your cell number." A touch of pink erupted on Ellen's cheeks.

"I came by your house a second time," Rueben explained. "Only I talked to one of your sisters that day. The reason you got my voice mail is because I accidently left my cell phone at my folk's house."

Her eyes widened. "You went to Pennsylvania?"

"Yeah. I stopped to see my folks first, and then I went to speak with Arie's parents."

Ellen offered Rueben a hopeful smile. "How did it go?"

"It went well, but I'd rather not talk to you about it here." He gestured to the store entrance. "How about we sit in my rental car, so we can talk privately?"

She nodded.

Rueben took a couple deep breaths and headed for the door. Seeing Ellen again made him wish even more that they could establish a permanent relationship. But if all she could offer was friendship, he'd take it.

✳

As Ellen slipped into the passenger's seat, her stomach fluttered. She'd never been this nervous with Rueben before. By the way his knees bounced, she figured he was apprehensive too.

He opened his mouth, then shut it.

"What did you want to say?" she asked.

He clenched the steering wheel and looked straight ahead. "I know you're being courted by some fellow name Ezra, but I—"

"Now where did you hear that?"

"When I stopped by your house Saturday night, your sister Lenore gave me the address of the place you'd gone." He let go of the wheel and swiped a hand across his damp forehead. "So I went there, and when I drove up the driveway, I saw you talking to a young Amish man near a buggy."

She nodded. "That was Ezra Bontrager. He works at my dad's shoe store."

"Yeah, I know. One of your other sisters told me that when I stopped by your house again this morning and found out you weren't home." Rueben paused. "Between seeing you two together, and a comment your sister made, I got the impression you and Ezra were courting."

Ellen shook her head so hard her head covering ties whipped across her cheeks. "Ezra and I are not courting. He's just a fellow I've known since we went to school."

Rueben released an audible sigh. "That's a relief."

She watched as his expression softened. When Rueben lifted his hand and stroked Ellen's cheek, her throat constricted.

"After completing my mission in Pennsylvania," he continued, "I came here to tell you that for the first time since Arie's death I feel free of the guilt. I asked God's forgiveness, her parents forgave me, and I forgave myself." He continued to caress Ellen's face. "I feel like a new person inside, and I'm ready to move on with my life."

"Oh?" The one word was all Ellen could manage. Her throat felt swollen, and her eyes stung with tears.

"I want you to be part of my life, Ellen. I know it's too soon to speak of marriage, but I love you, and I'd like to stay in Indiana so we can court. That is, if you're willing."

Ellen's body felt weightless. She could hardly believe Rueben was here and had confessed his love for her. "I love you too, and I'd be honored to have you court me."

As Rueben gazed at Ellen, she took in his brown eyes and the darkness of his hair. His skin, still tan, was smooth beneath her fingers as she reached up to touch his face.

Gently, Rueben pulled Ellen into his arms and kissed her lips.

Ellen melted into his embrace and sighed. What a wonderful discovery she'd made when she met this young man in Hawaii. She closed her eyes and offered a short prayer. *Thank You, Lord, for answered prayer.*

EPILOGUE

$\mathcal{E}$llen stood in the living room, with arms folded, watching delicate snowflakes swirling outside the window.

She released a contented sigh. It was hard to believe all that had happened in the last year. In addition to Rueben joining the church in her district and them getting married in the fall, they were now the happy owners of a bed-and-breakfast—the same one Mandy and Ken used to own. The couple who'd bought the business from Ellen's friends decided it was too much for them to handle, even with the help of their daughters. Their main complaints were not wanting to be tied down, and having to deal with sometimes picky clientele.

Ellen didn't mind staying close to home or dealing with a variety of people. She found running the B&B to be fun and rewarding. Her dream of owning a bed-and-breakfast had finally come true.

Rueben enjoyed running their new business too. They'd changed a few things back to the way the B&B had been before the previous owners made some modifications. Now, it almost felt as if she'd never left. Someday when children came along, Rueben might add on to the house.

Ellen's life seemed perfect, and daily she counted her blessings.

She shivered and put more wood on the fire. *I'll bet it's warm in Hawaii.*

Ellen had heard from Mandy the other day and was pleased to learn they were planning a trip to Middlebury in the spring. They would stay a few days at the B&B and spend the rest of their time with Mandy's parents.

Ellen couldn't wait to see her friends again, as well as their precious little boy. From the pictures Mandy had sent, it wasn't hard to see how much the little guy had grown. Ken had improved, although he still used a cane, and their bed-and-breakfast in Kapaa was thriving. Ken's mother was happy, and they'd enjoyed a recent visit with Dan and his wife.

Rueben stepped up behind Ellen, disrupting her thoughts as he wrapped his arms around her waist.

She leaned against his muscular chest and closed her eyes. "Mandy, Barbara, and I are all happily married," she whispered. "I hope that someday my dear friend Sadie will find someone who will make her as happy as I am."

Rueben turned her around to face him. "And you, my pretty fraa, make me happy too."

Hawaiian Lemon Chicken

Ingredients

1½ pounds boneless chicken
    breast cut into small pieces
1½ teaspoons soy sauce

1 cup cornstarch
½ cup milk
2 cups olive oil or coconut oil

Lemon Sauce

¾ cup water
¼ cup white vinegar
½ cup sugar or sugar substitute
2 tablespoons cornstarch

1 tablespoon lemon juice
½ teaspoon salt
5 lemon slices cut thin

Marinate chicken in soy sauce for 10 minutes. Dip in cornstarch, then milk, then cornstarch again. Fry in hot oil for three minutes or until golden brown. Drain on paper towel. Mix all sauce ingredients, except lemon slices. Cook in saucepan on medium-high heat, stirring constantly until mixture comes to a boil. Add lemon slices and cook another minute. Pour over chicken and arrange lemon slices for garnish.

Discussion Questions

1. Ellen left her home in Indiana to be with her friend Mandy in Hawaii because of an emergency. Have you ever been in a situation where you had to leave all that was familiar to help someone who lived far away? How did you deal with the feelings of homesickness?

2. How difficult do you think it was for Mandy and her husband, Ken, to sell their bed-and-breakfast in Indiana and move to Kauai to help Ken's mother? Have you ever had to make a sacrifice such as moving in order to help a relative?

3. Change was difficult for Ellen, and when the bed-and-breakfast where she worked was sold, she had to find another position that wasn't to her liking. Have you ever lost a job you really liked and had to take something you didn't enjoy? If so, how did you deal with the situation?

4. When Ezra took over for Ellen's father during his hernia surgery, he became an overbearing boss. What could Ezra have done to make things more workable between him and Ellen? Have you ever had to deal with an overbearing employer? How did you handle the situation?

5. Taavi reached out to Rob/Rueben when he didn't know him well and gave him a place to live. Have you ever helped someone you barely knew? What does the Bible say about helping strangers?

6. When Ken's accident occurred, Mandy's faith was put to the test. She was not only concerned for her husband's welfare, but worried that they would not have enough money to pay the bills. Between Ellen coming to help out and others donating money, Mandy and Ken's needs were met. Mandy accepted it with gratitude, but some people in similar circumstances are too proud to ask for or accept help. Have you or someone you know been in a comparable position? If you were on the receiving end, how did you respond? If you were on the giving end, how did it make you feel to help someone in need?

7. When Ken realized some of his injuries would hamper his ability to function in the manner he'd been accustomed to, he became depressed and withdrawn. How can we help someone whose life has been altered by sickness or an accident to rise above their circumstances and have a sense of self-worth?

8. Ezra thought he was in love with Ellen. If he had expressed those feelings and been kinder to her, what do you think the outcome would have been?

9. Rob/Rueben hid from his past and had become bitter and angry at God. He blamed himself for an accident that took someone's life and chose to deal with it by moving away and pretending to be someone else. What should he have done in order to deal with his guilt? And should he have been honest about his situation?

10. When Ellen found out about Rob/Rueben's deception, she felt betrayed. Have you ever been deceived by a friend? How did you respond to their deception?

11. Ken's mother, Vickie, suffered a devastating blow when her husband died. A short time later, her oldest son, Dan, unable to cope with his father's death, left Kauai and moved with his wife to California. This left Vickie with only Ken and Mandy's help in running her husband's business. She needed both sons, not only for their physical help, but for emotional support as well. How would you feel if an adult child or close family member moved away from you during a difficult time?

12. Did you learn anything new about the Amish by reading this story? If so, what was it?

13. Did you learn anything in particular about the Hawaiian culture you felt was similar to the way the Amish live?

14. Were there any verses of scripture in this story that spoke to your heart or bolstered your faith?

ABOUT THE AUTHORS

New York Times bestselling and award-winning author **Wanda E. Brunstetter** is one of the founders of the Amish fiction genre. She has written close to 90 books translated in four languages. With over 10 million copies sold, Wanda's stories consistently earn spots on the nation's most prestigious bestseller lists and have received numerous awards.

Wanda's ancestors were part of the Anabaptist faith, and her novels are based on personal research intended to accurately portray the Amish way of life. Her books are well-read and trusted by many Amish, who credit her for giving readers a deeper understanding of the people and their customs.

When Wanda visits her Amish friends, she finds herself drawn to their peaceful lifestyle, sincerity, and close family ties. Wanda enjoys photography, ventriloquism, gardening, bird-watching, beachcombing, and spending time with her family. She and her husband, Richard, have been blessed with two grown children, six grandchildren, and two great-grandchildren. To learn more about Wanda, visit her website at www.wandabrunstetter.com.

Jean Brunstetter became fascinated with the Amish when she first went to Pennsylvania to visit her father-in-law's family. Since that time, Jean has become friends with several Amish families and enjoys writing about their way of life. She also likes to put some of the simple practices followed by the Amish into her daily routine. Jean lives in Washington State with her husband, Richard Jr. and their three children, but takes every opportunity to visit Amish communities in several states. In addition to writing, Jean enjoys boating, gardening, and spending time on the beach. To learn more about Jean, visit her website at www.jeanbrunstetter.com.

Coming Next from Amish Country's Most Beloved Storyteller. . .

The Hope Jar by Wanda E. Brunstetter
What happens when making an elderly Amish couple very happy means going along with a lie that gets bigger by the day? Michelle is not who her new family believes her to be, but how can she tell the truth without hurting the ones she has come to truly love?

Paperback / 978-1-62416-747-8 / $15.99 / August 2018

The Christmas Prayer by Wanda E. Brunstetter
Bestselling author of Amish fiction, Wanda E. Brunstetter, takes readers on a journey in 1850 along the California Trail when a sudden snowstorm traps three wagons in the Sierra Nevada Mountains and forces Cynthia Cooper to evaluate the man she has promised to marry against two other worthy men in their party.

Paperback / 978-1-68322-657-4 / $12.99 / September 2018

Don't Miss Book 1, The Hawaiian Quilt!
A trip of a lifetime for Amish girl Mandy Frey is disrupted when she and one of her friends miss boarding the cruise ship after a stop on Kauai. But the adventure is just beginning as they make new friends and learn about the island. When it's time to go home, will Mandy leave a part of her heart behind?

Paperback / 978-1-63409-224-1 / $14.99